D1282236

Threads of Amarion

Threadweavers, Book 3

Todd Fahnestock

F4
PUBLISHING

Copyright © 2018 Todd Fahnestock

All rights reserved.

The characters and events portrayed in this book are
fictitious. Any similarity to real persons, living or dead, is
coincidental and not intended by the author.

No part of this book may be reproduced, or stored in a
retrieval system, or transmitted in any form or by any
means, electronic, mechanical, photocopying, recording,
or otherwise, without express written permission of the
publisher.

ISBN 13: 978-1-952699-30-6

Cover illustration and design by:
Rashed AlAkroka

Maps by:
Langon Foss

For Chris Mandeville, my avatar

CONTENTS

THREADS OF AMARION

Pronunciation Guide

Main Characters:

Medophae—ME-dȯ-fā
Mershayn—Mər-SHĀN
Mirolah—MI-rȯ-lä
Silasa—si-LÄ-sə
Stavark—STA-värk
Zilok Morth—ZĪ-lok Mȯrth

Other Characters / Places:

Amarion— ä-MĀ-rē-un
Ari'cyiane—ä-ri-cē-ĀN
Avakketh—ä-VÄ-keth
Belshra—BEL-shrə
Bendeller—ben-DEL-er
Buravar—BYÜ-rä-vär
Calsinac—KAL-zi-nak
Casra—KAZ-rä
Casur—KA-zhər
Cisly—SIS-lē
Clete—KLĒT
Corialis—KȮR-ē-a-lis
Dandere—DAN-dēr
Darva—DÄR-və
Daylan—DĀ-lin
Dederi—DE-de-rē
Denema—de-NĒ-mə
Deni'tri—de-NĒ-trē
Dervon—DƏR-vän
Diyah—DĒ-yä
Elekkena—e-LE-ke-nə

Ethiel—E-thē-el
Fillen—FIL-en
Grendis Sym—GREN-dis SIM
Harleath Markin—HÄR-lēth MÄR-kin
Irgakth—ƏR-gakth
Keleera—kə-LĒR-ə
Lawdon—LÄ-dən
Lo'gan—lȯ-GÄN
Locke—läk
Mi'Gan—mi-GÄN
Natra—NÄ-trə
Oedandus—ȯ-DAN-dus
Orem—Ȯ-rem
Rith—RITH
Saraphazia—se-ruh-FĀ-zhē-ə
Shera—SHE-rə
Tarithalius—ter-i-THAL-ē-us
Teni'sia—te-NĒ-sē-ä
Tiffienne—ti-fē-EN
Tuana—tü-ä-nä
Tyndiria—tin-DĒR-ē-ä
Vaisha—VĪ-shə
Yehnie—YEN-nē
Ynisaan—YĪ-ni-sän
Vullieth—VƏL-ē-eth
Zetu—ZE-tü

Mailing List/Facebook Group

MAILING LIST
Don't miss out on the latest news and information about all of my books. Join my Readers Group:

https://www.subscribepage.com/u0x4q3

FACEBOOK
https://www.facebook.com/todd.fahnestock

AMAZON AUTHOR PAGE
https://www.amazon.com/Todd-Fahnestock/e/B004N1MILG

Book 3

Threads of Amarion

PROLOGUE
MIROLAH

THE HUMAN FEMALE body sat facing the ocean with an unblinking gaze, and she was a part of that body, looking out from the inside. She felt with its senses, felt the sting as the icy air made crystals at the corners of her eyes, and the snow froze against her in drifts.

She was also a part of the waves below, rolling and crashing. The water that pushed against the wind, sending spray into the air and crashing into icy rocks.

She followed the wind, and she was part of that as well. The vigorous storm whipped at the last of the seagulls. He was a huge, stalwart fellow, smarter than the rest, driven to reach her even when his instincts screamed at him to seek shelter.

The storm would soon kill him, just as impassively as it would freeze the mountain peaks.

She seeped into the rock underneath this human body. That cold granite slept peacefully, and it enjoyed the storm. It enjoyed just about everything, even as it was slowly worn away, year after year, by the water below.

She became the falling snow, dancing along with its quiet song, loving to fly, loving to fall. Tiny flakes stuck to each other as they touched the earth. When the storm cleared and the sun rose the following day, most of them would melt away. Even the flakes in the highest reaches of the Corialis Mountains would only last the months of winter. They were all doomed. But the snowflakes were oblivious. They whispered their merry song, intertwining with the rage of the wind.

Stop it. A voice bubbled up past all of the sensations. *I am not these things.*

It was just one more voice in an endless cacophony of voices, and she ignored it, riding the raging wind again. She found the seagull a mile away, pumping his wings fiercely. He was at his breaking point. He—

The seagull's wing folded, broken at last, and the wind took him down in a spiral. He crashed against the side of the craggy mountain. His limp body fell to the shore and lay there, unmoving, and the merry snowflakes began to cover it.

It was the way of things. Life and death. Oceans crashed into the shore only to draw back and crash again. Seagulls were born and seagulls died.

Stop it!

She looked down at her naked body, half-buried in swirling snow. Her skin was turning gray. She flexed her hand, and it barely curled. This human body was dying, too. Dying again. Something about that annoyed her.

Like a cook kicking over a cauldron of hot water, she pulled GodSpill into this body. Her skin healed, filled with a rosy pink color, flush with the vitality of an eighteen-year-old woman.

She looked away again.

Yes! Said the voice. That was how it began. Now stop. Stop it!

Below her, she felt a huge, skinny dog scramble up the rocky cliff. He wanted to reach her, too, and he was determined. He had tracked her all the way from the place of human-made stones and towers.

He would not make it. He was a strong beast, far stronger than the seagull, but he, too, was at his limit. He had no fur and, like this human body, he was already beginning to freeze. His muscles were stiff and knotted. He could not hang on. Like the seagull, he would fall to his death in a moment.

She became the ocean again, rolling out, crashing in, but the voice pestered her again.

Help him.

She frowned, looked down at her skin. It had lost its pink vibrancy already. Frost collected on the hairs of her arms and the crooks of her elbows.

The skinny dog slipped, and his back legs scrabbled desperately on the snow and rock. But he was too slow, too cold. He went over the edge.

Help him!

His paws whipped futilely in the air. He yelped and plummeted—

She caught him, suspending him in the midst of the howling storm. He quieted immediately.

Why not? She had let the seagull die. She would let the dog live.

She brought him back and put him on the ledge next to her. He whined and sat down, shivering in the snow, then went silent, shaking uncontrollably as he watched her.

She reached out and found the essence of the cold air around the dog. She changed the color of the threads, warming the air. After a moment, the dog stopped shivering.

"And now what?" she murmured. Her voice sounded deep and ragged compared to the symphony of voices that spoke to her from the sea, the wind, the rock, the snow. The voice of this human body was crude and inept.

"Mistress?" the dog barked.

"I am not your mistress," she rasped. "I do not know who you are."

The dog whined miserably.

She considered letting the cold batter the dog again. She considered throwing him off the cliff, but she didn't. Something about that seemed wrong. A flicker of identity came and went.

Why? What is the difference between embracing death and killing? How can I feel this deep need to murder while at the same time feeling it is wrong? Why is it wrong?

The rocks of the mountain did not long to kill, nor the ocean nor the wind. They simply followed their passion and their purpose.

What was her passion and purpose?

"Do you know me?" she rasped to the dog.

"Yes, mistress," he barked.

"Why am I here?" she asked.

"You died," the dog whined. "They killed you."

For the first time, she blinked her eyes and turned this human body to face the dog, looking at him through the lens of human vision. He sat solemnly, watching her. The snow swirled between them. She could barely see him. Even when the snow cleared for an instant, he was blurry.

She realized her eyes were watering in the wind of the storm, and that was causing the blurriness. Annoyed, she turned her attention to the wind, to the cold, to the snow of the mountain. She changed these threads, changed *herself*, and a radius of summertime radiated outward from her, enveloping her human body and the dog. The snow melted away underneath her. She rejuvenated her dying skin, muscles, and tissues once more. There. That was better. Now she could see the dog clearly.

"I am dead," she mused. "I was this body."

The dog whined again and hung his head. "This one does not know. This one licked you, and you were cold like a fallen deer. This one does not know."

"Did you kill me?" she asked.

"No, mistress!"

"Then how do you know?"

"This one tried to follow you. They threw you from a window."

"They. They who?" Murderous images flashed through her mind. A man with black clothes and bright blue eyes. A boy with silver hair, white skin, and a shiny metal stick. A sword. He'd had a sword.

"Bad GodSpill. Bad man."

"Where are they?"

"Leave them, mistress. Bad GodSpill. Let us just go," he whined.

She contemplated that. "I do not understand."

"They will kill you again. Let us go."

"I do not think so," she said. "If I have died, they cannot kill me again."

"This one does not know," the dog whined miserably. He shifted from foot to foot, though he was no longer cold.

"Where would we go?"

"Back to the forest. Away from the towers, the bad man, and his bad GodSpill."

"Why not stay here then?"

The dog looked out into the storm that swirled a foot away from his face. "This one does not understand," he whined. "Not go to the forest?"

"Yes."

"Stay here?"

"Yes."

"But mistress, there is death here. All around. Too cold."

"You are not cold anymore," she said.

He shifted on his feet, looked at the blizzard. His tongue lolled out, and he panted. "This one does not know," he barked.

"Then we will stay here," she said.

"No food. You are not hungry?" he barked.

"If I am dead, do I eat?" she asked.

The dog whined, but he did not answer.

She considered.

"You need food," she said.

"Yes," he barked.

"Then we will get you food."

The dog stood. His long, bony tail wagged vigorously.

She pulled the threads. They both rose slowly into the air, floated away from the mountain ledge, and disappeared into the howling storm.

1

MERSHAYN

MERSHAYN RAISED his head as quickly as he could, which wasn't very. His lank hair hung in his face. Droplets of his sweat dotted the wet stone beneath him, mixing with droplets of red. His nostrils filled with the coppery smell of his own blood and the musky stink of his own fear. He hated himself for that.

The room was small, no furniture. There was a slit of a window, and in the far corner was the cage that held the limp quicksilver. A storm raged outside.

Sym's weasel face leaned close to Mershayn's. The big torturer next to Sym had taken off his shirt to show his thickly muscled torso and the scars on his arms and chest, like his bulging biceps were going to intimidate Mershayn even further.

My face feels like chopped meat. Your manliness doesn't impress me.

"There's defiance in his eyes," Sym said to the big torturer. "You said you'd bleed that out of him."

"It's early." The torturer flexed again. Mershayn would have rolled his eyes if they didn't hurt so bad.

Sym grunted.

Mershayn tried to straighten, but the pain of his shoulder lanced through his left side. So he tried to ignore it. It flared, and he almost passed out. He thought about giving up, just lying down. That would feel nice. He could stop struggling and join his brother Collus in death. They'd killed Collus. They'd killed Mirolah...

Lovely Mirolah...

I'll see you soon. In the next life, I'm going to kiss you. I'm going to steal a kiss from you....

Mershayn shook his head, trying to clear it. He wasn't going to quit. Sym had killed Collus and Mirolah, and Mershayn owed him for that. If Sym killed Mershayn, fine. But if there was even a chance at vengeance, Mershayn wasn't going to just lie down. He wasn't going to break. He was going to shove a sword through Sym's guts.

He spat at Sym, missed him by a good foot or so.

Split lip. Messed up my aim.

The big torturer hit him in the side of the jaw, hard. Mershayn's head slammed to the side.

Mershayn had to face the fact that he was on an unparalleled losing streak. He'd lost his freedom, his dignity. He'd lost his sword, his pride, and, finally, lost his brother and Mirolah.

He spat a tooth at Sym, missed again.

And that tooth. I lost that, too.

Sym had a threadweaver of his own, more powerful than Mirolah. Some foul spirit from beyond the grave named Zilok, who was even more powerful than the legendary Captain Medophae, apparently. It had taken control of Mershayn's mind, had wiped out Medophae's little army in about thirty seconds. Mershayn couldn't possibly beat something like that, but he might get the chance to gut Sym. That was all he lived for now.

"Do you know why I'm doing this?" Sym asked in a conversational tone. He crouched down next to Mershayn, keeping his boots just out of the pool of sweat and blood.

"Becss yrr pssa sht...." Mershayn mumbled, his words slurred.

The big torturer pulled back his fist, but Sym held up a hand.

"Did you hear that?" Sym said to Gael'ek, who stood by the

door with a stoic expression. Mershayn knew Gael'ek. He was a hack swordsman, relied entirely on his strength because he had no grace. Apparently he was Sym's top thug now. "I think he's insulting me."

Sym nodded, and the torturer stepped forward. Mershayn tried to move his head back, but he was abominably slow, and anything he did seemed to make it worse. The fist slammed down on the side of his ear. He gasped and fell to the stones. Consciousness slipped from him.

He awoke to a fine view of Sym's boots. The would-be king was talking, and it appeared as though Mershayn had only been out a second.

"...enough for today, I think," Sym told the torturer. "Let us leave him to the sting of his failure." The toe of Sym's boot slid under Mershayn's chin and lifted his jaw. Mershayn hoped his blood ruined the leather.

"Goodbye for now, *Lord* Mershayn." Sym's voice was smug. "I shall see you tomorrow." He let Mershayn's head drop back to the stones. The three men left. The door closed, and the massive tumblers clicked into place as they locked him in.

Lock the doors. Yes. Nice. As if I can even reach the doors....

Mershayn took stock of himself. After the long, arduous process of sitting up, favoring his tender shoulder, he decided he was intact where it mattered. There were no broken bones, just a lot of pummeled muscles and bruises. He wondered if he should thank the gods for small favors or if Sym was just saving the hard stuff for later. Maybe bone-breaking was tomorrow's entertainment.

He tried to get his eyes to focus on the far side of the room.

Stavark lay crumpled in a tiny, pitiful heap inside his cage.

Earlier today, just after they were hauled here from the audience chamber, two guards had attempted to extricate the quicksilver from the cage and chain him to the wall. They used long, iron hooks to grab a hold of his arms and legs. The first guard who hooked him received a broken wrist for his trouble. The moment the hook encircled his arm, the little quicksilver became a silver blur. Before the guard could react, Stavark yanked the guard's arm into the cage. In the next instant, the man screamed as his wrist snapped.

After that, Sym ordered huge buckets of water to be dumped over the quicksilver, one after the other in quick succession. While half-blinded and half-drowned, Stavark didn't see the blunt end of the metal hook that smashed into his head. He dropped like a stone.

When awake and moving, Stavark was a force of nature, unstoppable. But curled up like that, he just looked small, a white-skinned boy with silver hair. What the hell was he even doing here? Had Captain Medophae recruited this child for his personal war?

The wound in Stavark's calf leaked blood, but it wasn't gushing. He was still alive, and that injury would mend if they tended it. Mershayn shook his head. Despite Stavark's skinny appearance, he was the toughest little person Mershayn had ever seen.

Mershayn tried not to dwell on his recent failures, but like Sym had suggested, all he seemed able to do was take a long hard look at them. The hours dragged by. Hunger gnawed at him, and he had an increasing need to use the privy.

Soon, nature's call was like a hammer pounding his bladder. He winced and tried to ignore it. No doubt Sym would like for Mershayn to urinate all over himself, furthering his humiliation.

As he fought the growing need to relieve himself, Mershayn suddenly realized something odd. They had not taken him and Stavark down to the dungeons. Why? There had to be a reason.

Maybe Sym didn't like the idea of descending so many steps to witness the torment of his playthings? It was much easier to pop in for a quick bit of mauling before lunch and dinner. Or perhaps Sym hoped to loosen his prisoners up with the cold of the massive storm outside the thin window.

Mershayn looked at the whipping snow. It was daytime, and as the hours slid by, he could even guess at the time by how the sky darkened. That was nice. Useful. As a result, he knew it was about nightfall when he finally soiled himself.

He half-expected Sym to return and beat him some more that night, but the would-be king of Teni'sia didn't show his face.

Eventually, Mershayn succumbed to his bone-deep weariness.

Even the cold didn't seem to hurt by the time he slumped in a corner, barely separated from the puddles of water, blood, and urine, and went to sleep.

AT FIRST, Mershayn thought the rusty opening of the lock was part of his desolate dream. When the door slammed against the wall, though, it jolted him to his senses. One of his eyes was gummed shut, but he opened the other as best he could, slowly focusing on an enraged Grendis Sym.

"Who is he?" Sym growled.

Two burly guards entered behind Sym. Mershayn recognized neither of them, which either meant his vision was too blurry, or these men came from Sym's holdings in Buir'tishree.

"Who?" Mershayn croaked.

Sym's boot smashed into the side of Mershayn's head. He cried out, falling flat to the floor. He hated himself for showing weakness, but gods, that had hurt.

"Am I going to have to crack your worthless head?" Sym hissed, crouching next to Mershayn. He grabbed Mershayn's hair and yanked his head up. "I've been lenient with you, bastard. Tell me what you know."

"Perhaps if you give me a clue..." Mershayn mumbled. "I can help."

"Your assassin," Sym said. "Who is he?"

Assassin?

Mershayn swallowed and thought carefully before he answered. "What...sorts of assassinations?" he mumbled.

Sym growled, and Mershayn prepared himself for another thunderous crack to the head, but it didn't come.

"Is he one of my guards still loyal to you?" Sym asked.

"I don't...know. What...is he doing?"

Sym stood up and kicked Mershayn in the ribs. Mershayn rolled with it, taking only part of the blow. It was much better than the hit to the head.

Sym whirled and left with his guards.

Mershayn raised his head, looking out the thin window above him. Orange light lit a cloudy sky as the sun set. He chuckled, and it slowly rolled into a full laugh. It hurt his ribs, but he did it anyway. He thought he had run out of allies, but he'd forgotten one. Sym hadn't said so, but Mershayn would bet his life that this assassin had struck last night.

Oh Silasa, my monstrous beauty. If you were here, I'd kiss you on your cold lips.

He kept laughing as the sun fell.

2

SILASA

SILASA OPENED HER EYES. It was night again. Dirt and snow pressed against her face.

Disgusting.

She remembered when awakening was a gentle journey from one place to another, with sunlight seeping into her bedroom as dreams evaporated like mist. It took time, a shifting from one fading world to another filled with crisp clarity. As a child, she would blink, letting the dreams fade away, turning her thoughts to getting dressed, to breakfast, to her cousin down the hall, and sneaking away from needlepoint to splash in the ocean.

It wasn't like that anymore. Silasa did not dream. One moment she did not exist and the next she did. As far as she knew, she was stone-dead during the day. She would not be surprised if someone told her that her body vanished in the morning and reappeared at nightfall.

Frozen mud had collected in her mouth, at the corners of her eyes. Her arms, crossed over her chest, were trapped by the weight of earth and snow.

Disgusting. Disgusting. Disgusting.

She hated this part about traveling. She couldn't just stop and erect a tent. She had to bury herself or risk immolation. Just a touch of the sunlight's rays would light her body up like a bonfire.

She shrugged, pushing her hands apart like she was swimming. Dirt and snow moved around her, and she surged upward, breaking into the open air.

A blizzard whirled around her. Even with her supernatural senses, she couldn't see more than a few feet in front of her. It was as though the weather sensed the conflict in Teni'sia and mirrored it.

She brushed off her long, black dress—ripped and caked with grime—and fingered the haggard lace decorating the waist. The ruined strip hung to mid-thigh. With a quiet motion, she yanked it free and tried not to think about it. The lace at her cuffs, though grimy, was at least intact.

She delicately pulled her cuffs to length and let them fall stiffly from the sleeves of her half coat, as they were meant to.

She realized how pitiful it was, standing in the middle of a blizzard, adjusting lace cuffs of an ensemble that was ruined, but she continued anyway. When she was finished, she smoothed the front of her dress, faced the swirling storm, and picked up the thoughts that had been abruptly cut off when her mind "vanished" during the day.

She had been betrayed.

At least that's what Silasa assumed. She'd rushed north to help Bands and, just about the time the sun was rising, Bands flew overhead, back toward Teni'sia. Ynisaan had sent Silasa north, conspicuously removing her from Medophae's attack because Bands might die in a fight against another dragon. But the battle had ended before Silasa even arrived.

Now that Silasa thought on it, Ynisaan had never said "might" before. When she'd sent Silasa to rescue Medophae, before Mirolah returned GodSpill to Amarion, Ynisaan had said, "If you don't help Medophae, he *will* die." Ynisaan had sent Silasa like an arrow, sure and precise. There had been no doubt, no "might." And Ynisaan had practically known what the future would hold, like she'd read it in a book.

Silasa had breezed right past all the signals of deception because she trusted Ynisaan.

Silasa leapt down the snowy slope and ran toward Teni'sia with all the speed that her undead legs could muster.

It took the entire night to run back, through swirling snow and mountainous terrain. She approached from the north, where the cliffs splintered out of the sides of the mountain that eventually became the castle. Mortals would die by the dozens trying to come this way, falling from treacherous ridges, and even if one could climb those unclimbable walls to the Northern Walk, it would only take a pair of Teni'sian archers to pick apart an entire army. With a vigilant guard, no one could attack Teni'sia from the north.

But Silasa had strength enough in her undead fingers to cling to the smallest cracks and scale that wall. She had the storm at her back, howling against the stone, whipping snow around her.

With frost on her eyelashes and skin—and a braid that had become an icicle—Silasa climbed the snow-swept walls to the Northern Walk. The nearest guard was bundled in his cloak, shivering. His cowl was drawn so tightly that he didn't see her as she slipped past him.

With dawn less than an hour away, she raced through the castle's lamplit hallways, trying to discover what had happened to Medophae.

It didn't take long to realize that Medophae's invasion had failed. There was no revelry in the quiet palace, no celebration of a successful coup. Instead, guards dressed in Sym's house colors, green and white, roamed about. Those not freezing on the Northern Walk strode smugly down the hallways.

Silasa sneaked past them and descended the steps to the dungeons.

There were two guards on duty there, playing dice in the antechamber between the hallway and the cells.

They both looked up when they saw her, each making an "O" with their mouths. Silasa imagined she looked like death's bride with her frozen white skin and angry white eyes.

They both went for their swords, knocking over benches as they lurched to their feet, yelling. She dodged the first swing and kicked the guard into the wall so hard his ribs broke. He crashed to his knees, dropping his sword and gasping for breath.

The second guard was quick. Her sword flicked out at Silasa's stomach, ripping through a fold in her dress. Silasa spun up the woman's outstretched arm and grabbed her neck.

"No!" the woman shouted. Silasa tore her throat out, dropped the body, and turned to the gasping man.

"Who's in there?" Silasa rasped, suddenly realizing her throat was nearly frozen also. "Tell me, I let you live."

"What are you?" the man gasped, holding his side and squinting up at her.

She lifted him by his neck. "Too late," she whispered and sank her teeth into him. Hot blood rushed down her throat, and she gulped greedily. The run north had left her famished, so she feasted until there was nothing left, then dropped the corpse.

New strength rushed through her. She felt alive, voracious, even more hungry than she had just a moment before. The power of White Tuana coursed through her, lifted her up, filled her with thoughts of carnage. She wanted to leap upon the woman's corpse and tear at her throat, rip at her belly.

No, Silasa thought. I do what must be done. Only that. Never more.

She turned her head away and looked at the table. There were two plates of chicken bones, picked clean, where the guards had been playing dice. There were also two cups, two forks and two napkins. She picked up one of the napkins and dabbed at her mouth like she was at a royal ball.

I'm not a savage. I do not belong to Her. I am the master of my own flesh.

She stood over the dead woman, staring down at her until the bloodlust calmed.

Kneeling, she took the keys from the woman's belt, turned, and opened the doors to the cells. Her ragged dress whispered against the stones as she walked between barred rooms on either side. The last time she'd been here, she had come for only one prisoner, Mershayn. This time, the cells were filled with his soldiers. She could see them clearly in the darkness, recognized a few of them. They couldn't see her as well. She probably appeared like a black

15

wraith, a shadow slipping through shadows.

One soldier squinted and moved closer to the bars.

"Where is Medophae?" she asked.

He flinched back, finally seeing her and how close she was. "Gone," he blurted. "To find Sym."

"And King Mershayn?"

"Went with him."

"Silasa?" Captain Lo'gan's voice came from down the row. Silasa went to his cell. He had a cut on his forehead, and his arm was wrapped in a bandage obviously refashioned from someone's ripped tunic.

"What happened?" Silasa asked.

"Trap," Lo'gan said.

"We knew it was a trap."

"Well, they knew we knew."

"What happened to Medophae?"

"Whatever he tried, it failed. Captain Medophae, the king, the quicksilver, and that threadweaver, they all went to find Sym. That's the last I saw of them."

At a cursory glance, only about two dozen of Mershayn's soldiers were in these cells. They had started with fifty.

"Where're the rest?" she asked.

"Dead," he said grimly. "They were waiting for us. A hundred at least."

She unlocked Lo'gan's cell and handed him the keys.

What is your game, Ynisaan? Why send me away when I could have helped?

Lo'gan passed the keys to the woman at his right. The woman's head was shaved, and she had a scar on each cheek and on her forehead. Deni'tri was her name, Silasa recalled. Deni'tri immediately began unlocking doors and the soldiers of Mershayn's ragtag army emerged into the hall.

"You know your way around the castle?" Silasa said.

Lo'gan snorted.

"Then you're on your own." She turned and strode down the hall.

"Where are you going?" he asked.

"To find Medophae."

She sprinted into the guard room and back into the main hallway, taking the stairs down. She searched room after room deep within the castle, but none of them contained her friend. There were a good number of roving guards, though, and she left a trail of bodies in her wake.

Frustrated, she felt the coming of the sun. No matter where she was, she could always feel it, and this castle was not a safe place for her to spend the day. Sym would redouble his guards. He would search for her. And if they found her while she slept, that would be the end of any help she could give Medophae.

She found a lower balcony and jumped into the storm, which finally showed some signs of slackening. She waded through the drifts and climbed to a cave that looked like it went deep into the mountain.

She crouched in its entrance, watching as the storm slowly erased her footprints. The last thing she needed was to have a hunting party follow her straight to her temporary lair.

When she was satisfied no one could see she had come this way, she ran deep into the cave and found a cramped alcove where she could lie down on the uncomfortable rock.

Angry, dissatisfied, she settled herself, wishing she could spend time thinking about Ynisaan's order. She lay in the dark, seething, walking through the castle in her mind, thinking of where her friends might be. The night was such a long time away, but there was nothing to be done for it. If Medophae's group was still alive, they'd just have to stay that way until—

SILASA'S CONSCIOUSNESS RETURNED. She bared her fangs, rolled out of the thin, horizontal alcove and leapt to her feet. Night had come. It was time to hunt. And this time, she could do it right. She wouldn't have to spend most of the night running through a storm.

She emerged into a world of white mountains sparkling in the moonlight. The sky was clear, and freshly fallen snow covered the

17

landscape.

She jogged, stepping high back toward Teni'sia. Urgency thrummed through her. Too much could happen during an entire day. She might have missed the chance to help her friends, but by the gods, she was going to try. And if there was nothing else she could do—if Sym had hurt them—she would take a bloody revenge.

She took the same route up to the Northern Walk as she had last night and, as luck would have it, set foot upon the walk without a guard in sight.

Moving lightly along the castle's edge, she stopped as the walk curved around a turret. Her keen ears picked up a low conversation between two guards.

Their voices were tense, nervous, talking about the mysterious attack on the dungeons last night.

"...said the assassin broke his neck," one of the guards was saying. "Twisted like this." He paused, as though illustrating something. "Like the assassin was as strong as ten men."

"He was Wave-altered, you mark my words," the second man said. It was higher pitched and nervous. "It's gettin' unsettling in Teni'sia. The money's good, but gold ain't worth nothing if you're dead. Might be time to look for work elsewhere."

"You best not let Sym or Captain Gael'ek hear you talking like that," the first guard said. "You'll end up a head shorter."

Silasa reached into a pouch at her waist and withdrew a hand-sized rock she'd taken from the mountain. She threw it over the edge, close to where the guards were having their conversation. It clacked against the cliff, then thumped in the snow far below.

"Did you hear that?" the second guard said.

The first guard grunted.

"Well what was it?" the second guard pressed nervously.

"Don't get jumpy. Probably some dumb surf dragon trying to climb the cliff."

"In the snow?"

"Shut up."

She listened to their footsteps moving toward the rail.

Silasa strode across the icy stones, her feet making whispering sounds. One of the guards was tall and thin, and one was squat and solid. The short guard was looking over the edge of the rail. The tall one other scanned the walkway to the south, facing away.

Bad luck, friend.

She closed on them.

The tall guard spun just as her hand closed on his neck. His eyes went wide, and he choked, scrabbling against her arm.

She snatched the squat guard's neck next, then picked them both up. The short guard, obviously the more experienced, ignored her death grip and drew his sword. She pulled him close, fast, as he swung. His arm wrapped around her, the weapon thumping harmlessly against her back.

She plunged her teeth into his neck. Blood splashed on her chin. She drank deeply and quickly. The squat guard gave a thrash like a hooked trout, then went limp. She drained him, pulling his hot life into herself. Tuana's power surged through her, bringing vitality to her frozen limbs.

She dropped the ghastly corpse, its lips shrunken, its face white, and its fingers curled into thin claws.

The tall guard went wild, flinging himself like an animal caught in a snare. He tried to wrap his legs around her arm and pry her grip free, but he couldn't match her strength, not with both arms, both legs, and another three men to help him. His struggles became feeble as he ran out of breath.

She choked him unconscious and left him by the body of his partner. Sparing him reminded her of who she was, reminded her not to give in to her bloodlust. It was White Tuana's desire to kill, not hers. Never hers.

Silasa wiped her chin, headed south on the walkway, and entered the archway of the Northern Walk's guard house. Two of the three guards inside were awake. One of them saw her, drew a dagger, and threw it remarkably fast.

It sank deep into Silasa's chest, and it hurt. Rage flared inside her, and the power she had just drunk burst through her, moving her arms and legs. She leapt onto the guard, tearing open his neck and feeding hungrily. A red haze covered her vision, and the movements of the other guards seemed slow-and-quick, mismatched flashes from a frantic dream. A sword came at her, missed, sparked on the stones. A man leapt at her, trying to tackle her. Her fingernails sank into his soft flesh. Her teeth sank into his neck. Another sword sliced her leg, drawing her blood. She hit him in the chest, fingers like nails, and she felt his bones break. Her teeth sank into another warm neck.

Then it was over. Her right arm was bloody to the elbow, and she felt sticky wetness on her chin and chest, quickly growing cold. She stood over three drained corpses, and she vibrated with power, feeling like she could leap straight upward and burst through the roof twenty feet above her.

Stop it. Stop it....

On the other side of the guardhouse was a courtyard open to the night sky with extensive gardens covered in snow. She ran across the open ground, moving fast, and leaving bloody footprints. The double doors of the castle proper stood on the far side, protected by two more guards. One of them, an exceptionally alert woman, shouted before Silasa slammed into her. The woman smashed into the wall, dropped like a bag of sand, and lay unmoving. Silasa grabbed the second guard by the neck before he could yell. She moderated her strength and choked him into unconsciousness.

That was sloppy. The woman's shout would alert other guards, especially if there were more behind the door—

A huge shadow passed over her.

Silasa crouched, her gaze darting upward.

There was nothing there. She melted into the shadow of the wall and stood still for a long moment, listening. Thin clouds slid across the moon. Had it been a cloud?

She grabbed the keys from one of the fallen guards, snapping his belt like a piece of kelp, and fit the key into the door. The lock clicked, and she swung the door wide.

There were no guards on the other side. She entered, turned the corner, ready for another attack.

A crossbowman hid halfway behind a short wall, but he didn't shoot. Silasa waited, ready to leap into action. The man had to see her, but still he didn't shoot. She narrowed her eyes.

He was slumped against the wall like he had fallen asleep on his bow. Another guard lay stretched out farther down the hall as though he had turned to run for help, but then decided to take a nap.

A chill ran through her. That was a threadweaver's work.

Her first reaction was to turn and sprint away as fast as she could go. Zilok Morth was the resident threadweaver in Teni'sia right now, and there wasn't a damned thing Silasa could do against a being like Zilok. Her speed and strength was nothing to him. Morth would take her mind, make her dance like a puppet.

She froze.

Think. Don't do the first thing. Do the smart thing. Zilok had no reason to put Sym's guards to sleep. Why would he—

"Were you simply going to kill them all?" a woman's voice came from down the hall, a voice Silasa would know anywhere, a voice she hadn't heard in a century.

Bands's dove-blond hair and emerald eyes shone in the darkness, glowing with their own inner light. She stepped forward, and the shadows parted like a cloak. She wore a sleeveless green gown, floor length, as though she was going to a ball.

Silasa's voice caught in her throat. Her first instinct was to run to her friend, to wrap her up in a hug. Ynisaan had said Bands had returned....

Silasa's thoughts curdled like souring milk, and she felt icy fear in her gut.

This was exactly the kind of mind game Zilok would play. She hadn't felt him enter her mind, but that didn't mean he hadn't. Certainly, he wouldn't put his own guards to sleep unless it was part of a larger plan. Impersonating Bands to "befriend" Silasa was exactly the kind of thing Zilok would do.

Silasa backed up a step, trying to push down her fear.

Of course. It was Zilok all along. He took control of Silasa's mind before the battle. He projected Ynisaan's likeness into Silasa's mind. That was how he got Silasa out of the way before the battle. After all, which was really more likely? That Ynisaan, a creature who had proven to be dedicated to stopping Morth, had suddenly lied to Silasa to make sure Medophae failed...

21

...or that Zilok had crafted an elaborate trap, impersonating Ynisaan and manipulating Silasa like a marionette so she couldn't help Medophae?

She bared her teeth. "I see you, Morth," she said. "You fooled me. But you won't do it twice."

Bands stopped walking, her head cocked to the side, then she nodded. Her face softened into a compassionate half smile, that same smile Silasa knew so well, her best friend's smile. The expression hit Silasa like a punch to the chest. It was so perfect, so...Bands. How many times had Bands looked at Silasa like that when they were talking late into the night?

"The gods curse you...." Silasa said. Her stomach churned at the vile imitation, at how much Zilok knew, at how casually he could ravage Silasa's emotions. She took another step back.

"I am not Zilok," Bands said softly.

"Why not just kill me?" Silasa asked, but she knew the answer. It was amusement. Torture the poor, lonely vampire girl by taking Medophae away, then dangle a phantom of her best friend in front of her.

"Silasa..."

Silasa bared her fangs. "Do it, then. If this is the end, finish it. Stop this charade."

"Silasa," Bands repeated, like she was speaking to an unruly child who wouldn't listen. "When Ethiel captured Medophae, whose counsel did I seek?"

"Bands was inside Ethiel's gem. She wasn't around when Ethiel captured Medophae."

"Ah. My mistake. I'm not talking about his recent capture. I meant the other one. The earlier one. The first time Ethiel caged Medophae, in the Age of Ascendance, 1152. Whose counsel did I seek?"

"Do you think your knowledge of history will sway me?" Silasa asked. "Whatever it is you want from me, whatever fruit this is meant to bear, I'll make you choke on it."

"I did not ask you how I should go about freeing Medophae," Bands continued, unruffled. "Do you remember what I asked you?"

"I'll never tell you."

"I asked you if I should kill Ethiel," Bands said. "I knew I could get Medophae back. I knew I could beat her. What I didn't know was if that deluded woman deserved to die. Do you remember?"

Silasa's scathing retort died on her lips. That *had* happened. Bands had asked her that question. Silasa remembered it vividly. How could Morth know that? No one else had been there. Had Zilok spied on them?

"Medophae stayed in that cage for a day longer than he needed to," Bands continued. "Because you and I talked. We talked all night. Do you remember what you told me?"

"I remember." Silasa's voice was barely a whisper.

"You told me to kill her. You said that an ordinary woman deserved mercy, but Ethiel wasn't ordinary anymore. She was a force, too powerful to simple chide and turn my back on. You said she deserved the same pity I should give a rabid dog, destroyed for her own good and the good of everyone else."

Bands glanced down at her hand, turned it over. It was flawless. Long, slender fingers, perfectly cut nails. It always would be, of course, because Bands's human body was a construction of her imagination. "Do you remember what I said in response?" She cocked her head, looking back into Silasa's eyes.

"You didn't want to," Silasa whispered. "I argued with you."

"For an hour, you argued. And you were right." A tear welled at the corner of those emerald eyes with their cat's pupils. "And I paid the price for my mistake. A long and terrible price."

"Oh gods..." Silasa whispered. "Bands?"

"Yes."

Silasa ran forward and threw her arms around the dragon woman, and Bands clasped her tight.

"By the gods," Silasa said.

Bands released her and looked down at her. Silasa had forgotten how tall the woman was. "We have many stories to tell," Bands said, smiling that half smile. "First, we save a kingdom, eh? And then Medophae, again, from the looks of it."

Silasa laughed through tears, holding onto her friend's arms, afraid that if she let go, Bands might vanish. But no, she was here. She was solid and real. Everything was going to be all right.

"Teni'sia cannot be in turmoil," Bands said. "There is a danger greater even than Zilok Morth poised over Amarion, and we must meet it head-on."

"Worse than Morth?"

"Worse than Amarion has yet known. We must move quickly or we'll have no chance at all." Then she changed the subject. "Your friend, the one called Mershayn. He is alive."

Relief flowed through her. "I didn't dare to hope."

"He is in the western tower. Do you know what happened here two nights ago?"

"Medophae and his friends went to trigger Zilok's trap and remove the usurper Sym. That's all I know. It seems reasonable to think Zilok took them."

"And Grendis Sym now rules."

"Yes."

"And you believe the kingdom would be better off with Mershayn as king?" Bands asked.

"You're looking for the strongest king?"

"We will need a strong king in the days to come."

Silasa hesitated, trying to arrange her thoughts. Bands never wasted words. If she asked questions, they were important. "Sym is a killer and a schemer," Silasa said. "But he obviously knows how to take and hold power. If you need a strong king... Well, he might serve. I don't know what you're asking. Do you want a ruthless king?"

"I need strength. I need the kingdom to be unified. What about Mershayn?"

"Mershayn..." Silasa began. "I...I like him, but..." Silasa held up her hands helplessly. "I don't know. I'm not a kingmaker, Bands."

"You are tonight. What is Mershayn like?"

"Vain, cocky, self-absorbed, thick-headed, stubborn. He's a rogue and a philanderer, and too clever by half. He has no moral code, except..." Silasa trailed off.

"Except what?"

"Except he really did love his brother. He fought like a wild beast to save him. He would not be stopped nor reasoned with. I pulled Mershayn out of the dungeons, gave him the freedom to save his own life, but he wouldn't. He chose to go back for his brother against impossible odds. And he inspired others to help him."

"And did they save his brother?"

"They almost did."

"You like him," Bands said.

"If I was the sixteen-year-old girl I look like, I'd be head-over-heels for him. He's charming, good-looking, quick-witted. But maybe that's all he is. It's certainly all he *does*. He takes advantage of women whenever he gets the chance."

"Interesting."

"He'd probably make a horrible king."

"Do you like Sym?" Bands asked.

"Sym is a power-hungry weasel. But he'd probably make a stronger war king, if that's what you're asking. And he knows what he is doing, obviously. He's a political animal."

"Excellent," Bands said. "I think I understand. Let's have a conversation with Mershayn. If I agree with you, we'll put him on the throne."

"Agree with me...? But I said Sym would probably be better."

"No. You told me you like Mershayn, despite his shortcomings, and that you dislike Sym, despite his strengths."

"So we're going to topple Sym's regime—what Medophae failed to do—just like that?"

"Silasa, I can't afford to slink around hiding, influencing a little bit at a time. We have to move fast, otherwise all of this will be burning rubble."

"Rubble?" Silasa asked.

"In as little as a few days, dragons will be in this city, killing everyone they can."

"Why?"

"Stay close," Bands said. "Inform me. I've been gone a long time. I need your assistance."

"Of course. Whatever I can do."

"Good. Also, stop killing them," Bands said.

Silasa looked back down the dark hallway to the site of her last bloody battle. "I was...angry," she said softly.

25

"I need you, Silasa. Not White Tuana's vampiric slave. You play with fire every time you take a human life. Every gulp of human blood gives Tuana another foothold inside your soul."

Silasa bowed her head. "I'm sorry."

"Don't be sorry," Bands said, striding up the hall the way she had come. "Be better," she called over her shoulder. "Be yourself, not what that twisted goddess made you."

Silasa jogged past the sleeping guards, hurrying to catch up. "What about them?" Silasa said.

"Let them sleep. It may be the last deep sleep they have for a long time."

3

MERSHAYN

MERSHAYN OPENED HIS GUMMED EYES. At least he could see out of both of them this time. The pain in his body thudded rhythmically, his heart pounding out the surges of hurt. It never ended, but he kept his eyes open. Silasa was coming. The vampire had kept her promise, and that meant he had to hang on long enough for her to reach him.

"Why do you smile?" Stavark asked.

Mershayn swung his head around. The boy lay exactly as he'd fallen two days ago, but his eyes were open.

"Thalius! I thought you were dead." Mershayn let out a breath of sheer relief.

"I should be dead," Stavark said, his voice barely audible. "It is the only punishment for what I am now."

"Stavark..."

"I killed the *Maehka vik Kalik*. I am no *syvihrk*."

"That wasn't you," Mershayn insisted. "It was that thing, Zilok Morth."

"I stabbed her, over and over." Stavark closed his eyes. His

27

voice dropped so that Mershayn could barely hear it. "My hands... My blade..." he whispered.

"Stavark..." Mershayn began, but trailed off. He understood the boy's guilt. Mershayn had killed his own brother. Oh, he hadn't wielded the sword, but he'd been blind to the obvious signs of the coup until it was too late. He'd ignored his one responsibility: protect his brother. If Mershayn hadn't been more concerned with his own diversions than Collus's safety, the king would still be alive.

Mershayn's guilt burned like a hot coal next to his heart, a terrible pain that would never go away. Collus was dead because Mershayn refused to shoulder responsibility until it was too late.

So he knew how Stavark felt. But there was a difference between their two betrayals. Mershayn was actually at fault. Stavark was not.

Still, Mershayn knew there were no supportive, coddling words that could snap Stavark out of his self-loathing. He didn't need soft hands; he needed a hard slap. And then he needed a path to vengeance.

"Your sword killed her," Mershayn finally said. "But it wasn't you. That foul spirit took your mind just like he took mine. He used you, raised your hands, made them stab. If you see yourself as the villain, then you're a fool. The real villain got away. If you take the blame for him, if you let him get away with it after all, then maybe it *is* your fault."

Stavark glared daggers at Mershayn.

Mershayn saw that the words had burned through Stavark's self-loathing. Now was the time to give him a path to vengeance. "When we get free—"

"You're a fool, human," Stavark spat. "They will kill us here, just like they killed our friends."

The cell grew dark as drifting clouds obscured the moonlight outside. Mershayn shifted, trying to find a comfortable way to sit with the chains binding him. He'd tried to find that position for almost two days now without success.

"I want them to kill me," Stavark finally said. "I do not wish to be freed."

"Fine," Mershayn said. "Take the coward's way."

"A *human* cannot understand," Stavark snapped. "I cannot *kill* whomever I choose, as you do, and congratulate myself. I cannot slay the *Maehka vik Kalik* and still be a *syvihrk*."

"If a *syvihrk* can't take a hit get back up again, then fuck the *syvihrk*," Mershayn flared.

Stavark hissed. He turned his head away.

Something heavy thumped outside. Mershayn twisted. The lock clicked, and the door swung open.

Silasa entered. Her black dress, ripped and filthy with dirt and blood, rustled behind her, but her feet made no sound.

"Silasa!" Mershayn laughed, despite the sting in his cracked lip. He laughed again, filled with hope at seeing her, then said, "Where have you been? I've been waiting for you. What kind of person would make me wait this long?"

"What kind of person gets locked up in a tower bedroom instead of a dungeon?" she replied.

"Haven't you heard?" he said. "The dungeons are not secure. Guards dying left and right."

"Is that so?" She gave him a wry smile, then stood aside. Another woman entered the room.

Mershayn opened his mouth and had a hard time closing it. The woman was stunning. She was what a goddess might look like. She was easily as tall as Mershayn, and she wore a sleeveless green gown with white fur trim. Her bare arms were muscled like a warrior woman's, but her poise was that of a queen. And her eyes were brilliant emerald green, and they had...pupils like a cat's.

"By the gods..." he murmured.

Stavark turned over on his side, flicking a glance at the blond woman. His eyes narrowed, then widened. He sat up.

"No," he whispered. "*Kaarksyvihrk! Vekisk syvihrk syt quavakar. Syt syksekkin,*" he murmured in a language that sounded like a rock skipping across water. He clenched his teeth, and tears welled in his eyes. His fingers closed over the bars and gripped them so hard Mershayn could see the boy's straining tendons.

"*Ket syksekkin, syvihrk,*" the goddess woman said in Stavark's language. She turned to Mershayn. "My name is Bands."

"Bands?" He flicked a glance at Silasa, who smirked at him. She

29

nodded as though confirming his unspoken thought. He looked back at the blond woman. *"The* Bands? From the Wildmane legends?"

Bands waited patiently.

"You're Wildmane's..." He almost said "lover," then stopped himself. It was too crass a word to use with this...goddess woman. "You're his... You're the dragon woman?"

"I am a dragon, yes," Bands said.

That took a moment to digest. He felt that, with threadweavers and demigods and vampires running around, a dragon shouldn't phase him. But it did. Dragons existed only in stories! With some effort, he recovered his composure.

"Is he with you? Medophae?" he asked.

"Lord Mershayn, as much as I would like to sit around and discuss my beloved, we have much to accomplish and very little time. I am told that you are the man who can do what needs doing."

Mershayn glanced at Silasa.

"That wasn't what I said," Silasa said drily. "I said you were vain, cocky, self-absorbed, thick-headed, and stubborn."

Mershayn looked back at Bands, confused.

"Are you that man?" Bands asked, ignoring Silasa.

"Vain, cocky, and stubborn?" he said. "Yes."

"You came here to be a king," Bands said. "You failed. I can change that, but I need to know if you can be the king Teni'sia needs." She paused. "Can you?"

He hesitated. "Look, I didn't come here to be king. I came to kill Sym because he killed my brother. A tiny band of ragtag guards called me king for a day and a half. I led them. We got slaughtered."

She didn't react.

He rolled his eyes. "You want me to be king again? Sure, I'll be your king. Give me a sword and show me where Sym is, and I'll be your king for as long as it takes."

She narrowed her eyes. "I realize that you have been through an ordeal, but I am not joking with you. I do not make empty threats, and I do not make empty promises. I need you to rule this kingdom. Can you?"

"Teni'sia doesn't need a king. It needs an executioner."

"No, it needs a king."

"Look, I'll be your executioner, but I would make a horrible king. I have done nothing but fail since I got here."

"So Silasa has told me," Bands said.

"Well, there you have it." He waved a hand. "Besides, I'm not even a noble. I can't rule. But if you free me, I'll kill Sym or die trying."

"I don't need a man with a vendetta."

Mershayn slammed his cuffed hand on the stone. "I came here with one purpose: to protect my brother. And he's dead now! I don't do responsibility."

"I see." Her eyes narrowed like she was trying to see through him. "It is a horrible thing, to lose one you love. To know you might have stopped it. Can you get up after such a horrible thing and do what is right?"

"What's *right*?" He snorted. "Let me tell you what's right. If someone pushes you, you push them back. If a weasel kills your brother, you chop its head off. How is that for a kingly code?"

"That's the code of a grieving brother, of a guilt-ridden man seeking absolution. A king thinks of others first. Silasa told me how you thought of your brother first. Before yourself. Before anyone. So you have the ability. The question is: Can you turn that same passion to serve others besides your brother?"

"I doubt it," he said.

"If I made you king and I asked you to spare Sym, could you do that?" she asked.

"Why in the world would I want to do that?"

"For Teni'sia. If the kingdom needed him, could you stay your wrath?"

"No one needs Sym."

"If you are to be king, then *you* will need him." She cocked her head. "Or can you not see that?"

He wanted to rage at her, but he saw what she was saying. If he really was king, he'd be a fool to kill Sym out of hand, before he wrung the little weasel for all the information he could give, before he could assure that all those nobles who followed Sym were brought to Mershayn's side. If the king of Teni'sia killed Grendis Sym, the crown would lose the lords of Buir'tishree out of hand, not to mention at least two of the other noble houses. It would spark a rebellion.

But that wasn't Mershayn's problem. He wasn't king and he could never be king. The nobles would never accept him. There were dozens of purebloods who should take the throne before him, and Sym was at the top of that list. The most Mershayn could do was avenge his brother, then go back to Bendeller and his old life.

"You're in this up to your neck now," Bands said softly, as though reading his mind. "Do you think if you killed Sym, the rest of the nobles would simply allow you to leave? Let you go back to your drinking and wenching?"

He opened his mouth, but couldn't find anything to say.

"You stepped into the flow of power, Mershayn. You're either a king or a traitor now. There is no middle ground. You either go up and take control or you go down, and they kill you. There is no leaving the game."

He sat with that for a long moment, and he realized that his fate had been sealed the moment he came north with Collus to this god-forsaken castle. She was right. There was no way back.

"What if I told you," Bands continued, "that, mere days from now, Teni'sia will be ashes and rubble?"

"What?"

"What if I told you that the only way to prevent this was your ability to unite the kingdom, including making a bridge to Sym?"

"What are you talking about?"

"Dragons from the north, thousands of them, each so powerful that just one of them could level this kingdom."

"Why would..." he trailed off. "Dragons?" he asked incredulously.

"The dragon god wants you dead. All of you. He wants to take Amarion for his own, and he will get what he wants, because that's what happens when you're a god, unless we find a way to stop him. That means that we must do everything possible, take every chance, to beat him. That means you must step up to the throne and lead."

Mershayn glanced at Silasa. "Dragon god? What is she talking about?"

"She's telling you. You should listen," Silasa said.

Mershayn had never believed in the gods any more than he'd believed in dragons. He would concede that they might have once been real. But more likely was that humans had invented the gods to feel better about themselves, to feel like there was some order to the world, to feel like they weren't alone. But there was absolutely no evidence of a human god save his name and some stories about him. Mershayn used Thalius's name to curse or to emphasize a statement just like everyone else, but that was the extent of his religious devotion.

Except now he had seen Silasa throw guards as if they weighed nothing. He'd seen a mythical quicksilver move like a bolt of lightning. He'd been brought back from death by a threadweaver, and he'd witnessed the legendary Wildmane shoot a column of gold fire from his chest.

Suddenly, a dragon god didn't seem so out of bounds.

"I don't believe it," he said.

The smallest curl turned the edges of Bands's mouth. "Yes, you do." She glanced at Silasa. "That's a start, I suppose."

The goddess woman Bands looked back at him, then knelt down in front of him. "You fought a usurper for your brother's life," she said. "Would you fight a god for all the other lives in Amarion?"

He looked around the room. Stavark and Silasa watched him with serious faces.

"You want me," he asked incredulously, "to fight a god?"

"Yes," Bands said.

He didn't speak, and the silence stretched. Despite himself, excitement flooded through him. And hope. Long ago, when Mershayn was a boy, he'd imagined himself leading—a king, shining in his armor, beloved by his subjects. He had been young and foolish, but at this moment when everything else was ludicrous, maybe young and foolish was a perfect fit.

"Okay," he said.

"Okay, what?" Bands pressed, her dragon's eyes glittering.

"I'll be your king," he said.

"Why?" Bands demanded.

He almost said, "because you asked me to," but he stopped. Leaders did not have thrones given to them. They fought for them.

He cleared his throat. "Because I can lead."

"Why?" she persisted.

He stared into those captivating, unearthly eyes, and he understood the trap. A leader didn't convince others he was strong enough to lead. He led. Others followed, and those who followed either believed or they didn't.

"Because you need me. Because your alternative is Sym, and if you think he'd make a better king, then go ahead. You deserve what you'll get."

After a moment, the dragon woman smiled. She turned and gave Silasa a nod. "Okay, I see it now."

Bands gestured and spoke an incomprehensible word. The locks on his manacles creaked open and fell away.

She murmured again, making a small circle with one finger. Three bars of the quicksilver's cage turned to mist, rising up toward the ceiling. She pointed at Mershayn, still murmuring. His body tingled—his face, his arms, his ribs.

He sucked in a breath and fell back against the cold wall. He stared down at himself, miraculously healed once again. He would never get used to that.

Bands let out a slow, tight breath, as though in pain, then she looked at him. "I embrace you, Your Majesty. Embrace the rest of the people in this kingdom. Embrace the people throughout Amarion."

Mershayn stood up.

"Come, Your Majesty," Bands said. "It's past time to set this play in motion. We take the stage an act too late."

Silasa wrinkled her nose and said, "If he's climbing on stage, he'll need a new costume. No one is going to follow that stench."

"Thanks," Mershayn said wryly.

"My pleasure, Your Majesty," Silasa said.

4

GRENDIS SIM

As Grendis Sym lay down for the night in his royal bedchamber, he felt everything was going fairly well. With the help of the spirit, Zilok Morth, Sym had routed the rebels. The bastard was locked away, and the formidable Captain Medophae was gone. Even the feral little silver-haired monster was in a cage.

In addition, this morning he took Lord and Lady Vullieth prisoner as conspirators against the crown. He put Vullieth in a private chamber for questioning, but he'd stripped Ari'cyiane bare and chained her to a column in the throne room for all to see while Sym held court. Anyone in the kingdom who wished to gawk at the bastard's whore could do so. It was an effective deterrent to any other Teni'sians who might have treason in their hearts.

Of course, he'd unchained her when the day was done and chained her up in the bedroom on the other side of these royal chambers. Sym wasn't so cruel as to risk the lady's health on a cold dungeon floor all night in winter, not when she could be a deterrent to possible traitors.

He looked forward to the morning, to the moment when he

told her she was going to spend another day chained naked to that column in the throne room.

Satisfied, he lay back and drifted off to sleep.

THE CLINK of metal awoke him with a start. Cold fear prickled his scalp, and he sat up. He'd told his guards not to disturb him. Sym touched the sword hanging from his bed post, then slid the blade from its jeweled scabbard.

He got up silently. The stones were cool on his bare feet as he moved toward the archway of his room.

There was another clink of metal and whispered voices, and this time he could pinpoint them. The intruders were in Ari'cyiane's room, which was on the far side of the royal sitting room next to his bedchamber. Who dared sneak into the king's own chambers? How had they slipped past his guard? He silently swore that Captain Gael'ek's head would adorn a pike tomorrow.

The sitting room was silent. The shapes of the desk and the two sitting benches seemed undisturbed. He strained his ears to catch even the smallest sound—

Ari'cyiane gave a muffled cry in her room, and someone else whispered to her, telling her it would be all right.

Sym moved into the sitting room quickly, sword raised. The intruder would soon find this blade in his back.

He drew up short. Scant moonlight outlined a tall woman in a sleeveless gown standing by the arched window of the parlor. Somehow, Sym had overlooked her at first glance. She murmured something, and his muscles bunched, freezing up. He remained where he was, fixed to the floor, sword up and unable to move.

The room was nearly full dark, yet he could see the green of her eyes. They glittered like emeralds.

"Leave my chambers this instant!" he demanded.

"You are responsible for the lady in the other room?" the tall woman asked calmly.

"She is a traitor to the crown."

"The punishment for treason is execution," she said. "Why is she bound and naked in your rooms?"

"She required something more creative."

"Humiliation?"

"I demand to know who you are!"

"You are done demanding, I think."

Abruptly, Sym began to move, but not by his own command. He drew a surprised breath as he clomped awkwardly toward Ari'cyiane's room. The tall woman fell in behind him.

The bastard knelt by Ari'cyiane's bed, whispering softly to her. Standing behind him was a frightening woman in a ragged black dress. She looked dead. She had smears of blood on her chin and neck. Her skin was as white as alabaster, her hair as dark as night, and her eyes were filmed over like she was blind. His heart began to race when she moved, turning a hungry gaze on him.

Another figure moved in the shadows, and Sym spied the damned silver-haired boy. This was a nightmare! They were all loose, in his rooms. He struggled against the invisible force, but all he could do was grunt. The quicksilver struck flint on steel and lit a lantern.

"Let me have him," the dead-looking woman said.

"No," the tall woman replied in a calm tone. "We talked about that."

"We didn't talk about *this*." The white-eyed woman pointed at the softly sobbing Ari'cyiane.

"Silasa—"

"I'll use a dagger if it makes you feel better," Silasa said.

"Let Mershayn decide," the tall woman said.

The bastard helped Ari'cyiane sit up, wrapping the blanket around her.

"Stavark, please help her," he said. The boy went to the bed and helped Ari'cyiane to her feet.

The bastard turned to Sym, and orange light played across his dirty, bloodied features. Only a few hours ago, Sym had kicked that face, but it didn't seem swollen or scraped at all. The fury in Mershayn's face made Sym struggle again. The bastard was going to kill him.

Mershayn wore one of Sym's swords belted around his waist,

obviously lifted from the sitting room. He drew it and walked toward Sym, and he braced himself for the sickly punch of steel through his flesh.

"Let him go," Mershayn said.

Suddenly, Sym's limbs obeyed him. He stumbled backward, holding his sword in front of himself, stunned.

"Defend yourself, if you can," Mershayn growled. Sym felt a moment of elation. The bastard was going to give him a "fighting chance" through some skewed sense of honor.

The bastard launched his attack, slashing down. Sparks flew as Sym blocked the swing, and he smiled tightly. Everyone knew the bastard was talented with a blade, but almost no one knew how good Sym was. Unlike the bastard, Sym didn't flaunt his skill. Instead, it was a secret he guarded selfishly. Sym had been trained by the best swordmasters in Teni'sia since he was little. There wasn't a single person in this castle he couldn't best with a blade.

Mershayn roared and attacked again. His sword flicked left and then right. Sym blocked the first, but barely got to the second. It had come at him like a flicking finger, almost too fast to see.

Sym emptied his mind as he had been trained, stepped back, and focused on his technique. Mershayn attacked again, and Sym parried, then parried again. He readied to attack, then had to parry again. Sym pivoted, trying to gain room, but Mershayn followed, slashing, thrusting. Sym parried, blocked, parried again. He tried to stab back, but the man never let up. Sym tried a stop thrust, and Mershayn leaned to the side like a tree in the wind, dodging the strike, then slashed Sym's forearm. Sym hissed.

Mershayn watched him with glittering eyes. He swung overhead. Sym blocked, but the blow numbed his entire arm. He felt the vibration in his teeth. With a grunt, he switched hands and made a desperate attack.

Mershayn switched hands and parried. He cut Sym on that forearm, a perfect match to the first slice. Sym gasped, almost dropping the blade.

Mershayn swung overhead again. Another crashing blow. Sym rocked under it, suddenly realizing with cold horror that Mershayn was playing with him. The bastard knew a blade like a hawk knew the wind. Mershayn wasn't just a master of the sword, he was an artist.

Sym's heel hit the wall. He had been pushed back across the entire sitting room without realizing it. It distracted him, and Mershayn poked his wrist. Sym cried out, and his sword clattered to the ground.

Mershayn shouted in rage and smashed the flat of his blade into Sym's cheek. Sym crumpled. His vision swam, then he felt the sharp steel tickle his throat.

Mershayn stepped on Sym's stomach, reducing his breaths to short little gasps. Mershayn's lips twitched over his teeth as he breathed heavily.

Sym held still, watching the fury play across the bastard's face. Sym knew if he moved, if he even whimpered, he was a dead man. He waited in anguish as his heart beat painfully.

Finally, Mershayn removed the blade from Sym's throat.

Silasa snarled, but Mershayn ignored her and looked at the tall woman. She watched him calmly; Sym couldn't read anything on her face.

"The kingdom is in chaos," Mershayn said, breathing hard. "A king has already been slain. Nobles have died. Adding another to the pile isn't going to help."

The tall, regal woman nodded.

"So you're going to live," he said to Sym in a low voice. "And you're going to do your part. And you will serve me as your king."

Sym reeled with how quickly the fight was over... It was already over! He'd been utterly outclassed. He had heard of Mershayn's prowess with a sword, of course, had even see him practice once or twice, but Sym couldn't possibly have known the man's true ability. And his fury... Sym had never experienced anything like it. After all he'd done to Mershayn, the bastard should have killed him. But he hadn't. Sym was still alive. That meant there was a chance to come back from this place, to take this foolish kindness and use it.

As a rule, Sym did not underestimate people, and tonight he had. He had not expected Mershayn's overwhelming skill. Sym would never make that same mistake with Mershayn again. The next time Sym had Mershayn helpless, he would gut the bastard.

"Of course…Your Majesty," Sym said, panting. He fell back on his ingrained social graces. Speak in a calm voice, and people calm down. Tell them what they want to hear, and they trust you.

Mershayn's lip curled, and his hand gripped the sword tighter. He cleared his throat.

"You're leaving a snake at your breast." Silasa shook her head. "He will kill you if he can."

"Then let's find out who is more clever." Mershayn crouched, getting closer to Sym. "If you can kill me, you win," he said. His voice dropped to a sibilant whisper. "But if you try, and you fail, then I'm going to give you to Silasa."

Sym looked at the bloodied woman. She smiled, her lips peeling back to reveal long fangs.

"Yes, Your Majesty," Sym said. Tell them what they want to hear. At this moment, Sym couldn't imagine what he needed to kill each of the people in this room, but the answer was out there. Given enough time, Sym was going to find it.

Mershayn turned his back on Sym. Sym considered snatching up his sword and stabbing it into the bastard right then and there. His humiliation was large enough that it might almost be worth his life, but he glanced at Silasa. Her white gaze held him like she was a cat and he the mouse, promising all the horrors of dismemberment and bloodletting indicated by her grisly chin and neck. All she needed was for him to dash into the open, and she would pounce. She wanted him to do it. Sym licked dry lips and did nothing.

"Silasa," Mershayn said. "I charge you with watching this man. If he tries to escape, if he schemes, if he so much as calls me a bad name to another noble, eat one of his fingers."

The dead-looking woman raised an eyebrow and looked at Mershayn.

"He is to have no contact with his previous advisors," Mershayn continued. "I want him isolated except when we need him to communicate. Bands, I want you to find his inner circle and round them up. Silasa, you'll be in charge of getting that list from Sym. They'll replace anyone Sym has put in the dungeons. Be creative if you need to."

"It shall be done, Your Majesty," Bands said.

"It's going to be hard to be near him and not want to drain him," Silasa said.

"Rise to the occasion," Mershayn said. He took a deep breath, then faced Sym again. "We may need each other before this is all done, Lord Sym. And that need may be more important than our desire to kill each other."

Bands put an arm around Ari'cyiane and led her from Sym's chambers. Sym watched Lady Vullieth leave, and it seemed to represent his absolute failure. But Sym had failed before. Life presented opportunities when you least expected it. All he had to do was stay alive long enough to find those opportunities.

He swore to himself that, once he turned the tables, he wouldn't make the mistake of mercy. Not for the bastard or any of his monsters. They would die so they could never threaten him again.

Silasa smiled at Sym, revealing those hideous fangs. "You," she beckoned with one long, white finger. "Come with me."

"Of course, my lady. I am at your disposal." He kept his voice smooth. He kept his tone mild.

Let them know I am beaten. Let them think they have the power. And I will wait....

5

MERSHAYN

WITH THE LIST Silasa procured from Sym as well as an incredibly intuitive list of her own, Bands rooted out Sym's most loyal allies on the first day.

The next day caused Mershayn's head to swim. It only took him a few hours to realize he had been better off as a neglected bastard than as a king. Kingship was a complicated, responsibility-laden, thankless job. No one seemed happy with his decisions, not the ones who supported him nor the ones who seemed to hate him. Those who had sided with Sym wanted to oust Mershayn. The nobles arrayed against Sym didn't want a bastard on the throne. Lord Vullieth, the one noble who might have supported Mershayn openly, was absent, recovering from wounds he had received at the hands of Sym's torturers.

Mershayn called upon Sym as often as he could manage. Silasa could not guard the weasel during the day, so Sym and Mershayn went everywhere together. Mershayn would have loved to spend his time seeking pleasure in the arms of a willing lass, but he was stuck with the one person he hated the most.

Every time Mershayn looked at Sym, his blood boiled, but he suppressed it. Instead, Mershayn made certain that Sym stayed useful and, strangely, Sym seemed willing to cooperate. He seemed to sense—and rightly so—that he was only half a step away from a swift execution. The useful part was that Sym seemed to know everything about the kingdom, and Mershayn developed a grudging respect for his knowledge. Collus had not been half so informed as Sym.

Sym tried to misdirect Mershayn once, but Bands caught him. Mershayn had asked about the origins of each group within Teni'sia's guard, and Sym had lied about a secret group of Buir'tishree loyalists—the group that had attacked and captured Ari'cyiane. The lie would have slipped right past Mershayn, and those loyalists would have continued operating within the castle, conspirators waiting for Sym to call upon them.

When Sym finished giving his report, Bands looked at him with those beautiful, catlike green eyes of hers and said, "This is your only warning, Lord Sym. Lie again, and I will inform Silasa."

Sym went deathly pale. He cleared his throat and painfully related the truth about his followers within the castle.

Mershayn had no idea how Bands could know Sym was lying. It indicated that maybe she could read people's minds. While that spooked Mershayn, it scared Sym to his core. Up until that point, despite his captivity, the Lord of Buir'tishree had carried himself with a kind of muted self-assurance. Perhaps Sym thought that, with just a little time, he could turn the tables on Mershayn. But having someone like Bands at his side—someone who might see every scheming thought in Sym's head—caused Sym to wilt.

In addition, on that first day, Bands caught a larger fish: Lord Baerst. Mershayn had always thought Lord Baerst a stern and humorless man, but one who despised Sym and kept his passions under tight rein. Bands discovered that it had all been a facade to keep the other nobles off balance and to win confidences among Sym's opponents.

Bands recommended immediately that Mershayn send Lord Baerst and his closest retainers, along with a contingent carefully chosen by Bands, north to Corialis Port as an advance lookout for anything strange. She didn't tell Baerst that he was looking for dragons, but any evidence of them would surely bring Baerst hurrying back to report.

After Baerst's exile, the name, "The Bastard King," began circulating throughout the kingdom. Though the moniker had obviously been started by the nobles who were Sym's supporters, according to Bands, the nickname was said with a great deal of affection in the lower quarters of the city, and that encouraged him. He wasn't doing this for the nobles, after all. Let them jump into the True Ocean, for all he cared. He was doing this for the people of Teni'sia. Bands's words made him feel better.

She was like that. When she told Mershayn something, he wanted to believe, and her words left him feeling larger than he had before. When she stood near him, he felt confident. He could not have held the reins of the kingdom, even a day, if not for her. Nobles blushed or quailed under her gaze. She rarely spoke, but when she did, her words were the right words, her tone took control of the room, and the conversation inevitably turned in Mershayn's favor. He took mental notes about how she commanded respect and tried to emulate her.

Never say three sentences when one would work. Stay calm, no matter the flurry of emotion coming at you. When you give a command, make it sound like it is the *only* answer.

He wasn't very good at it yet, but he tried.

And Silasa was a force of nature. She showed up each night just after sundown to take Sym, giving Mershayn his respite from the man's odious company. She, too, was a pillar for Mershayn to lean upon. Each time Silasa appeared in his rooms, he knew he had survived another day.

Petitioners came with demands. They came with advice. They came with questions. Mershayn denied, agreed, or supplied answers, as the occasion warranted.

He thought often of Collus. Mostly, he thought of his brother as a reminder of what *not* to do as king. Still, Mershayn wished Collus was here. These strange, supernatural creatures who supported him were indispensable. They stopped problems before the problems even arose. They seemed to know what Sym's allies would do before they knew. In two days, they had completely confounded the nobles opposing Mershayn and moved to put strong supporters in positions of power. Bands seemed to be calmly checking items off a list, as though she had overthrown a dozen kingdoms before.

But he couldn't tip a beer with any of them. And he certainly wasn't going to ask them to carouse along the wharf and flirt with willing wenches.

He missed Collus fiercely—the history of common experiences, the camaraderie of someone who actually liked him. Neither Silasa's unfaltering loyalty nor Bands's calm wisdom could replace that.

On the third day of Mershayn's reign, Captain Lo'gan and his band of guards resurfaced. Mershayn breathed a sigh of relief. Lo'gan had been willing to trade his life for Collus's, as had Deni'tri. And they were flesh-and-blood mortal humans. Their mere presence made his rule more normal, and Mershayn began to relax a little. Lo'gan was reinstated as Captain of the Royal Guard. Guards with questionable loyalty were bucked down to menial work.

Mershayn barely slept those first four days, but by the end of them, Teni'sia had a workable monarchy in place. The wagon was bumpy, but the wheels were actually turning.

That evening, Mershayn walked into the royal sitting room with a spring in his step.

"You don't seem very talkative tonight," Mershayn said to Sym, who sat at the empty table as usual. Mershayn had removed all of Sym's belongings from the royal rooms and moved in. He didn't want to stay where Sym had once lived, but Bands told him appearances were important. If he was to be king, he must live where the king lived.

"What would you like me to say?" Sym asked laconically.

The last sliver of the sun slipped below the horizon outside the arched window. Mershayn looked at the beautiful sunset over the Inland Ocean. A dolphin surfaced near a jagged promontory of rock on the calmer side of the bay. Its shiny skin reflected the orange light for one moment, and then it was lost amongst the sparkling waves.

Mershayn smiled into the sea breeze. "You spoke a great deal in the beginning," he said.

"That's when I thought I was an advisor."

"You are an advisor. A damned useful one."

"I am a slave."

"Are you upset because we uprooted your greedy little fingers from the workings of the kingdom? Or is it that..." Mershayn paused for effect, "the kingdom is still working without you? That must sting. It's almost as if Teni'sia doesn't need you in charge."

Sym tried to mask his sullen look.

Mershayn was feeling particularly jaunty because Lo'gan had also installed a proper nighttime guard for Sym, which freed Silasa for other work. A knock sounded at the door. The guard standing behind Sym glanced up, but did not move from his post. The man's job was to ensure that Sym didn't stick a knife or a sharp stick into Mershayn's back when it was turned. Mershayn always had a guard when he was with Sym. The more frustrated Sym became, the more likely he'd try something desperate.

Deni'tri spoke through the door. "Your Majesty, Silasa is here."

"Good," he said.

Deni'tri opened the door, and Silasa entered. He'd survived another day as king.

She wore a dark burgundy dress, old of fashion as was her habit. Ladies' fashion these days did not have lace, but Silasa preferred such dresses. The more lace at the cuffs or sown into the hem, the more she liked it. He wondered where on earth she'd found it.

Deni'tri motioned to Sym and escorted him out, closing the door behind her.

"Have you slept?" Silasa asked. That was always her first question.

"I spent a leisurely moment looking at the ocean. It was absolutely decadent."

"Did you sleep?"

"I had a nap."

"You lie. Bands says you did not."

"Then why ask?"

"To see if you would lie."

He waved a hand and turned away from the window. "I'm not tired."

"You look tired."

"And you look sixteen." During one of their chats, she had told him that she had been a sixteen-year-old princess in Belshra before she'd been turned into a vampire.

Silasa wasn't amused by that, though Mershayn thought it was terribly clever. He sat down in the nearest chair and put his feet up on the table. "See?" he said. "I'm relaxing."

"Relaxing is not sleeping."

"There is much to do." He pointed at the stack of papers on his desk, a number of mundane decisions and decrees that needed making. Bands had suggested finding others who could review such paperwork, but he'd declined. He wanted to know everything that was happening in the kingdom before he delegated it.

"There will always be much to do," she said. "That is part of being king. If you let it, it will eat you alive."

"Eat me alive? You should show your fangs when you say such things. It heightens the tension."

"You're not funny." She frowned.

"I'm actually very funny. You just have to have a sense of humor to get the jokes."

"They say that Queen Tyndiria went to bed every night exactly two hours after sunset," Silasa said.

"She had a gorgeous demigod waiting between the sheets. Who wouldn't?"

"Still not funny."

"Try smiling first. It leads to laughing, they say."

"Hmmm. Perhaps I *am* more serious than most. It comes from drinking blood, I imagine. You know what else comes from drinking blood?"

"Red lips?"

"My victims go to sleep. It happens almost immediately. So you see, there are other ways to put you to bed."

"Are you flirting with me?"

This time, she did crack a smile. "You are a stubborn ass."

"And then some." He paused. "Has there been any word of Medophae?" Mershayn changed the subject.

She shook her head. "Bands has searched with her threadweaver's sight. Medophae is not anywhere near Teni'sia. She promises as soon as you are thriving as king, she will go looking for him."

"Thriving as king," he repeated. "See, *that's* funny. At least Bands has a sense of humor."

She frowned. "One benefit to a missing Medophae is that Zilok is also missing."

"It's hard to imagine Zilok Morth besting Bands. That woman exudes power. You say she's also a threadweaver. Could she not simply do away with him?"

"Perhaps you were not paying attention when you met Zilok Morth."

Mershayn recalled the horrible weight on his mind, clenching his brain like a hand. "As you say." He suppressed a shiver, and let out a breath. "Well, this light-hearted conversation is enough to make me slit my wrists. If I was not tired before, I am exhausted now."

"Then perhaps my presence has rendered some small benefit." She paused. "Now, do I bite you, or will you allow me to take you to your room?"

"Only if you carry me like in the old days."

"Perhaps it *would* be better if Sym were on the throne," she murmured under her breath.

Mershayn walked around the table and put a hand on her shoulder. As always, he forced himself not to recoil at the coldness of her skin, at the...revulsion that touching her sent through him. "To bed I go. Are you to see me to the threshold?"

"Yes."

"Did Lady Bands give you orders to knock me unconscious?"

"She told me to be creative if I needed to be."

"I tell you what," Mershayn said. "Let's pretend I'm not the king. Let's pretend I am the once carefree bastard of Bendeller. Let's pretend you are a Belshran princess who has come to me for the sole purpose of sating her lust."

Her pale lips curved upward at the corners.

A second smile! Mershayn considered that a win.

"To bed, Your Majesty," Silasa said, and the smile vanished.

"I love it when you're forceful—"

A knock sounded at the door. Silasa's brow wrinkled in annoyance.

"It would be rude not to answer," Mershayn said, slipping gracefully past her and opening the door. He stopped, stunned.

Lady Ari'cyiane stood in the hallway, her blue eyes glinting like ice.

"I would have a word with you, Your Majesty," she said.

6

MERSHAYN

MERSHAYN HAD AVOIDED Ari'cyiane this past week, and the last place he'd expected to see her was at sundown in his rooms. He hesitated, then opened the door wide for her.

"My lady," he said, bowing and standing to the side.

She entered the room, dressed as if for court in a light blue gown strung with pearls. A white shawl covered her shoulders, a creamy cloud against the blue dress, her stylish concession to the chill weather. Two locks of her strawberry blond hair had been braided and pulled back from her temples to hold back her artful mass of curls in a kind of crown. She appeared recovered from her ordeal, at least physically. The color was back in her cheeks, and she was as lovely as ever. She stood, poised, but her eyes flashed with something feral.

Silasa stepped back silently, arms at her sides, her white eyes watching impassively.

"You can go, Silasa," Mershayn said. "Lady Vullieth and I should...speak alone."

Silasa gaze flicked over Ari'cyiane, and the vampire didn't move.

"Your Majesty, she has a knife."

Mershayn was surprised by that, but he tried to keep the surprise from his face. He looked where Silasa was looking, but couldn't see the knife. How did Silasa know?

"I'm not in danger of assassination from Ari'cyiane," he said.

Ari'cyiane's gaze smoldered, and she didn't confirm Mershayn's words.

"I would rather stay, Your Majesty," Silasa pressed.

Mershayn held the door open for her.

Silasa glanced at Ari'cyiane once more, then left. Mershayn closed the door.

With everything swimming in his head, Ari'cyiane was the one person he had not thought about over the past few days. He had done the right thing with Sym, but Mershayn felt he had betrayed her by not killing the Lord of Buir'tishree. One look at her told him she felt the same. He held her gaze without speaking, waiting. He knew that whatever words he might use would be the wrong words.

She finally broke the silence. "I waited for you to come see me."

"I apologize, my lady," he said. There were days in this last week when he had dreamed about losing himself in her arms as he once had. But everything had changed now. He was not the same and neither was she. "There have been more demands on my time than I could have imagined. I would have come if I could."

"You didn't want to see me. I understand."

"How is Lord Vullieth?" He turned the conversation.

"He mends," she said as though they were just talking about the weather. "He will fully recover in time. It was only his body they broke."

"I am glad to hear it."

"Lar'eth is a good man. He is..." Her voice caught in her throat, and she stopped speaking. After a pause, she continued as though nothing happened. "Despite all he knows about what went on between us, he supports you as king."

"I am gladder still to hear that."

She glared at him.

"What happened with you...in the throne room..." He could

51

find no delicate way to ask the question. "He knows?"

"Of course he knows, Mershayn. Everyone in the kingdom knows. Every single person who wanted to see me naked and helpless needed only attend Sym's court."

He bowed his head.

"It was all I could do to convince Lar'eth not to challenge Sym," she continued. "Even healthy, Lar'eth wouldn't last a minute against Sym. That snake is one of the best swordsmen in the city."

"Yes," Mershayn said, his heart thundering.

"But he's not better than you." The accusation was deadly soft. Her nostrils flared, and he felt her contempt. "Why didn't you kill him, Mershayn?"

"Ari'cyiane..."

"No one would blame you. The court would applaud you. I would have sung your praises. Instead..." Her voice caught, and she stopped speaking again. She held his gaze, tears in her eyes as she waited for her voice to steady. "Instead, I find myself wondering if I ever really knew you. Where is the passionate man who would give his life for what he loves?"

"There are more important things than my desire just now. I have to rule—"

"He killed your brother. He..." Her face reddened, and this time, she pushed through the catch in her throat and whispered, "He *humiliated* me, Mershayn. He chained me like an animal, ripped the clothes from my body, and you..." She let out a sob, then turned her head away. She put a hand against the window sill.

Mershayn gently put his arms on her shoulders—

She spun, clawing his face. A stinging pain fired into his cheek, and her nails came away with blood. He staggered back.

"Don't touch me!" she said. "I do not crave your pity or your hands on me. There is only one thing you can do for me."

"Ari'cyiane—"

"Kill him."

"I cannot."

"You are king." Her voice was as unbending as iron. "You can."

He swallowed hard. "Then...I will not."

"I despise you," she hissed.

He felt a trickle of blood slide down his jaw. He was overwhelmed, struggling to succeed in this impossible role he'd been given, saddled with the knowledge of a dragon invasion. He craved her approval. He wanted her love. He wanted it to be easy again, to casually lay in her bed as they whispered to each other, full of their own passion and cleverness.

Ari'cyiane had loved him when he was only a wry bastard. She'd loved him *because* of it. And he had lost her forever.

The irony of the situation hurt, because if he was in her place, he would feel exactly as she did. He would demand justice.

"I do not expect you to understand," he said.

Her lips pressed into a hard line. "Do not expect anything else of me, either. Sym is a traitor and a murderer. Do you know what a real king would call that? A criminal. Criminals must be punished."

"He is being punished. Justice must be—"

"Your justice is a sham. If a fisherman murdered another man, you would execute that fisherman. But you fear what others of the Buir'tishree line will do to you if you kill Sym. You fear for your own position." She shook her head. "I believed you were brave, Mershayn. And at this test of tests, I see now that you are a coward."

A dot of blood fell on the flagstones between them.

"I must have all the nobles behind me, even the Buir'tishree line," he said hoarsely. "Do you think I could manage that if I killed their lord?"

"Sym will never be your ally," she hissed, and now he saw the dagger clenched in her trembling fist. "He will scheme. He will plot, and when your back is turned, he will stick a knife in it. Sparing him has not made him love you. It only makes you weak!"

He wondered if he would stop her if she chose to plunge that dagger into his chest, or if he just would let it happen.

She flung the dagger to the floor at his feet. It clanged against the stone and spun past his foot.

She strode to the door and flung it open, but she stopped. Her profile was outlined by the lamplight in the hall. "Think over this decision well, *Your Majesty*. You will have no friend in me until Sym is dead."

She slammed the door.
He let out his breath, then raised his hand to touch his cheek.
Blood and tears.
All hail the king.

7

MEDOPHAE

MEDOPHAE BLINKED.

Mirolah...

The conflagration in the throne room rushed back to him. Zilok had killed her. He had taken Stavark's mind and made the quicksilver stab Mirolah over and over. Medophae had flown into a rage, and Oedandus exploded within him. He'd shot golden fire at Zilok, then suddenly black fire had mixed with the gold... And then there was only pain.

Somehow, Zilok had turned the tables on him, using that crown artifact to turn Medophae's attack back on him.

He wanted to rise and slash about himself, raging at yet another failure, at yet another loved one lost. But if he knew Zilok Morth, the vengeful spirit would be close by. He would linger to gloat. Medophae might be alive, but the fight wasn't over.

Cautiously, he opened his eyes.

The blurry room came into view, dark and gray. Moonlight shone in through the windows on either side of him. The air was warm, and there was no snowstorm. This wasn't Teni'sia. Zilok had transported him elsewhere.

He was in a hut with a flagstone floor. The walls were clean and made of what looked like slender trees. The logs were blond in color, hollowed out in the center, and vertical. There was a cot in the corner, a well-crafted wooden frame with a mesh of fine fabric strung across it. Above it hung two waterskins and a cloak with a fur collar. On the opposite wall was an iron stove. One pot and one pan hung on the wall above it. There was also a waist-high, square basin built into the wall across from him, with mortared tile. A groove for draining water trailed from the basin to the edge of the door and underneath—a waterbox. It was for keeping fresh water inside the house, for cooking and drinking and washing inside the room. It was fed by a natural spring that had been diverted to feed clean water to this hut. But people on Amarion didn't use those. The only place Medophae had ever seen waterboxes was on his home island of Dandere.

He rolled over onto his side, and the pain of it made him gasp. His muscles were feeble, mortal. Oedandus was gone. His mind was quiet, his god's dark voice gone. There was no unearthly fire raging in his belly. For fourteen hundred years, he'd been practically invulnerable. Now, in less than a month, he'd been stripped of Oedandus twice.

He sat up, and his skin prickled as he sensed another in the room. He looked behind himself.

Zilok sat in a chair in a corner of the room. He wore the black clothes he had preferred in life: a blousy black shirt beneath a black vest, black breeches, and black leather boots. His blue eyes glowed. On his head rested that enormous crown adorned with spikes of uneven crystals that he'd worn in the Teni'sian throne room. The crystals were quiescent now, but Zilok's smile was assured.

Medophae sat up, crossed his legs as though preparing for a civilized conversation, and straightened his back. He tried to cover his stiffness and pain. He was thirsty and hungry, and he wondered how long he'd been unconscious.

"I thought you were going to kill me," he said.

Zilok studied Medophae with those unnaturally blue eyes. In reality, the only substance the spirit really had was those blue eyes.

His real form, so far as Medophae could tell, was just a pair of floating blue fires the size of eyeballs. He conjured the body, Medophae supposed, because it made him feel more real. The illusion was convincing, but just one look at those glowing blue eyes, and anyone could tell they were in the presence of a supernatural creature.

"I was going to kill you," Zilok said with that cultured accent his parents had drummed into him when he was alive.

Medophae reached deep inside himself, tried to feel Oedandus. If this was the same spell Zilok had cast on Medophae before, then Oedandus was still around, somewhere, but Zilok had created a barrier between Medophae and his god. Barriers could be broken. If Medophae could find it, bash through it, maybe he could even the odds of this confrontation.

But he couldn't find anything. Everything in his body felt staggeringly normal.

"The idea of slaying you while you slept didn't appeal," Zilok continued. "I want you looking at me when you die, just as I looked at you when you killed me."

"I'm looking at you now," Medophae said.

"Are you in such a rush to die?"

"Being near you makes me ill," Medophae said.

"Charming, as ever," Zilok said. "I think you're searching inside yourself, looking for Oedandus. I think you're wondering how I did it. How I took him away from you a second time."

Zilok always could read him. They had been best friends for so long, back when Medophae was young, back when Medophae's soul was fresh, and having a best friend meant everything. How sour it had turned in the end. Medophae had found his calling, and Zilok became more and more twisted until finally, he had become this aberration, this thing bent on manipulation and death.

Zilok shook his head. "You won't figure it out. You're a twig floating on the ocean. You have no concept of why the waves move or how. You never have because you never cared enough to know."

"It's laughable, you talking about caring."

"I won't make you strain your mind." Zilok ignored the insult.

"You're on Dandere, where you were born."

So the construction of this hut wasn't a coincidence. There would be many huts like this on Dandere, and it explained why Medophae couldn't feel any barrier between him and his god.

Zilok hadn't ripped Oedandus away from Medophae; he'd ripped Medophae away from Oedandus.

Oedandus's power didn't extend past the continent of Amarion. It was part of how he'd been nearly destroyed. Long ago, Oedandus had been ambushed by three other gods. He'd been defeated, and his life force had been stretched thinly across the continent of Amarion, reducing his sentience to an animalistic level and nearly ending him. The only way he could form even rudimentary thoughts and feelings was to push his life force into a living creature with Oedandus's own blood: Medophae. Medophae became a lightning rod for the god's power, and Oedandus filled him up. It made Medophae almost impervious to the workings of threadweavers, but Zilok's new crown had somehow circumvented that invulnerability.

Medophae's mind whirled with questions. "So now I'm on your little prison island," he said.

"My island?" Zilok said. "You're home. You should thank me."

"I should have killed you."

"You did," Zilok said with icy calm.

Medophae paused. This was going to end in his death. There was no point in dancing around it. Zilok finally had Medophae at his mercy. Medophae had to think, to figure out a way around the inevitable.

Medophae shook his head. "You could have been remembered as a great man, Zilok. Chapters in history books would have been written about you and all the good you did for humankind. But instead, you chose to become...this." He gestured at Zilok's illusory body.

The blue fire in Zilok's eyes flickered, and he was silent for a moment before answering. "Remembered in history books? Like you, you mean? Those so-called histories are stories. They're sweet, gossamer lies, told by puffed-up dullards. These *histories* linger because they are cherished by those who have no interest in truth, only in what they wish to see. You were beautiful and immortal, on the arm of a beautiful and immortal woman. You were what they *wanted* to see, so when you murdered, they wrote their stories and called you a hero. When I murdered, they called me a monster."

"I didn't murder."

"Your body count speaks otherwise."

"We are not the same—"

"No. We are not. I am honest. You are a deluded child who bumbles about, defecating on those he pretends to care about."

Medophae raised his chin.

"Tyndiria... Mirolah..." Zilok continued. "Bands... Seldon Tyflor... Vlacar..."

Medophae's fists tightened. But his anger was impotent, and Zilok knew it. What was Medophae going to do? Knock the crown off Zilok's head? Swing through his insubstantial body? The only weapon Medophae had ever possessed against Zilok was the power of Oedandus.

"Shall I continue? There are so many others. Malacye Gorros... Vitrio... Cuinn... You brought them all into danger," Zilok said. "You brought them under the knife, and then you walked away. Shall I go on?"

"Talk until you're blue for all I care."

"How about Zilok...? How about that one?"

"Your death wasn't an accident."

Zilok went silent, and he was completely still except for those glowing eyes, which flickered now like they were on fire within.

"I've been thinking about killing you for more than a day now," Zilok said. "Just waiting here, watching you sleep, thinking about it."

"You've taken all the people I loved...." Medophae choked on the words. "Why not just end it? You can. I can't fight you."

"I..." Zilok leaned his head forward, eyes glowing, "...took from you?"

"Mirolah did nothing to you. Tyndiria only wanted what was best for her people. And you tore them apart to hurt me." He put his arms out to his sides as though Zilok had an arrow trained on his chest. "Finish what you started. There are no innocents to block your way now. No gods. Do it."

"I...took from you?" Zilok repeated, his voice vibrating with incredulity. "I loved you like a brother. I followed you into a chasm of nightmare to do the impossible. I saved your life. It was because of me that you could kill Dervon the Diseased. I gave you *everything*."

"Don't recount our history like I wasn't there. You broke my heart when you turned evil. You enslaved an entire kingdom. How much did I beg you to stop? To turn from that path? How much did I—"

"You *abandoned* me!" Zilok said. "You gained your god's powers, your hero's status. You stood on the corpses of Vitrio and Cuinn. You stood on the shoulders of Bands and Saraphazia. You stood on *my* shoulders, accepting the accolades of an entire generation, and then you left us all behind without a backward glance. All save *her*. You went gallivanting around the countryside on the back of your dragon lover, imposing your brand of butchery and calling it justice." Zilok shook his head. "And everyone *loved* you...."

"That's not how it was."

"Tell me again the story of the Deitrus Shelf."

It was as though Zilok had punched him in the stomach. Uncounted hundreds had died at the Deitrus Shelf, all because Medophae lost Oedandus's temper. Both the army that Medophae had come with and the army they'd come to fight had all been buried under an avalanche that Medophae had accidentally started. "That was an accident. That—"

"More 'accidents', more sweet lies."

"I lost control! I would never do that on purpose. Not like you. You've murdered innocents with cold calculation." He didn't know why he was arguing with Zilok. This creature was insane; he'd lost his sanity centuries ago.

"Are you saying, then, that you're not responsible? That you flung your giant's fist about, smashing, destroying, and that it's not your fault?" Zilok's voice dropped to a whisper. "Oh, you cried every time you killed an innocent. I know you did. But then you got back up, and you did it again. And then, four hundred and thirty-seven years ago, your arrogance finally felled someone you *do* care about: Bands. Only then did you feel the horror of what you are. Only for *her*..." Zilok shook his head. "It's time to stop believing the minstrels' breathy tales, Medophae. You're a false hero. You're a murderer."

The words slashed at old scars. This was how Zilok tormented his victims, by twisting their minds.

"You're a foul beast from beyond the grave," Medophae growled. "You wear the face of someone who was once my friend, but you're an abomination. I won't listen to your acid accusations."

Zilok laughed. "Acid. I like that. The words do burn, don't they? But it's not acid you feel. It's truth. That's what sizzles in your heart."

"Then why am I sitting here still?" Medophae asked. "A threadweaver with half your power would have peeled and cored me by now. What are you waiting for?"

Zilok nodded. "It's a good question. I've been pondering it, but now I think I know."

Medophae waited for the inevitable strike.

Zilok watched Medophae. Finally, Zilok said, "I loved you, Medophae Roloiron. I want you to know that before I pass my judgment on you. I loved you more than my parents. You were the brother of my soul. You were *my* hero. I wanted to walk the world by your side, help you accomplish great things. I drove myself to exhaustion learning threadweaving so I could be worthy to work with you, at your mighty level. I married Kondra de'Lar because it gave me what you had with Bands, or at least I thought it would. I would have died for you, and you abandoned me. You took your immortality and your dragon and you left me behind like an autumn leaf fluttering to the ground, spent. And when I chose the course of my life without you, when *my* power rose, did you return to congratulate me? Did you clap me on the back like a brother should and tell me my kingdom had been hard won? No. You passed your righteous judgment, and you stabbed that crackling sword through my guts."

"You had gone too far," Medophae said. "You...slaughtered hundreds, just to install yourself as king of Ostern. It was horrible."

"It was war. Do you know how many men King Harrelith's grandfather slew to make Ostern his kingdom before me?"

"I would have stopped him, had I been there," Medophae said. "It doesn't make it right for you to do the same."

"I was your friend," Zilok said. "*That's* what matters. That's what should have mattered."

"You don't just get to kill those in your way."

"Like you do?" He shook his head then, holding up a hand as Medophae prepared to reply. "I have decided what to do with you. I'm going to abandon you like you abandoned me."

Medophae was barely able to comprehend what he was hearing. It was like facing a volley of arrows that had thunked into the ground at his feet. "You're just going to leave me here?"

"I believed you were a hero, Medophae, but you're not. You're ordinary. There is nothing special about you except the accident of your birth. On Amarion, you were the great Wildmane. But I want you to end your days as you should have been. I want you to dig ditches for your food, convince others to take care of you without your glamour. I want you to grow old, and wrinkle, and then I want you to die. I want you to feel the vigor slip from your body."

Medophae felt a sliver of hope then. Was Zilok just going to leave him here?

Zilok made a curious face then, and he looked down at his right foot. It was slowly disappearing, as if the boot had been formed of mist that was evaporating. Medophae couldn't remember a time that Zilok's illusion had ever done that.

Zilok paused, perhaps concentrating on making his foot return. It didn't. He frowned, then the expression vanished, and he focused on Medophae.

"Here is my parting gift for you, a memory of our friendship." He gestured, and an invisible blade chopped through Medophae's wrist.

He screamed as his right hand spun away, thumping onto the flagstone floor. Blood spurted from the stump. He sucked in a breath, doubled over, and tried not to scream a second time, but it came out as a muffled whimper. He pushed the stump against his armpit, trying to stop the blood.

"Even as a mortal, you're an excellent swordsman," Zilok said. "I don't want you earning your living from your centuries of unfair experience. I want you to start over. I want you to start with less than nothing, just like you left me." Zilok stood on one good leg and one leg that had faded even further. "I would say farewell, but instead I will say: Fare poorly, Medophae. Spin in a cesspool of your own mediocrity. I'll return in fifty years to see what has become of you. Until then, for the first time in a millennium and a half, I plan not to think on you at all."

Zilok Morth vanished, leaving Medophae bleeding.

8

MEDOPHAE

MEDOPHAE WASN'T a stranger to death. He'd seen hundreds of men and women fall in battle, too many to count. He knew pain. He knew wounds. The cut was clean and razor sharp. No blunt trauma, no cauterizing fire to stanch the wound. There was nothing to stop his life from leaking away in a matter of seconds.

He took his wrist away from his armpit and yanked his tunic roughly off his head. More of his life drained onto the floor. He put the now-bloody tunic into his teeth at the seam and ripped it, yanking a strip away from it. It was long, misshapen, but it would have to do. He didn't have time to make a perfect cord.

Quickly, he twisted the cloth into a makeshift rope, wrapped it around his wrist and cinched it tight, creating a tourniquet. The blood flow slackened to a drip, and he bound his wrist with the rest of his tunic.

His vision swam, and he was already beginning to feel cold. That was a bad sign. Many warriors who died of blood loss talked about how cold they felt just before the end.

He staggered to his feet, pressing his poorly bandaged hand

against his side to keep the pressure on it, and stumbled to the door. He needed to find help. If he passed out, he was done for, and sparkles already appeared at the edges of his vision. If he couldn't stay awake, it would be the end of him.

The door opened to lush trees and a path directly ahead, leading down to the black ocean, sparkling with moonlight. The boughs of the trees formed a dark canopy overhead. He lurched down the steps and down the snaking path. His vision became like a tunnel. It was so cold, and he was having a hard time feeling his legs now. Five steps. Five more...

He emerged from the trees onto a beach. He blinked at a campfire not too far away, burning low against the waterline. Three figures huddled around it, and a fourth stood ankle-deep in the water a short distance away.

"Who goes there?" The sarcastic voice came from beside him. Medophae whirled to see a man standing at the edge of the trees. Medophae must have staggered right past him without noticing. The man had short hair that pushed up in ten different directions—like he'd slept on it and had just awoken—and a patchy black beard. He wore sailor's clothes—brown pantaloons and a dirty white tunic open at the front. He pointed a short sword at Medophae's chest.

"I always wanted to say that," the man continued, smiling a lopsided smile. His eyes took in Medophae's condition, and the smile widened. "What's in the pouch, friend?"

Medophae glanced at the coin pouch at his side, and he backed down the beach. The sand made his footing unstable, and he almost fell. He blinked and tried to stay upright, trying to keep the man in his sight as he glanced to his left. The figures around the fire rose and began walking toward him.

"What ya got, Kendrin?" one of them called.

"Not sure yet," Kendrin said. Then, to Medophae, "Give us the pouch, big man, and you can be on your way."

Medophae fumbled with the ties on his belt, pulled the pouch free. He held it up. "It's yours," he said. "As payment."

"Payment?" Kendrin said. His friends had almost reached them.

"Food," Medophae said. "And a new bandage. Help me, and it's yours."

"I have a better deal, friend. How about I gut you, and then keep the pouch? Less effort for me. And I get the money quicker."

Medophae swayed, staggered back a few paces, then forced his legs to stay put. Water skimmed up the beach, splashing around his boots, then withdrew.

"Better yet," Kendrin said. "I just leave you standin' until you fall. Then I take the pouch anyway." Kendrin's friends arrived, fanning out behind him. There were four altogether. Medophae looked for the fifth, the smaller figure that he'd seen standing in the water, and spotted him.

No, not him. It was a young girl. She wore the same kinds of clothes as the other ruffians—blousy tunic and pantaloons—but she'd worked her way up the surf to stand behind him, the waves rolling softly up to her knees.

Medophae narrowed his eyes. These people were predators, looking for the weak. The only language they understood was strength.

"Come for me, then." Medophae growled. "I'll be on my feet long after you're dead." He held his arms wide. There were three bare-handed methods of taking a weapon away from someone. They were all dangerous, but effective if the weapon wielder was taken by surprise. Medophae was pretty sure this man didn't know any of those techniques.

The man lunged, and Medophae pirouetted to the left. The sword whispered past his belly, missing flesh. Medophae aligned his body with Kendrin's, hip to hip, and curled his left arm under Kendrin's, grasping the thumb of his sword hand. With a hip check, Medophae launched Kendrin forward, stripping the sword and breaking his thumb. Kendrin cried, pitching headfirst into the shallow surf. His sword spun up into the air, end over end. Medophae reached out to snatch it with his right hand—

—except Medophae didn't have a right hand anymore. His stump passed through the air, and the sword splashed into the water.

Kendrin's friends shouted with alarm, drew their swords and ran at Medophae.

He crouched, grabbed the sword with his left hand and stumbled to his feet. The quick bob made him light-headed. He saw the first sword coming at him, and he thought he saw his own sword raised to deflect it...

...then he was falling. His vision went dark. There were shouting voices. His back slapped the shallow surf, and salty water splashed into his nose and mouth. Slender fingers closed over his temples.

Then there was nothing.

9

ZILOK MORTH

WHEN ZILOK REALIZED he had lost control of the illusion of his body, it unsettled him, but he assumed the problem was with the island of Dandere. It wouldn't do to show weakness in front of Medophae, so he left Medophae with his first challenge and left the hut, floating through the trees down to the beach.

Since the destruction of Daylan's Fountain, the GodSpill in Amarion was thick and plentiful. Every thread of the great tapestry was soaked with it. But not on Dandere. Here, the GodSpill was diffuse and weak, and that made threadweaving more difficult, even maintaining the illusion of his body. After all, Zilok used GodSpill to keep himself alive, to tie himself to the crown so he wouldn't float up through the Godgate.

He needed to return to Amarion where the GodSpill was plentiful. And while he hadn't planned to leave Medophae quite so soon, he wasn't concerned. Oedandus could not reach Medophae here, and hundreds of miles of ocean separated him from Amarion. No humans sailed farther than a mile from any coast on the True Ocean. Only the bravest pirates even tried to "jump the teeth," the straight between the south and north peninsulas of The Jaw, a daring jaunt that only put a ship on the deadly waters of the True Ocean for half an hour, yet still only one out of three ships ever made it.

Saraphazia did not think much of humans. If she saw a boat on the True Ocean, she destroyed that boat, and she was always looking.

Medophae wasn't going anywhere.

Zilok pulled a substantial amount of GodSpill from the nearly dry threads around him, then tried to replace the illusion of himself.

It didn't work.

That should have had some effect.

He investigated further and realized that his spirit was being eaten away as well, not just the illusion. Was this some kind of attack?

He needed to return to Amarion and investigate this in the flush of his own power. It had taken Zilok every ounce of Oedandus's stolen power to squeeze Medophae's physical body through the threads and bring him this far without killing him. But it would only take a fraction of that to send Zilok back. One advantage of being a spirit was that he could travel the threads at will.

He reached into the threads of Dandere and pulled more GodSpill into himself. The trees, the sand, the undergrowth, and the very air around him resisted this time. All things clung to the GodSpill, especially when there wasn't a lot of it. The GodSpill was, really, the essence of life, and all creatures fought to hold onto a certain core amount of it. But Zilok tore away as much as he could, struggling until he felt full.

But the GodSpill drained from him like he suddenly had a hole in his soul, as though his attempt to pull more into himself accelerated his disintegration. Icy fear grew in his ethereal heart.

He looked overhead. As always, the ever-present swirling maw of the Godgate hung impassively over him, waiting, but now it was closer, stronger.

What was happening?

He reached into Natra's Crown, the artifact he had stolen to redirect the power of Oedandus, but it was empty, drier than the threads around him and...

Zilok realized with horror that the drain he felt was coming from the crown. Just as it had sucked the life force of Oedandus into it, it was now sucking GodSpill from him.

No...

He recalled the curse that had been written on the wall of Natra's treasure room, a warning to her fellow gods and goddess, and to any who might attempt to steal from her:

My love my dedicated bind, take these up and all unwinds.
Brother, leave these peaks untouched or face the fear you fear so much.
Zetu, father, keep your place, it's not with these to join the race.
Dervon, if, for greed's sweet sake, you wield my tools, your soul will break.
Saraphazia, endless toil, touch these and your waters boil.
Thalius, my jaunty son, dance with these, your dancing's done.

Those who seek, please walk away, take your pleasure in the day
I've made it, and it's free for you. A joyous life with simple truths.
But touch these items, flesh will rot. In decaying throes you're caught.
These, my children, let them be. Or lose all this that makes you free.

If these warnings you can't heed, if wisdom is subsumed by need,
Then breach the threshold, do not wait, and face the horror of your fate.

ZILOK REMOVED THE CROWN, looked at it, and made his decision in an instant. He didn't need it anymore. Let the crown stay here. Then, once he understood what was happening and how to counter it, he could return and claim it.

He threw the crown into the sand and floated away from it, out over the True Ocean, until he couldn't see the crown anymore.

He reached into the dry threads again, pulling GodSpill into himself. This time, it filled him up to bursting, and he pushed himself into the threads of the air over the ocean.

His perception elongated. He shrank and dove down a narrow tube of blue and white, whisking through the threads like an otter down a slippery stream. It was a long way to Amarion, but traveling the threads only took a few—

Something latched onto him, like there were suddenly a hundred hooks in his ethereal flesh. They yanked on him, draining him, hauling him backward.

No!

His swift progress halted, and Zilok popped out of the thread. He felt the terrible call of the crown, though the isle of Dandere was now far away. Zilok could even see the coast of Amarion, a thin brown and green line against the horizon. He felt the strength of the greater GodSpill and pulled it into himself, but he was a leaky bucket again. There was a hole straight through him that funneled into the distant crown. For every cupful of GodSpill dumped in, most drained out.

Zilok screamed and forced himself back into the threads. It was excruciating. Rather than an otter whisking down a stream, he was a rat crawling down a hole pierced by a thousand daggers, all cutting into him.

But finally, feeling like he was bleeding from horrible wounds, Zilok pulled himself out of the threads at his destination, deep in a secret passage beneath the wintery Corialis Mountains. His former anchor, Orem, was bundled up and sitting by a fire he had made to ensure he did not freeze. The man, still dulled by Zilok's spell, stood up at the back of the cave, waiting obediently.

"Come closer," Zilok gasped.

"Yes, my master," Orem said, obediently walking to him.

Zilok cut his connection to the crown, reaching out with a hundred ethereal fingers and latching onto Orem's life. He felt better instantly. Orem became Zilok's vitality once again. Let the damned crown rot. Perhaps he wouldn't ever go back for it. Let some other fool stumble across it and be eaten.

"That was unpleasant," Zilok said.

"Yes, my master."

"I must convalesce."

"Yes, my master."

That had been a very near thing. Zilok reached into the rich threads of Amarion, the threads that composed the rock, the air, the snow outside. He let the rich GodSpill flow into him.

71

...and it trickled out of him again.

"What?" he demanded aloud. Orem only stared at him.

Zilok spun. At the mouth of the cave, half sunk into the snow as though it had been dropped there, was Natra's Crown.

10

MEDOPHAE

MEDOPHAE BLINKED HIMSELF AWAKE. The salty smell of the sea was all around him. His eyes were heavily crusted with sleep, and dawn was beginning to light the sky down the beach where his feet were pointed. A wave came in, thinning as it rushed up the beach to tickle his arm and the right side of his body. The raging pain in his wrist had died to a quiet throb, and the stump had been sewn up with some slick cord that looked like sinew. The top and bottom edges of the stump had been punctured by thin shark's teeth.

"By the gods!" He yanked his arm up out of the water. Each shark tooth had been whittled to a needle, each with a hole bored through one end of it, connecting it to the sinew. He'd never seen thread like this, but the stitch job was masterfully done. Every stitch looked just like the last, and they were tight. Even a ghastly wound like this could heal with barely a scar with stitching like that. And it was already well along with its healing, as though he'd been lying here for days.

"You should leave it," a girl said.

73

He craned his neck around. Behind him, the ruffian girl stood ankle-deep in the water. She was maybe ten or eleven and, aside from the sailor's pantaloons and tunic, she looked more like a girl he would see living in the Teni'sian palace, rather than a girl living rough with seaside ruffians. She had clean skin, big eyes, and hair that looked well-brushed. It tumbled down her shoulders to her waist in waves. It was hard to tell if it was light brown or blond. It was difficult to see by the pre-dawn light, which gave it a blueish cast.

The other ruffians were nowhere to be seen.

"Where are your friends?" Medophae asked.

"They went away," she said. "You should keep your arm in the water. It's good for it."

Actually, the quickest way to bring on infection was to put an open wound in seawater, but who knew what this little girl had been taught by those men? Medophae stood up. "Went away?" He looked up and down the beach, but there wasn't any sign of them. "Where?"

"I gave them your pouch. It made them bigger. That's what they really wanted."

"Bigger?"

"Everyone wants to be bigger."

She had the oddest way of speaking. Her accent wasn't Dandene, nor from any other kingdom on Amarion. "The pouch wasn't what you wanted?"

She looked straight up at the sky, which was slowly turning blue, then she looked back at him with a lopsided smile. One lone dimple appeared on her left cheek. "People are funny about rocks, aren't they?" she asked.

"Rocks?"

"Gold. Silver. Rocks. Well, melted rocks." She paused. "And gems. Also melted rocks."

"Those men just left?"

"They got bigger. That's what they wanted."

"They were going to kill me."

"So they could feel bigger."

"So they could steal my money."

"You're so big and strong. If they killed you, they'd feel bigger and stronger. That's why they were going to kill you."

"I don't think that's the reason."

"That and their dream."

"Dream?"

"To make themselves bigger with melted rocks."

"You're a strange girl."

"But I do know how to knit things." She made a motion with her hand like she was sewing.

"*You* sewed me up?"

"Well it wasn't the ocean!" She giggled.

He looked at her, and she stared back like he was a puppy about to do a trick.

"Are they your family?" he asked.

She laughed as if that was the funniest thing. Then she stopped like someone had slapped her face. She sobered. "Well, yes."

"Your father?"

"No."

"Uncle?"

Her large eyes widened. "Oh no," she whispered. "I don't talk about my uncle. Ever." She looked frightened. "Mother never talks about my uncle, and she forbids me to."

"Okay," he pacified her. "Well, thank you for helping me."

She glanced at his stump, then back up at him. "It's what you wanted, right? You came looking for help. You were going to give them money to help you."

"Well... Yes."

"But I helped you instead."

"You certainly did."

"Well... Do you feel cheated?"

"What? Cheated? No." He raised his stump. It made him queasy to look at it, so...short. No hand. But without her, he would have died. "Is there something I can do for you in exchange for your help?"

"Yes!" she said emphatically, as though she'd been waiting for him to ask that question. She clapped her hands.

"Oh," he said. "Well, I will do what I can. Tell me."

"I will," she said. "But not yet. I did you a favor. And you will do me a favor in the future, right?"

"You're saying that I owe you."

"Yes." She clapped her hands again. "You owe me."

"Very well." The rising sun illuminated the girl further, and he suddenly realized her hair was *actually* blue. The bluish tinge was not a trick of the light. A chill ran through him. Medophae had met the goddess of the True Ocean many times. Like all gods, she could look like whatever she wanted. She could look human, or dragon. She could even be a talking wave, but she almost always appeared as a whale. She loved her whales, cared for the denizens of her ocean, and barely tolerated everything else. She made an exception for Medophae because he had killed Dervon, whom she hated above all others. Dervon had killed her daughter, Vaisha the Changer.

"Saraphazia...?" he murmured.

"Oh goodness!" She held up a hand like she would cover his mouth, but she was about ten feet away from him. "Don't say her name, silly!"

"Who are you?"

"I'm Vee," she whispered. "Don't say her name again, please. She listens for her name. And she's probably looking for me already...." Vee raised her head and looked down the coast toward the sun, as though hearing something he couldn't hear. "Oh no. It's too late." She bit her lip, then said to him. "Don't tell her I was here. Please?"

"Who are you?"

"You mustn't tell!" She ran into the surf and dove into the face of a wave. He waded after her, but she was much faster than him.

"Wait!" he shouted. The waves pushed at him, and by the time he was waist-deep, he couldn't see her anymore.

To the left, where Vee had looked, a huge swell rose on the ocean, coming his direction.

11

MEDOPHAE

THE SWELL APPROACHED QUICKLY, the ocean bulging like a blue blanket over some vast creature. Medophae backed up the beach, shielding his eyes as the water exploded and rushed up the beach. It took his legs out from underneath him, swirling him all the way to the trees.

The water receded, spinning him and pulling him back down the sand until he came to a stop right in front of the giant, dark blue whale.

Its head was as big as a castle, and its enormous fins—each the size of a ship—had propped it up so that it could look down on Medophae. Its girth had crushed a trench in the beach, and water sluiced around the giant body as it raced back to the ocean. The rest of its body extended so far back it disappeared into the waves.

Every god Medophae had met, save Tarithalius, intimidated mortals with their size. It was possible they just couldn't help it, being as powerful as they were, but Medophae suspected it was just because they were bullies. They enjoyed seeing fear in the faces of mortal creatures.

Medophae coughed out water and shoved his stump into the sand in an attempt to push himself to his feet. He hissed at the pain and yanked it back out, falling on his side again. It still felt like his hand was there. With a hundred needles stabbing it, but still there. He was going to have to get better at that.

Using his left hand, he pushed himself to his feet and faced the goddess. The giant eye on her left side tracked his progress.

"Saraphazia." He bowed low. "Thank you for coming."

Giant waves rose and crashed behind her, along the length of her monolithic body. They were so big they should have obliterated the beach and the forest for a hundred yards, but they crashed against an invisible barrier a dozen feet away from Medophae. It was all he could do not to flinch.

Intimidation. All part of the show.

The whale's mouth opened, revealing millions of long, white fronds that were her teeth. "Who were you talking to?" The voice emerged from the cavernous depths.

Vee's words rang in his head: Don't tell her I was here. You mustn't!

"I'm in need of assistance," Medophae said.

"Who were you talking to?"

"I was calling you."

"Are you telling me that you weren't talking to anyone before I arrived?" The voice boomed, vibrating his chest.

"Yes," he lied. "I came here for you." Part of that was true, at least.

The pupil of the eye, nearly as tall as he was, narrowed to half its size. "Something has happened to you. You no longer walk with Oedandus."

"I have been attacked." He held up his stump. "And now I need your help."

"You need my help...."

"Oedandus is trapped on the continent of Amarion. He cannot reach me here, but I must get back to him. Events are moving that—"

"And what do you think I can do for you?" The sepulchral voice vibrated through him.

"A trifle, for you. I beseech you to take me back to Amarion."

"A trifle?" She said, an edge to her voice. "I do not suffer humans in my ocean."

"Humans...?" Medophae said. Her tone was different than the last time they had spoken. Saraphazia had always been rather cold, but in the times she'd spoken with him, she had been warmer than this. Finally, he said, "You once told me that when I needed your aid, you would come. When Dervon lay dead at my feet, you swore you would—"

"I swore to Oedandus. I swore to the vessel of my mother's consort. I did not swear to you, human."

Medophae's mouth hung open. "You're joking."

"Take caution in your tone, mortal. I suffer your presumption because you were once part of Oedandus. You are no longer, and I have tolerated you about as far as I will." Her thick head raised, glancing past him at the island. "This is where you were born. You can thrive here. Be grateful."

He held up his stump. "My hand has been chopped off!"

Those giant eyes blinked, uncaring.

Medophae ground his teeth. He wanted to rage at her, to call her a faithless oath-breaker, but he had no leverage to move her. Not only did she not care about his "mortal troubles," but she might actually just kill him. He wouldn't be the first human she had simply decided to kill because he'd offended her. With effort, he reined in his outrage. He had to be smarter than that.

"Then I'll trade information," he said calmly.

"What could you possibly know that I don't?"

"Avakketh," he said.

That stopped her. Saraphazia hated Avakketh, god of dragons, almost as much as she had hated Dervon the Diseased before Medophae had killed him. The god of humans, Tarithalius, had told Medophae that, long before humans were created, the whales and the dragons had fought each other in a conflict called the War of the Behemoths. Back then, dragons had no wings and whales did not swim in the oceans. They were both land-bound creatures carving out their territory in the world.

Avakketh had joined the conflict on the side of the dragons, Saraphazia on the side of the whales, and their war nearly destroyed the other sentient races of the world. So Natra, the mother of the gods, sent the dragons to live in the northern mountains of Amarion, transformed them into airborne creatures, and gave them dominion over the skies. Natra then transformed the whales into hulking creatures with fins and gave them dominion over the True Ocean.

Avakketh went with his dragons to the north, and Saraphazia went with the whales. Thalius said that so great was Saraphazia's hatred for her uncle that she cast a spell over the whole of the ocean, making it like acid to any dragon who dared set foot in the water.

"What about Avakketh?" Saraphazia rumbled.

"He is planning to attack the human lands of Amarion. He's going to wipe out humanity. Once he realizes I'm gone, he'll begin. There will be nothing to stop him. Every moment I'm away is dangerous. If he comes south... No one else can stand against him."

"You?" Saraphazia said with disdain.

"I'm the same person!" he blurted without thinking. "I am the only way Oedandus can stop him. Surely you see that?"

Saraphazia said nothing.

"Well?" He demanded.

"Let Avakketh destroy the humans. They were a mistake, anyway."

A hollow fear fluttered in his belly. "You can't mean that."

"Humans should never have been created in the first place. It was Thalius being Thalius. He thinks he's funny when he does such things, but Natra never approved of a fifth sentient race. It's ridiculous. It always was."

"But you can't...just let them die."

She just watched him.

He suddenly realized what he really was to her. Humans were annoying flies to Saraphazia, to be slapped when they touched her ocean, and otherwise to be ignored. His mind raced.

"He'll come for you next," Medophae said.

"I think not."

"Once he eliminates humans, he will dominate the continent,

from the Spine Mountains to the True Ocean. How long after that before he decides he wants your domain, too? When he comes for you and your whales, you'll wish you'd helped me."

"If Avakketh or his dragons enter my ocean, I will destroy them."

"And if he enlists White Tuana? You ripped her eyes out. You helped kill her father. She would jump at the chance for revenge. If they also bring Zetu..." He let the statement hang in the air a moment. It was Zetu, Dervon, and Tuana who'd nearly destroyed Oedandus, made him into what he was now.

"Zetu has vanished. He no longer walks the world."

"Oedandus was also sure that Zetu wouldn't rise against him. He thought Zetu was an ally."

Saraphazia was utterly still. He hoped she was working out in her head what he had worked out in his. He hoped that—

"Goodbye, Medophae. Farewell in this protected haven your god made for you. He ensured that you and your kind could fish the waters for a mile around the island, and I honor that agreement to this day. Take it as a blessing." Water rose around her, lifting her bulk high into the air. The spray drove him backward. He stumbled and fell, again trying to break his fall with a hand he didn't have.

He shouted through the pain, tried to rise, but got tumbled again by the water as she submerged and the wave rushed up the beach. As the water receded, he staggered to his feet.

"Saraphazia!" he yelled.

The wind and sea spray died. The ocean withdrew, and Saraphazia was gone.

"Saraphazia!"

Only a giant swell, moving quickly away, showed where the goddess was. Then that, too, flattened against the ocean, and the waves rolled in as they had before.

Medophae fell to his knees at the edge of the surf.

12

MEDOPHAE

MEDOPHAE SHOUTED at the ocean for another hour before he finally fell to his knees in the water and bowed his head.

The thudding thump of his mortality beat in his wrist, a pulse that whispered how feeble he really was. His stomach growled. He'd been too long without food now, and those mortal hunger pangs had begun. Ever before, he could ignore that feeling for as long as he needed to.

Medophae was going to have to start paying attention to mortal necessities now. He was going to have to start accepting his situation.

The reality was this: He was trapped here. Whether a thousand years ago, a hundred years ago, or right now, no human ship had ever sailed across the True Ocean. Not once, not ever. It was impossible. The only way to cross was with Saraphazia's blessing.

The despair Medophae had lived with for hundreds of years hung over him, thick and heavy. He'd spent those centuries twisting with indecision, not knowing what to do. Ironically, he now knew what needed doing, and he was barred from doing it.

Avakketh was coming south. While Medophae languished here bantering with a stubborn goddess, humankind was threatened with extinction, and Medophae was the only one who could stop it.

That was why Avakketh had sent those nightmares to Medophae, to threaten Medophae's loved ones, to force him out of Amarion, and Avakketh had dredged up Medophae's weakness: Bands. He'd told Medophae that Bands was miraculously free of the gem, that he'd unwittingly solved the riddle by falling in love with Mirolah.

It was an insidious lie. It was the sweet fiction Medophae longed to believe above all else, the one thing that could throw his mind into chaos. And Avakketh knew it.

His insidious ploy it had worked its damage. The notion of Bands being free had consumed Medophae's mind, had thrown his relationship with Mirolah into doubt, and had distracted him when he charged headlong after Zilok Morth.

Soon after those dreams, Medophae had begun to twist every little thing into a sign that Bands had somehow returned. He started looking for his beloved around every corner. When Stavark's friend, Elekkena, spoke to Medophae in Denema's Valley, it was like she was speaking the way Bands had once spoken. When Mirolah revealed that Elekkena was a young threadweaver, Medophae wondered if the girl was somehow Bands in a new form. Then, after Elekkena mysteriously vanished, Mirolah mentioned the quicksilver girl had murmured words while threadweaving. Bands always murmured words in dragon speech when she threadweaved.

In that moment, the fantasy had grown beyond Medophae's control. He fought it, didn't tell anyone his hidden thoughts, but suddenly Elekkena *had* to be Bands in disguise. She talked like her, threadweaved like her. Choosing to look like an adolescent quicksilver girl would have been easy for Bands.

Medophae's heart had ached because his beloved had come and gone, that she had traveled him without revealing herself.

But it was a lie. Medophae knew that now. That kind of emotional turmoil was exactly what Avakketh wanted. Longing for Bands had been Medophae's undoing for three hundred years. He gave up on trying to be a hero. He had floated along, nothing more than a powerful ghost, doing only what was well within his vast capability, shying away from anything at which he might fail.

And at the end of that dark stretch of years, Mirolah had come to him like a light. When he was at his lowest, when Zilok had stolen Oedandus and Bands's gem, and a mortal fever had taken Medophae, he'd finally given up. He'd lain down to die.

Mirolah had pulled him out of that despair. She had stoked his identity with a question, had rekindled it.

"What did you want to be?" she had asked. "When you were my age, what did you want to be?"

He had been so busy looking into the teeth of his fears, so busy seeing his own flaws, that he'd not thought to look into the past for his missing answers. But Mirolah had been right.

"I wanted to be an adventurer like my mother," he had said. "I wanted to do what others thought was impossible."

I wanted to do what others thought was impossible...

He thought back to his first quest, when he went looking for his lost god. Everyone believed it was impossible. But he'd found Oedandus.

He thought about his second quest, to seek out the god Dervon the Diseased and kill him. Everyone believed it was impossible. Gods couldn't be killed. And yet, one step at a time, one lucky or destined step at a time, Medophae had marched across Amarion and brought death to the unkillable.

Medophae called his memories back to him, back from a time when he'd made his choices without hesitation. That second quest had slowly gathered friends, slowly gathered momentum. Medophae had made one possible choice at a time, each one stacking on the last until finally he climbed over that wall of impossibility.

Medophae stood up. It started with just one step, one lucky or destined step at a time. He looked down the coast, and he pushed Saraphazia's crushing dismissal from his mind. He stopped thinking about the deadly True Ocean. He thought about only what was in front of him, and he took that first step up the beach.

There was a real threat to Amarion. Humankind needed him to

be the hero of the legends, and he wasn't going to let them down. Not this time. He wouldn't allow Avakketh's mind games, Saraphazia's intransigence, or a stupid ocean to stand in his way.

I am still breathing. I can still wield a sword. No arrogant goddess is going to dictate where I stop. There is a way off this island, and I'm going to find it if I have to sail straight into her teeth to do it.

He started up the beach, cradling his throbbing hand. He walked for an hour, trying to ignore the growing hunger in his belly, before the shore curved inward, creating a placid bay. A seaside village nestled against the curve of the shore—dozens of structures.

He had grown up on this island, but that had been fourteen centuries ago. Nothing looked the same. He wasn't even sure where on the island he was. He had no recollection of this bay.

When Medophae's father, Jarod Madis Roloiron, was king of Dandere, the capital city was on the south side of the island as was most of Dandene civilization. Based on the position of the sun, this was the north side.

Huts similar to the one in which he'd awoken lined the shore of the bay, climbing up the slope in a stairstep, replacing the ubiquitous trees. There were also larger houses, built in the same style, with those slender trees cut and shaped to make the vertical slats of the walls, but these houses were more extensive. Many had balconies overlooking the ocean. They had thick, double-built walls and thick glass windows that opened on upward hinges.

Dandere had seasons even more pronounced than Amarion. In the summer, it was warm enough that one could walk around in little more than a loincloth. Winters were brutally cold. The True Ocean delivered ice storms one after the other. Every few years, even the ocean froze. Waves brought spikes of ice with them, smashing docks not made of stone. Every house had outer shutters that protected the glass and could be shut tight against the storms.

Medophae glanced at the azure sky and wondered how long it would be before the ice storms came. In Dandere, fall was like a deep breath before a jump. It was short, and fall had to be nearing its end. In Teni'sia, it had just turned to winter. If he was going to get over the ocean, he couldn't delay.

85

He turned his worry away from ice storms and looked at a row of three stone docks sticking out into the quiet bay. The ocean's waves broke on a distant reef that protected the bay, keeping it placid. Medophae looked at the docked ships bobbing gently.

He spotted a sailboat on the right-hand dock that was small enough to be manned by one person and large enough to make the trip across the ocean. He started toward it.

Two people worked on the dock. One old man bent over a basket that looked like it had fish in it. The second, a woman in wide pantaloons, knee-high boots, and a tunic that reached almost all the way to the edge of the boots, paused at a rope she'd been tying, then stood up straight. She put her hands on her hips and regarded his approach. As he came closer, her eyes widened at his missing hand and the blood on his tunic.

He didn't make eye contact with her, just kept walking toward the boat. She stepped back in fear.

He boarded the ship like he owned it.

Please have water and food.

There was no point in taking an unsupplied ship. He'd never make it across the entire ocean. He ducked down into the cramped hold.

Two water kegs were stacked against the starboard bulkhead. Medophae smiled. There were also three fishing rods hanging on the wall. He opened two boxes and found one of them half filled with stale bread in burlap sacks and a basket with dried meats. That was enough. With this to get him started and the fishing rods to supplement it, he could survive. He pulled a twisted strip of meat out and tore a chunk off with his teeth, his mouth immediately filling with saliva. His stomach rumbled, and he strode up the brief stairs to the deck, chewing.

The old man was still leaning over his basket of fish, but the woman was now far away at the beginning of the dock, talking to three new sailors. She pointed at him just as he threw the lines off the boat.

"Hey!" one of the men said, running up the dock toward him. Medophae threw off the second line and kicked away from the pylon. The sailboat drifted out into the water. He went over and released the mainsail. It unfurled, caught the light breeze, and yanked the boat farther away from the dock.

"That's my boat!" the running man shouted. "He's stealing my boat!"

Medophae tacked, swinging the sailboat out into the bay and angling toward the reef. There was an animated discussion on the dock, but Medophae knew they wouldn't organize anything quickly enough to catch him.

He was free to pursue his folly. One possible step at a time.

He turned the bow toward open ocean, cutting across the placid bay. He had spent a decade sailing the Inland Ocean with Bands, and had become an expert sailor during that time. Doing it with one hand presented problems, but he wasn't going to stop.

The moment Avakketh knew Medophae had left Amarion, he would begin his attack. He might even be starting now. Every moment Medophae wasted was another moment the continent of Amarion could be engulfed in dragon flame.

He hit the waves breaking on the reef head on. The boat climbed, tipped, and raced down the other side. He hit the next wave, hauling on the tiller to cut the water directly, and made it over the second wave. The sea spray hit his face, and Medophae found himself grinning as he bore down on the third wave. He hit it and laughed as he burst through the reef break onto the swells of the True Ocean. His blood rushed, and for a moment he felt like he was eighteen again, when nothing mattered but the adventure.

Take away my hand. Throw every obstacle in my way. I'm going back to Amarion.

In moments like this, it didn't matter what he faced. All that mattered was the struggle, pitting everything he was against the challenge in front of him. He'd felt this way when he first left Dandere on Bands's back and went searching for his god. He'd felt it when he dared hunt Dervon. He'd felt it when Mirolah pulled him back to life in that little town of Gnedrin's Post and they'd decided to escape Zilok Morth.

He felt it now, facing the vast expanse of the True Ocean with two barrels of water and a fishing pole.

Bring every challenge you can throw. Bring them all.

The little sailboat passed the danger of the reef and gently climbed and slid down one swell after the other. He checked the wind and the sun, then fixed the sail to send the boat in a southwestern direction. It would be better to sail at night, when he could get a fix on the stars, but for now, southwest would do. Breathing hard and grinning, he put his hand on the gunwale to rest.

His grin faded as he looked across the ocean.

A swell the size of a mountain rolled his way. Saraphazia. He glanced back the way he had come. Dandere was now barely a bump on the waterline, roughly the same size as the swell headed his direction. There was no time to get back to the island.

"Then let's do this," he muttered under his breath. There were no clouds in the sky, but Saraphazia didn't need a storm to make deadly waves.

He leapt to the rigging and let out both sails to catch all the wind he could. The little boat lurched forward, moving fast toward the swell. At the last second, he cut to port, putting the stern into the swell as it picked him up. Sea spray rushed at his face, but he clung to the tiller and fairly flew down the wave.

With a shout, he came off the swell and hit the level ocean, instantly cutting to starboard. The timbers creaked, but the ship was nimble and well-built. It held together as he cut a neat semi-circle around the giant swell.

"You owe me!" Medophae shouted at the swell, knowing that Saraphazia could hear him. "I killed Dervon for you. I do not ask your assistance, but you will let me pass!"

A wave arced over the rail, slamming into Medophae and taking him off his feet. The ship tipped dangerously, and he slid over the planks like a greased pig. He snatched the rail at the last second with his good hand, dangling into the water as the ship laid on its side. He submerged, and the ship dragged him through the water. He hung on with a death grip.

Suddenly, the boat tipped the other direction, yanking him out of the ocean. He shouted into the salt spray and hauled himself onto the deck. The boat continued tipping, flopping over to the other side. He slid the other direction and caught the tiller, held himself, then turned to face the wave—

It crashed down, cracking the middle of the ship and sending Medophae launching straight upward into the wave's face. He hit it, and it engulfed him. He spun like a twig in a river. Water was everywhere. A splintered piece of the mast shot by him, almost impaling him, and he swirled past it. He struggled to find out which way was up, but he couldn't. The sea just kept spinning him.

He looked for light, and saw it below him. His lungs had begun to burn, and he desperately wanted to take a breath.

Fight for it. Upward. Fight.

He reoriented himself, putting the light above him and kicking that way, using his good hand to cup and push. He kicked and kicked, but it was too far. The huge wave had taken him deep below the surface, and it felt like it was still pushing him.

His legs were weak, and his chest felt like it was going to explode. Sunlight dazzled the surface, now overhead, but he was too far down.

Just as he was about to give one last kick, knives stabbed into his back. He gasped, letting go of what little air he had left and inhaling seawater. The knives raked across him as the waves spun him.

The reef! The wave had taken him all the way back to the shore.

The reef shredded his back. He tried to turn, tried to get away from it, but he was helpless. The waves pushed him down, rolled him, then lifted him up again. He broke the surface and gasped, getting half a breath before being tumbled down again. The coral stabbed at him, and this time his head hit, and everything went black.

13

BANDS

THE ROYAL GARDENS of Teni'sia were beautiful under the starlit skies. Trees as old as the castle loomed over ivy-covered walls, creating random patterns against the azure sky. The maze of tall shrubs, leafy trees, and subtle flower beds also showed the thoughtful planning of the garden's architect. It reminded her of Calsinac, and she wondered if the Teni'sian gardens were known in other kingdoms, renowned for their beauty.

The air smelled crisp and clean after the storm. Bands ran her fingers lightly over the top of a hedge, and the snow clung to her skin, began to melt immediately. She watched the crystals collapse into each other until they were beads of water. The frigid air that came with last week's storm had mellowed to a mild warmth. Snow still covered green lawns and green trees, but it was melting, bending the leafy limbs with its wet weight. It was a summer garden cloaked in white. Already, superstitious murmurs raced through the kingdom that the storm hadn't been a normal winter storm. They said it was a product of the unnatural Wave.

Bands inhaled the beauty around her. Her heart hurt, but this kind of beauty salved her, reminded her of what was important. She could stay her course if she could visit places like this garden, this intertwining of humanity and nature's grace. It reminded her of her guiding principle, which had made her fall in love with Medophae, which had made her forsake her own people.

Those with power must sacrifice for those who did not have it.

Medophae knew it. It was written on his soul, and she loved him for it. People like her, like Medophae, they had to be the protectors of beauty, whether in the smallest human or the largest dragon. There was no other use of power that mattered more.

Avakketh had forgotten that, if he had ever known it at all. Zilok Morth did not understand that. Bands liked to believe that Natra, the goddess who had created the world, had known it, though. Bands liked to believe that Natra, if she was here, would have agreed.

Bands drew in another breath of cold air, let it chill the fire burning within her. Since the moment she had returned from her fight with Zynder and found that Medophae had been abducted by Zilok, Bands had wanted to pursue the evil spirit. Since Zilok had found a way to strip Medophae of Oedandus once, he could do it twice. That meant every instant Medophae lay within Zilok's clutches was another moment Medophae could be dead.

Bands had to push that from her mind. She could not cleave to her principles if she put her own needs over the needs of humankind. Avakketh was coming, sooner rather than later. He would know she had slain Zynder soon, if he didn't already. He would know Medophae was gone soon.

And once Avakketh knew that, there would be nothing to stop him from coming south and incinerating humankind. Medophae was the only deterrent, the only real protection for humankind. Bands knew what even Medophae probably didn't: the gods were afraid of him. Aside from the great Natra, Oedandus had been the strongest of the gods. Now Medophae had that power.

So she needed to get Medophae back. He was the only true hope for Amarion, in the end. Her heart and her mind had been aligned in that, and she'd almost bypassed Teni'sia altogether to throw herself into the hunt for Medophae, but she had looked deeper into the details, searched for those subtleties that immediate action might trample over.

Finding Medophae could take a long time, and Bands needed to buy that time. What victory if Amarion fell to Avakketh's dragons while Bands searched for her beloved? And that meant preparing Teni'sia to fight.

Her first task was accomplished. Mershayn sat the throne. It had taken a full week to do it. It had been, of necessity, ham-handed and crude. It was a miracle, really, that the kingdom hadn't erupted into chaos in that short time. A week was a shakily short time to transfer kingly power, but a week was all they had. In fact, it was probably seven days more than they really had.

Happily, it was working. Mershayn was a diamond in the rough. He was unorthodox. His methods were surprising. He was contradictory, sometimes compassionate, and sometimes ruthless. He was utterly charming; it was hard not to like him. He was the kind of person you found yourself rooting for, despite yourself. In the end, his personality and command style was perfectly suited to the chaotic mood of the kingdom.

His easy charm instilled his allies with confidence. His unpredictability kept his enemies constantly tottering off balance. He had been known as a hedonistic ne'er-do-well before this week. Allies and enemies alike were stunned at his sudden competence, and Mershayn exploited their uncertainty like an expert swordsman finding the weaknesses in his opponent's guard. Bands couldn't have planned it better if she had tried.

Now, she dared to hope that Mershayn actually could rally this kingdom to war in time. She didn't know when Zynder would be considered overdue to report to Avakketh, but she did know that a week was stretching it. Bands was on alert for any signs of a dragon impersonating a human. That might be Avakketh's next step: to send a spy to find out what had become of Zynder. But Bands had seen nothing suspicious so far. She kept her well-known human shape so that, if a dragon had shapeshifted and walked the palace halls, he or she would be drawn straight to Bands. But so far, nothing.

Now that Mershayn was installed, she must turn her attention to her second task. Medophae. The defense Bands had planned would slow her god, but she could not best him. Only a god could kill another god. She needed Medophae.

Or possibly Tarithalius. He wasn't a paragon of reassurance, but the god of humans might choose to fight Avakketh if the mood took him. At the least, a war between dragons and humans would be fascinating to Thalius.

She paused on that, thinking. Most likely, Thalius was here already, lurking in Teni'sia as a sailor stinking of fish, a mischievous street urchin, or some garrulous guard. Thalius derived great pleasure from his perpetual masquerade, appearing as the unknown warrior who turned the tide of a battle or as the mysterious scribe who delivered crucial information to an indecisive king. Yes, he was likely here somewhere. Unfortunately, she couldn't count on him to help. If she was to effectively brace Avakketh, she needed Medophae.

Despair snuck through her defenses, and the whispered thought *Zilok has already killed him...* rose in her mind. She calmed her thumping heart. No, Medophae was alive.

She looked at the stars overhead, felt the chill breeze lift the tiny hairs on her arms. She drew a clean breath and exhaled, let that doubt flow out of her.

There was always a way. She must continue to think and act until she found that way. Medophae was alive. That was a simple fact until she had evidence that—

She felt the shift in the threads, the use of GodSpill. Hope and fear thrilled through her.

She recognized the subtle finesse, the meticulous grace of the manipulation of the threads. Zilok Morth coalesced behind her. Was he testing her? No, it was simply in his nature. Why approach an enemy from the front when you could approach from behind?

Stilling her tumultuous thoughts, Bands freed her mind for action. The time for contemplation and worry was over. The time for action, for intelligence, was now. She couldn't afford to trip over her own concerns when fencing with Zilok. She needed to look for opportunity. The two of them had circled each other for centuries, throwing minor threadweavings against each other during Zilok's schemes and Medophae's retaliations, but they had always been like spears glancing off shields. They had never engaged in a full threadweaver battle. Zilok was powerful, but so was Bands, and neither knew which was the strongest. She suspected Zilok, like her, wasn't in a hurry to have that duel. But Zilok knew, as did she, they must inevitably clash. Perhaps today was that day.

"Have you come to gloat?" she asked, holding perfectly still. She didn't turn to face him, letting him know that she need not see him with her eyes to know exactly where he was. His glowing spirit showed like a figure of knotted blue threads in her threadweaver's sight. The centuries of the Devastation Years, when Amarion had been bereft of GodSpill, had not dimmed him. He was as solid and powerful as ever.

"You assumed I would come at all?"

"You always do."

"I wouldn't want you to think I am predictable. Shall I leave?" he asked.

She let the silence stretch. He had found her. He had come to threaten, torture, manipulate, or perhaps even to get something from her. He would not quit it until he got what he came for.

Bands desperately wanted Medophae's location, or at least an indication he still lived, but her need was a weapon in Zilok's hand. If he could force her to show emotion, he would use that weapon against her. She could almost feel his longing to see her weakness, but Bands was a dragon. She had a patience that Zilok Morth could not comprehend.

She waited, saying nothing, and was rewarded.

"I find your game curious," he said. "And so I came to see what you are about."

"My game?" Her words were bait on a hook. The longer he stayed, the more certain she was that he wanted something, and that was like gold in her hand.

"Your grand revolution in Teni'sia. The instatement of the Bastard King. You've done a breathtaking job, I'll grant you. Of course, you have plenty of practice in building empires. Are you also building another hero? Will you coach this one along as you

THREADS OF AMARION

coached the Wildmane, sand his rough edges, and polish him? A hundred years from now, will you have the minstrels singing praises of the Bastard King?"

And that was *Zilok's* bait, dangled for her. He was trying to draw out her emotion, trying to see how her heart constricted at the thought of Medophae in Zilok's claws. Zilok was implying that any hero would do for Bands, that Medophae was unimportant as an individual, only as a purpose.

This was the tricky part. What to tell him? What to show?

"I am preparing," she replied.

"So cryptic. You were always soft-spoken about the big things. But for you, I'll bite. What are you preparing for?"

"Why have you come, Zilok?"

"Are you simply going to talk to me with your back turned during our entire conversation? Some might consider that rude."

"If you wanted to talk to my face, you would have appeared in front of me." She didn't turn around.

"You've not asked about Medophae. Did I hit the mark? Is Mershayn your new hero? Could you be *that* fickle? Has the Bastard King captured your heart as well as your attention?"

"You didn't come here to return Medophae," Bands said.

"I've come to help you."

"I see."

This time, he stayed silent. It was typical of Zilok to banter with his prey; he'd done that for as long as she'd known him, but something was off here. His rhythm lacked its usual elegance. He seemed...in a hurry, but that made no sense whatsoever. He already had what he wanted most: Medophae as his prisoner, helpless. If Zilok wanted something from Bands, his best play was to wait her out. Yet here he was, engaging her. What urgency could drive Zilok to be in a hurry?

"You've wrested this kingdom from Grendis Sym," Zilok finally said. "My former ally. I've come to congratulate you, and, as a favor from one threadweaver to another, to tell you that I will stay clear of Teni'sia. I will honor that you have become this kingdom's protector, and won't try to take it from you."

"You think I'm trying to protect this kingdom?"

95

He hesitated.

"Then you really don't know." She paused contemplatively. "Surprising." Vast information about a multitude of subjects went hand-in-hand with the name Zilok Morth. He was a threadweaver from the Age of Ascendance. He had the ravening thirst for knowledge, the same thirst that possessed every threadweaver, and he'd had hundreds of years to accumulate that knowledge. There was no greater insult to Zilok than to imply he didn't know something.

His reply was silence.

"You have not felt it, then?" she pressed.

"There have been many changes in the lands. To which do you refer?" His tone was flat.

"A dragon stalked the halls of Teni'sia until very recently," she said. "You didn't notice?"

Again, silence.

"Do you remember the strange lights over the mountains the night you took Medophae?" she continued. "Or were you so preoccupied with your revenge that you missed the larger picture?"

"Did one of your fellows come south to free you from your gem prison?"

"He came south to kill me. I killed him instead."

Zilok hesitated again. There wasn't a record in human history where dragon fought dragon. Not in any of the legends passed down verbally, either. That was because dragons didn't brawl with one another. They followed the will of their lord god, Avakketh. If one dragon killed another, it was not a fight, but an execution performed by the elites, and only at the express command of their god. Zilok wouldn't know about the elites, but he knew about the rest. No doubt he was putting together all the pieces in a flashing instant.

"And here I thought all the surprise had gone out of my life," he said, and she could tell that he was aching to ask questions.

"Wait and watch."

"You think Avakketh is coming south," he said.

"There's no reason for Avakketh to send an elite into Amarion, except as a prelude to war." She deliberately threw out the word "elite" again for him to chew on. His threadweaver's insatiable mind would want to know what that was, and every little tidbit that distracted him was a benefit.

"And he wants you dead because of what you know about dragon culture," he said. "Their weaknesses. And you side with the humans. You hold great and dangerous knowledge in your pretty, human-seeming head."

There it was. He'd dropped his line in the water. He wanted her knowledge, something she knew that he didn't. Her own mind gnawed at that, wondering what it could be. It was something arcane, almost certainly. He might be the superior threadweaver between the two of them, but she had lived longer. Did he seek a spell that had been performed before his time? Some threadweaver technique he wished to master that only she might know about?

"My knowledge doesn't belong to Avakketh anymore. It's free to humankind and any who would ally with them in this war." *Take it, Zilok. Pick it up.*

"Clever," he said. "It is refreshing, matching wits with you again. Yes, I have a curiosity about something. You might know a little about it."

She turned to face him at last. Usually, Zilok preferred projecting himself to mortal eyes as he had looked when he was in his fortieth year of life. But this time, he was just two blue flames in the shapes of eyes, hovering at head height above the snowy path of the garden. That told volumes. He'd been in some kind of fight, and it had diminished him. Had Medophae done this to him?

No, she suddenly knew that wasn't the case. If Medophae had done this, Zilok wouldn't come to Bands for help. In fact, that he had come to her at all strongly indicated that Medophae was alive. Zilok had spared him, for now at least. Yes, that made sense. In Zilok's mind, he'd see Medophae's continued existence as a reason for him to deserve help from her. And that would open up the gate in his mind, allowing him to seek her out.

She spoke her thoughts aloud. "You spared him."

The burning blue eyes narrowed. "Yes."

"Then I will help you, if I can."

"I won't give him to you," he said.

97

"What is your question?" she asked.

"The Crown of Natra," he said. "What do you know of it?"

Bands's eyes widened before she could stop them. Her mouth opened to respond, but she realized she didn't know what to say first.

"What did you do?" Her mind raced. She had met Natra, the Breather of Life, twice in her life, long ago when she was barely more than a hatchling, just before Natra disappeared from the lands forever. But Bands would never forget the crown at Natra's brow, with its tall, rough-hewn crystals, and she would never forget what Bands's mother had told her about it. The crown was how Natra controlled the other gods. It could take the power of any god and use it against them. And none of the gods would steal it because it had some horrible curse on it.

That was how Zilok had defeated Medophae. Somehow, he'd unearthed the Crown of Natra. It was impossible to contemplate, but then, it wouldn't be the first impossible thing that Zilok Morth had done.

"Where is he?" she asked.

"No."

She turned and began walking toward the castle, hoping that she was playing this right. Everything balanced on a knife's edge. He needed what she knew, but she would never willingly give him the key to such power as the Crown of Natra would give him. That would make Zilok a god. And she needed Medophae to fight Avakketh, but Zilok would never let him go. She couldn't finish this negotiation on a whim. She had to have time to think.

"'Never trust a dragon...'" Morth said as she walked away.

"'...unless you are a dragon,'" she finished the old saying, pausing on the snowy path and looking over her shoulder. "Obviously, I'm the exception to that rule," she said. "And you've tampered with something that's eating you. I will help you, but I need to do some research."

"Smoke and mirrors," he said. "I know these games. All you care about is the return of your lover."

"Come back tomorrow." She walked away, and this time she didn't stop.

Zilok did not call out to her again.

14

MERSHAYN

MERSHAYN SLUMPED against the wall beneath the arched window of his sitting room. His sword lay across his lap, nestled in its scabbard.

You and Collus. You were the only friends I ever really had. And now you're what's left. My one, true friend....

He grabbed the cup at his side, missed the handle, and tipped it. He snatched the cup before it fell, spilling only a drop.

I'm so fast. Did you see that? Fast enough to become king and lose myself, lose my brother, lose Ari'cyiane, lose everything I love at the same time. So...very...fast.

He downed the rest, refilled it from the keg of Cirienne lager Lady Mae'lith had given him at his coronation, which sat with him against the wall. He didn't stop after two cups, didn't stop after four.

My lovely Lady Ari'cyiane...

He kept seeing the look of pure loathing she'd given him. Once, her smile had been his to feast on, to warm him in his quiet moments.

What is the point of being king if everyone you care about hates you?

He had left the window open to the chilly air. A cold breeze ruffled his hair, tickled the back of his neck, but he ignored it. With a grunt, he stood up, catching his sword and keeping his cup from spilling.

Masterful work, swordsman.

The voice in his head took on the accent of the swordmaster who had instructed him when he was ten years old. Master Debarc had been a once-great master swordsman from Buravar who made his living teaching out-of-the-way country lords who didn't know—or didn't care—about his reputation as a drunk. But the man had been the most natural swordsman Mershayn had ever known.

Any idiot can memorize footwork, Master Debarc would say. Your reflexes are your ally, your gut feeling is your captain. A real swordsman feels the fight like a dance. He hears his legs and arms speak to him with the voice of the gods. Your head serves you before the draw, but once your blade leaves its scabbard, cut your own head off, as they say. Listen to your arms and legs in the fight, swordsman. Listen to your heart. Never to your head.

"Arms and legs," Mershayn said, flicking his wrist and throwing the ale into the air in a thin column. He focused, following the ribbon of suspended ale and scooped it up neatly in the cup as it dropped. Another little drop escaped, dotting the floor. "Not drunk at all, see?" he said to no one, looking out the window. The moon was obscured by overcast, but Mershayn guessed it was just after midnight.

He shivered and pushed himself away from the window, went into his bedroom and opened his wardrobe. He needed a cloak, but his old, faded green cloak had been taken away. Instead, he had the ridiculous royal thing Lord Balis had given him with its thick, black fur trim.

I'm a king now. I have a fancy cloak. That's what I have. I have no sweet praises of adventurous ladies, no soft fingers to run through my hair. No kisses for me. I have a dragon taskmistress and a humorless dead woman for an advisor. I have a fancy cloak and cold women. That's what I have now. Huzzah.

He set the cup on top of the wardrobe and threw his sheathed sword into the air. As it sailed up, he hooked the cloak with two fingers, yanked it from the wardrobe and flung it over his shoulders. The cloak flared out impressively, settled perfectly, and he caught his sword by the middle of the scabbard before it hit the ground.

Masterful work, swordsman.

Mershayn deftly retrieved his cup of ale and left his bedroom, then headed for the door, an idea forming. Yes. He was going to take his fancy doublet and his fur-trimmed cloak down to The Barnacles. He was going to drink by the docks until he fell down on the wet stones, far away from this palace, far away from where anyone knew who he was—

A voice came from the window. "Do I know you?"

Mershayn spun like a spooked cat. His hand jumped from sword scabbard to hilt, and he twitched his wrist. The scabbard rang as it slid off the blade and hit the floor with a clatter. Ale spilled on his fancy cloak, but his sword came up, ready.

Mirolah stood in front of the tall, arched window, naked as the new snow. That monstrous beast of a dog stood at her side, his back easily as tall as her shoulder. The grotesque dog—its teeth had to be as long as Mershayn's little finger—let out a soft sound like a cross between a howl and a growl, then sat down. His pink tongue lolled out, and he panted.

"By the gods," Mershayn spluttered. "Mirolah!"

Her eyes were no longer the dark brown they had once been. They swirled with rainbow colors—no whites, no iris, no pupil.

"That is my name?" she asked. The monster beside her whined. Then, she nodded. "Yes. That is my name."

"By the gods, I thought you were dead." He came toward her. "We looked for you, but there was nothing. Just...blood on the rocks."

"I don't like those." She gestured at his sword.

The hilt was torn from his grip, and the sword hovered in mid-air as the scabbard rose to join it. The blade slid home with a clang, spun, and clacked on the table. The monster dog gave a short growl, as though approving.

This was surreal. Mirolah stood there before him, but

everything about it was wrong. She shouldn't be naked. She should be reaching for something to cover herself. And those eyes...

Mershayn's instincts screamed at him to get away from her, to go find Bands or Silasa and bring them here. This was supernatural. He needed them to help him navigate it.

Instead, he took Master Debarc's advice, and "cut off his own head." His legs wanted to go to her. His arms wanted to protect. He strode forward and wrapped his cloak around her bare shoulders.

She watched him like a cat watches water. Neither her face nor her rainbow eyes gave any indication what she was feeling. He stepped back. She made no move to fix the clasp. It was freezing in the room, but she didn't seem to notice.

"It's cold.... Are you... Are you cold?"

"Am I cold?" she repeated, not seeming to understand the words.

"It's freezing outside, and you have no...clothes." His fingers itched to close that cloak.

She shook her head. "I am not cold."

"Would you like to sit?" he asked.

She frowned as he took her elbow, then allowed herself to be led to the padded bench. As he sat her down, he managed to wrap her more snugly in the cloak. The monster dog whined, then lay down on the floor and put his giant head between his giant paws.

"Yes," she said to the dog. "I think he can."

Mershayn looked to the dog, then back to Mirolah. "Did you just talk to it?" he said.

"Sniff said I should come here."

Sniff. The dog. The dog was talking to her, and she was talking to the dog. Mershayn stepped back, trying to come up with words. Nothing was going to sound right, so he just started talking. "You're..." He let out a breath. "Well...by Thalius, you're alive."

"Who is Thalius?" she asked. "Do I know him?"

"Mirolah, I need to know what happened to you. You were dead. I saw you stabbed. Am I...am I dreaming?"

"Perhaps we are both dreaming."

"They threw you out a window."

The big dog whined.

"Sniff says I died," Mirolah said.

Mershayn opened his mouth, then closed it. "But you're...here...."

"If I'm talking, does that mean I am alive?" she asked.

Mershayn licked dry lips. He thought of Silasa. "Of course it does," he said slowly, but not very convincingly.

Those unnerving rainbow eyes narrowed. "You do not believe your own words."

He let out a little laugh, and realized he wanted to laugh again. He wanted to just keep laughing and laughing. Dragons and vampires and demigods and dead threadweavers coming back to life, and he was stuck in the middle, like he could do something about any of this.

Gods, he wanted to laugh, but he knew that once he started, he would never stop. He choked himself off by swallowing, cutting off the laughter that bubbled up.

He was out of his depth. He really should call for Bands, and yet...

She stood up. "Tell me how I died," she said. "I was stabbed. I was cast out a window. That window?" She pointed. The cloak slipped from her shoulders and piled on the floor.

Mershayn cleared his throat. "We must get you dressed. Stay there a moment."

She watched him without emotion. He went to his wardrobe, pulled out one of his doublets. It was far too large for her, but he wasn't trying to make a fashion statement tonight. He turned to find her standing in the doorway to his bedroom.

"Here." He handed her the doublet. "Put this on."

She looked down at her naked body. "I am not cold," she said.

"There are other reasons." He tossed the doublet on the bed, then had an idea. He snapped his fingers. "Or wait. Wait a moment here." She cocked her head.

He turned sideways, slipped past her and crossed the sitting room to the room where Sym had kept Ari'cyiane. Collus had mentioned the chests of Tyndiria's clothes that had not yet been moved, and sure enough, they were still there. Three chests against the wall. He opened one and discovered a pile of dresses. Thank the gods. He pulled the top one out, a yellow dress. He turned and found Mirolah standing in the doorway again.

"Sniff doesn't wear clothes," she said.

"Sniff is a dog. Dogs don't wear clothes."

"Ah," she said. "It's a human thing. And I am human." She blinked, and the rainbow colors bled from her eyes, revealing a glimpse of their normal brown color. "Modesty," she said slowly, as though dredging a long-lost memory. "It is shameful to be naked among other humans."

"Well...it's uncomfortable, at least." He held the dress out to her.

"But not all of the time."

"Yes, all the time. People wear clothes all the time."

"Not all the time...." she murmured, blinking with her normal brown eyes. "There was a man with golden hair. It is the only pleasant memory I have." She frowned, looking at the dress in her hand. "The other memories have fled. They hide from me, and the GodSpill speaks so loudly." She walked toward him, dropping the dress, and the rainbow colors began to swirl across her brown eyes. "Help me remember. When are clothes not uncomfortable?"

He held her shoulders as she advanced on him. "I will help you. I'll do whatever I can to help you."

"I remember it being pleasant. I need...something pleasant," she said, and suddenly Mershayn's arms moved without his command. They pulled her against him, tightened around her. It was like he was a puppet. He eyes swirled with rainbow colors again, the brown vanishing beneath.

His head craned forward, and she kissed him.

"Stop..." Mershayn gasped. "Please..."

Sniff whined nervously, got to his feet.

Mirolah's lips came away. She turned her head to the side, regarding the dog.

"But I am remembering," she said to him.

The dog gave a short bark.

"I do not wish to wait. The GodSpill is going to take me. If I don't remember, it will rip me away from this body."

Sniff emitted a high-pitched, supplicating whine.

She closed her rainbow-swirling eyes, her brow furrowed in frustration. "Very well," she said in a monotone.

The compulsion vanished, and Mershayn could control his own body again. He cried out, staggered away from her, and fell to the floor. He stayed there like a crab, breathing hard.

Mirolah looked at the yellow dress on the ground. It rose like an invisible person was inside it and went to her. It rose as she lifted her arms, dropped over her head and molded to her, lacing up the back on its own.

"Very well," she said. "Then tell me how I met you, how I know you. Tell me everything you remember about my life."

Mershayn got to his feet, calming his heart. He smoothed his doublet to let his mind settle, then he went to the table like he was entertaining some foreign noble. He pulled out a chair for her. "Please," he said. "Sit down."

She flicked an annoyed glance at the chair. Sniff whined, and she sighed and sat. Mershayn drew up a chair and sat opposite her.

"When I first met you," he began. "You saved my life...."

15

MERSHAYN

AT FIRST, Mershayn thought his story would fall upon the ears of a statue, but Mirolah's stony expression changed many times during the rise and fall of the related events. By the end of it, Mershayn began to get some idea of the pain Mirolah experienced in every moment. Her reserved demeanor shut away a tremendous turmoil. He talked, and she asked questions until the sun lightened the overcast skies outside the window, and his hangover began to push into his head.

A knock came upon the door. It was morning. The king's life was starting again. No doubt that was Casur, his page, knocking so politely on the door.

"There are five people outside the door," Mirolah said. "A young boy, a man with no sword." Her face darkened. "Two men *with* swords." She cocked her head as though listening to a sound far away. "And a woman...who is not really a woman."

"A moment, Casur," Mershayn called. He stood, regarded Mirolah. "I do not know what your return will mean to those who knew of your death. Are you prepared?"

She shrugged. "How should I prepare?"

"I don't know. I just... You've been through a lot. Are you sure you want more people asking you questions?"

"The woman who is not a woman, do I know her?"

He hesitated. "You, um, you know *of* her. Everybody knows *of* her. I...don't think you've ever met her, though." Mirolah and Medophae had been together before her death. Bands was Medophae's beloved from every legend he'd ever heard, but from centuries ago. "If anyone could help you, it's her."

Sniff shifted on the rug and gave a brief, lazy yowl. He looked up at his mistress with sleepy eyes and settled his nose between his paws again.

"I—" Mirolah began. A ghost of a smile flickered on her lips. "Yes, I would like to meet her. But..." She took his hand. "I need something first."

A rush of vitality swept into him from her fingertips, power like he had never felt before. His exhaustion burned away as did the beginnings of his hangover. Next, a thousand little hooks pierced every muscle in his body. He hissed, jerking back. But her hand was unbelievably strong. She held him.

The pain vanished, but the vitality remained, swirling inside him. He felt like he could sprint all the way to Buravar.

"Thank you," she said.

"What...what did you do to me?" he asked.

"I am sorry. I did not mean to hurt you," she said. "But I need..." She trailed off. "I need you."

"What did you do?" He felt like she had invaded his body with some threadweaver spell, but the feeling of invasion had gone. All that was left was the rush of energy that made him want to grin. He felt like someone had punched him in the stomach and then kissed him.

Casur knocked at the door again. "Your Majesty?"

"Just a moment," Mershayn said impatiently, then turned back to Mirolah. "How do you need me?"

"I...connected to you. I have...put a little bit of myself inside you. Like an anchor. So that I don't...drift away."

The thought that she had somehow altered him was frightening,

108

but he mastered himself. He reminded himself that, without her, he would be dead. If she wanted his life, it was hers to take.

"Good," he said. "Of course I will help you. My life is yours, if you need it."

The rainbow swirls receded a little, revealing her natural brown eyes. "Thank you," she said softly.

Casur knocked again. "Your Majesty," he said more urgently. "Are you all right? Lady Bands and Lord Sym await you."

Filled with such strength that he felt could snap a tree in two with his bare hands, Mershayn stepped to the door and opened it. Casur stood on the other side, his hands held anxiously at his sides. Behind him, Sym waited with his perpetual frown. Mershayn's two guards stood on either side of the door, watching Sym carefully.

Bands lingered just beyond the throng, her green eyes narrowed. She cocked her head questioningly. He'd never seen her make that face before.

"Good morning, everyone," he said, and he dismissed the guards and Casur. When only Bands and Sym stood with him, he said. "I have a guest who visited me this morning." He opened the door wide. Sniff saw Sym and got to his feet. The monstrous dog's lips pulled back over those crooked teeth, and he growled. Sym's jaw dropped. He looked back and forth from Mirolah to Sniff, and he backed up into Bands. She put a hand on his shoulder and stopped his retreat.

"Mirolah..." Bands said.

The two women studied each other, and the room fell silent. Even Mershayn, who felt perhaps he should try to control the situation, could think of nothing to say.

"Do I know you?" Mirolah asked.

"I looked for you myself, but I found no trace," Bands said. "I couldn't even sense any threadweaving where you had fallen. How are you...?"

"My first memories are of Sniff," Mirolah said. Sniff padded forward, thin eyes focused on Sym. He turned his great head toward Bands, who flicked a glance at him, then returned her gaze to Mirolah. The dog lowered his head, sniffed at her leg, then backed away. He gave a long whine that petered out into a faint growl.

"Sniff says you smell the same as the quicksilver girl, but you do not look the same."

"What quicksilver girl?" Mershayn asked.

"Elekkena was Stavark and Mirolah's companion before they met you, Your Majesty," Bands said.

"Then you do know me," Mirolah said.

"Yes."

"Tell me."

"Very well, but not here." Bands abruptly turned and left the room. Mirolah narrowed her eyes, then slowly followed into the hallway with Sniff at her heels.

Bands's abruptness was out of character. Mershayn knew her well enough to know that she was upset, possibly even scared, though that was impossible to know.

"Please follow me." Bands made an elegant gesture, and Mershayn made to go with them, but she held up a hand. "Not you, Mershayn. You stay with Sym."

"But I..." He trailed off at her look. It was urgent, and it brooked no argument. He'd never seen her look anything other than calm, but she was rattled.

"I...yes," he said. "I've got a lot to catch up on."

Mirolah looked back and forth between Bands and Mershayn, sensing the unspoken communication, but unable to decipher it.

"Please, Mirolah," Bands said gently. "Come with me." She led the way down the hall.

"I will come back," Mirolah said to Mershayn, then she and Sniff followed.

Mershayn stood there, thinking about Bands's look. It was all he could do not to run after her and ask her what it was all about. But he trusted Bands. She had never failed to deliver on her promises, and each had been for the best.

Threadweavers are her area of expertise, and I'm the king now. I need to trust her to take care of this. If Mirolah is dangerous, Bands is the best equipped to understand that and, if needs be, to deal with that danger.

Mershayn had to admit that he was relieved. Being with Mirolah was like trying to solve a complicated puzzle that kept changing.

Clearing his throat, he turned Sym. "We have a long day ahead of us."

"She died." Sym's hands were shaking. "She shouldn't be alive."

"Yeah," Mershayn said, doing his best to sound casual, as if dead women walking around in his room was a normal occurrence. "Those threadweavers do things differently. If you're afraid of them, Lord Sym, I suggest that you don't make any more of them your enemies."

Sym breathed hard, tense. His eyes darted frequently back to the door.

"What are you going to do? Run away?" Mershayn asked.

Sym's shoulders slumped a little, and his gaze went from the door to his boots.

"Come on, we have much to do," Mershayn said.

"Y-Yes."

"Yes?"

"Yes, Your Majesty."

"That's right."

Mershayn left the room and headed for the throne room. Petitions would begin soon.

His seneschal, a thin, impeccably dressed man named Vo'Dula who had been hand-picked by Bands, tracked him down and made him eat breakfast in the antechamber next to the audience hall. Vo'Dula wore the same disdainful half smile all the time. Mershayn couldn't figure the expression out. The man was competent, obedient, and—if Bands had chosen him—certainly loyal, but he didn't seem to approve of anything Mershayn said or did. Poking fun at Vo'Dula did nothing to draw out an explanation of his sour expression; the man could verbally spar with the best. Mershayn's probing jokes always ended up turning back on him.

After the inevitably unsatisfying banter with Vo'Dula, Mershayn spent the morning wrangling with the Buravaran trade consul. Sym was actually helpful during the talks, giving Mershayn information about previous agreements. It was like the Lord of Buir'tishree had an entire library inside his head, and he could just flip open books to whichever page he wished, whenever he wished.

Mershayn also listened to a dispute between a merchant and the sailing ship captain who transported his goods. In the late morning, Mershayn argued with Galorman Balis about what to do with the Wave-altered. They did not see eye-to-eye on the subject. Balis didn't see the Wave-altered as people anymore, but rather creatures that should be chained up in a dungeon like rabid dogs.

At noon, Vo'Dula reappeared and stood politely at Mershayn's right until Mershayn acknowledged him. The officious man led Sym and Mershayn to the antechamber to eat lunch and informed him that Lady Bands had put all the other petitioners off until the following day.

"And where is Lady Bands?"

"To my knowledge, Your Majesty, she has left the castle grounds. She did not inform me where she was going."

"And...was there someone else with her?" he asked.

"There are quite a few 'someone elses' in the castle, Your Majesty." Vo'Dula said sourly. "Did you have a specific someone else in mind? Or would you like me to decide?" The man somehow managed to sound deferential and snooty at the same time.

"Specific," Mershayn said, trying to sound snooty, too. He couldn't do it as well as Vo'Dula. The man's nasal voice just naturally dripped with disapproval.

"She spoke for a short time with a young woman in the garden," Vo'Dula said. "Then she left the castle. She said she had an errand. Shall I have her trailed?"

Mershayn narrowed his eyes, not sure whether Vo'Dula was poking fun or not, which was probably the seneschal's intention. "What about the young woman? Where did she go?"

"I do not know. Shall I have her trailed?"

"Never mind."

"Very good, Your Majesty."

"Is it?"

"If you say so, Your Majesty."

"What would you say?"

"'Will that be all, Your Majesty?'"

Sym snickered.

"Clever," Mershayn said.

"Thank you, Your Majesty."

Mershayn waved a hand. So far, it was impossible to verbally out-fence Vo'Dula, but he intended to keep trying. "What's next?"

"Lady Bands scheduled a sweaty altercation for your afternoon."

"A sweaty altercation?"

"With Captain Lo'gan, Your Majesty," Vo'Dula finished.

"You mean sword practice?"

"Of course, Your Majesty. What else could I mean?"

Vo'Dula was baiting him. Mershayn pointed a finger at the seneschal. "Did Bands put you up to this snide repartee? Or does it just come naturally?"

"I don't know what you mean, Your Majesty," he said in his nasal voice. "Could you be more specific?"

"No. I don't think I can."

"As you say, Your Majesty."

"So it's on the north practice ground?"

"I believe they do have some sticks and clubs there, Your Majesty."

"Thank you."

"I live to serve, Your Majesty."

Mershayn waved the man away and stood up. He hadn't practiced his swordsmanship for a single day this past week. He had made mention of it to Bands in an offhand comment yesterday, telling her that if being king meant he gave up swordsmanship, then he'd hand the crown to someone else. He'd be damned if he was going to end up one of those kings whose bulging belly spilled over the arms of his throne.

After leaving Sym at the guardhouse, Mershayn headed for the northern practice yard. He had no wish for Sym to watch his fighting style. Sym had proved that he could take small bits of information and use them to great advantage, and Mershayn had to acknowledge that Sym was probably one of the better swordsmen in the castle. No need in giving him any advantages, just in case he ever did get a blade into that hand.

Mershayn wound through the halls that seemed so familiar now. He took the stairs to the third floor, went to the far northern side of the castle, and went through the double doors that opened onto the circular flat arena that had been carved out of the mountainside. Snow melted on the cobblestones, succumbing to the warm sunshine and creating delightful little puddles between miniature snow hills.

Lo'gan and Deni'tri were already there, early as usual. Deni'tri leaned against the stone rail, watching Lo'gan swing a practice wooden sword back and forth.

"This is a pleasant surprise," Mershayn said. "I didn't think they were going to let you swing swords at me anymore." During Collus's tenure as king, Mershayn had come here often, and tested his prowess against Lo'gan as often as he could. He was the best swordsman in the guard, and the only one who could challenge Mershayn. So far, Lo'gan had legitimately won one or two of every ten matches.

Lo'gan didn't say anything, merely nodded politely. Mershayn liked to think that Lo'gan liked sparring against him, but he really couldn't say. It was possible that Lo'gan didn't like anything. He was driven by duty, so much so that it was possible he'd forgotten how to like anything, only how to follow the orders he'd been given and give the orders he knew needed giving, as duty dictated.

"Prepared to lose again?" Mershayn taunted him. Here, at least, he could pretend he wasn't king.

"Prepared to do my best, Your Majesty," Lo'gan replied.

"This could be your lucky day." Mershayn picked up the first wooden sword on the rack. They were all constructed to be the same, but each was just a little different in weight and balance. He swung the blade back and forth, getting the feel of it.

"As you say." Lo'gan paused. "Will you wear the pads today, Your Majesty?" He nodded at the sturdy shed against the castle wall.

"Not today or any other day." Pads were unrealistic. They were good for beginners, but they could only dull the edge of a real swordsman. Master Debarc had scorned pads. Of course, Master Debarc was a bitter, reckless drunk, but...

Mershayn and Lo'gan walked onto the snowy practice yard, and the moment Mershayn crossed the arena line, marked by thin, white flagstones, he drew in a deep breath and relaxed. No troubles could find him when he did this. This was what he was born for.

"I'm not much for preliminaries today, Lo'gan."

Lo'gan saluted in response. Mershayn returned the salute, then ran at Lo'gan. He slid to a stop in the slush, then lunged with the last bit of his momentum. Lo'gan parried the bold strike and came back with a speed that belied his age. Mershayn spun, batting the hardwood away. He backed up, feigning that he had lost his balance, then locked his step and thrust again. Lo'gan was waiting for it, though. He blocked the light strike and riposted. He'd long ago discovered that Mershayn liked to be tricky. The wood whistled by Mershayn's ear, but that had been the real set-up. Mershayn tapped Lo'gan on the side.

Lo'gan nodded, backed up a pace.

"Point," Deni'tri said.

"Where is your fire, Lo'gan?" Mershayn swung his blade negligently back and forth.

Lo'gan saluted again, walking toward him.

"Ah, the direct approach. I like your style." Mershayn watched Lo'gan's approach keenly. He liked to give his opponents the feel that he didn't care, that he was sloppy and reckless. It wasn't going to fool Lo'gan, of course. He knew Mershayn was meticulous when it came to swordsmanship. Still, Mershayn had gotten used to keeping up a bit of banter while he hammered at his opponents. It relaxed him, and that made it a hard habit to break.

Lo'gan attacked quickly, swinging low to Mershayn's left. Mershayn blocked. Lo'gan's sword bounced off the block, and he used the momentum to bring it around low right. Mershayn blocked, backed up a step. Like clockwork, Lo'gan used the momentum again to come back around at the left.

Too predictable, my friend.

Mershayn blocked. It was almost pleasant. This was the kind of workout he needed. Bands seemed exceptionally good at identifying that sort of thing.

As expected, Lo'gan, let the bounce take his sword around to the right—

He locked his stance, let out a grunt and came straight down for Mershayn's left shoulder.

Mershayn barely had time to get his sword up. The strength of the blow shocked his arm, knocked the sword down, and whacked his right forearm solidly.

"Point," Deni'tri said.

Wincing, Mershayn shifted the wooden sword from right to left and shook out his hand. "Ouch."

"You could use the pads, Your Majesty," Lo'gan said, and Mershayn wasn't sure if that had been a jab, or a serious statement. Probably serious, knowing Lo'gan, but maybe not....

"Going for my fighting arm. I see. I see," Mershayn said, making a fist and rotating it. He was going to have a bruise.

"I was going for your left shoulder, Your Majesty. Your block deflected it to the right."

"Thanks for the play-by-play," Mershayn said.

"You're welcome, Your Majesty."

See? That sounded like a joke.

Mershayn saluted, and they moved toward each other again. They exchanged a few token test strikes, swords clacking together, then Mershayn went all-out. Like Lo'gan had come after him, Mershayn returned the favor, thrusting left, then right, then straight at Lo'gan's face. With an intent wrinkle in his brow, Lo'gan blocked each. When there was the barest window of opportunity, he thrust at Mershayn's face. It was a long stretch, and it left Lo'gan over-extended. Mershayn swung sideways at Lo'gan's head—

But Lo'gan had planned it from the beginning. He ducked. Mershayn's wooden blade swung over Lo'gan's head, and the captain's sword swung into Mershayn's exposed belly with all the momentum of his spin.

The air whooshed from Mershayn's lungs, and he doubled over. His knees hit the slushy stones.

"Point," Deni'tri said, her voice worried.

Lo'gan dropped his sword in the snow and knelt Mershayn's side. "Your Majesty? Are you all right?"

Mershayn gaped like a fish on a riverbank, but his lungs wouldn't work. Finally, they started, and he sucked in a gulp of air.

"I apologize, Your Majesty," Lo'gan said.

116

Mershayn took another two deep breaths. "For what?" he wheezed. "For me taking a nap? That was a clever move." He took another few deep breaths and managed to recover himself. "I'm going to have to remember that. It was damned risky, though. If I'd decided to thrust at your chest, I could have had your eye. Even a stick can poke out an eye."

"Without risk, there is no victory. Especially against a superior opponent."

"For a practice session?"

"Isn't that why you wear no pads, Your Majesty? Because if we are to improve, we must dare some risk?"

Mershayn gave a coughing laugh. "Well said."

The small door that led from the practice arena to the castle burst open. Vo'Dula's page, Bimeera, burst through. She stumbled on the snow, gained her feet, and sprinted across the courtyard. Deni'tri, ever alert, stepped in front of the child. Bimeera slipped in the snow, and Deni'tri deftly caught her arm, held her upright.

"Hail, little one," Mershayn said, but he felt the tension that came with the breathless child. Something was wrong.

"Your Majesty!" She gasped, spent from her long run. "Lord Baerst has returned. They're burned. His soldiers. All of them. Dragons, Your Majesty."

"What?" Lo'gan asked sternly.

"Dragons. They've destroyed Corialis Port!"

16

BANDS

BANDS LED Mirolah down the hall, down the stairs, around the common room reserved for visiting nobles, and out into the royal gardens where she had entertained Zilok Morth only hours ago. Mirolah followed, and the giant skin dog trailed last, always a few paces behind her.

Bands moved quickly, because the woman behind her was more dangerous than anything in the kingdom at the moment.

In the garden, the melting snow still lay across everything like a white blanket. Bands navigated through the hedges and snowy, manicured trees, but her heart was racing.

It had taken Bands many years to learn how to threadweave like a human, using GodSpill to alter the saturated threads of Amarion rather than pulling it from what dragons considered to be the source of all power: Avakketh. In that time, she had developed a threadweaver's sight. She could see the great tapestry of the world. She could see how those threads made up all things.

What she saw in Mirolah was frightening.

A normal human was comprised of more threads than Bands

could count. An arm, for example, had thousands of threads twisting into the shape of bones, muscle and skin. Those threads were comprised of even tinier threads, and those tinier threads were saturated with GodSpill, the substance of creation from which the gods were made. That loose GodSpill, spilled from the Godgate millennia ago, was what threadweavers used to alter the world.

In addition, humans were connected to everything around them: to the air, to the ground, to the plants and animals around them. It was called the great tapestry because everything was interwoven. Humans were attached to everything, and yet they stood out as they moved. Threads shifted as they slid across the great tapestry of life, like the raised bump of a mouse under a sheet.

Everyone had a mixture of different colors.

Rocks, water, and other inanimate elements had muted colors. In Bands's vision, they were mostly shades of gray, with some earthy tones. But humans and animals were woven in bright, moving colors. Once-living creatures—corpses, bones, and the like—looked similar to the elements; they were gray once life left them.

All humans were predominantly one color or another. Medophae was almost pure gold. Zilok Morth was predominantly blue. Ethiel had been predominantly red, hence her nickname "The Red Weaver".

Mirolah's body was a corpse being flooded with pure GodSpill. One moment, it faded to a dead gray, the next it was full of colors. A rush of rainbow colors invigorated the threads, then leaked away, the color draining until another wave rushed in, filling her again. The colors cycled through her like the crashing tide of an ocean.

And the connecting threads, the ones that bound Mirolah to everything around her, were huge and grotesque. They converged on her in a nightmarish parody. Bands had never seen anything like it. The stones of the castle, the gravel of the garden path, grass and hedges to the sides, the trees looming over them, the very air around her, all bent toward Mirolah like gnarled, flexed muscles.

Mirolah was not the bump of a mouse under a sheet like normal people; she was a porcupine who had speared the fabric of reality,

119

balled it up, and pulled it with her as she moved.

I don't think she's actually alive.... Bands suddenly realized. She died, and somehow she's holding herself together by her own will and...power. By the gods...the sheer power it takes to do that!

It staggered Bands's imagination. Mirolah was forcing the GodSpill to suspend the natural order for her. Bands had seen powerful threadweavers, like Zilok Morth, live beyond their mortal years by lashing their spirits to an anchor, which was typically a significant object or person, but even Zilok couldn't keep his physical body alive once it had died.

Bands led Mirolah deep into the garden, as far away from anyone who might get hurt as possible, to a secluded circle of paving stones with two benches, backed by tall hedges. Bands hadn't survived thousands of years of death-defying adventures by being hasty, and she thought carefully about what she would say. Her first question had to be the right question. To a non-threadweaver's eye, Mirolah might seem strange with those rainbow eyes and her stilted manner, but they didn't see that Mirolah was a catastrophe about to happen.

As Bands's swirling mind tried to put together all the pieces—at least the pieces she could understand—she came to three realizations in quick succession.

First, as she had surmised earlier when she was posing as Elekkena, the GodSpill spoke to Mirolah in a way it didn't speak to other threadweavers. The GodSpill was...sentient for her. It talked to her. For other threadweavers, the GodSpill was a resource like water, or stone, or wood. But not only did the GodSpill seem sentient for Mirolah, it related to her like a tempestuous lover. All-giving. All-demanding. Irrevocably bound to her.

Second, Mirolah was unbelievably powerful, easily the most powerful threadweaver alive. She could even be at the mystifying level of Daylan Morth, who was akin to a god.

Lastly, if Mirolah was like a god, she might be indispensable in the battle against Avakketh. If she didn't explode first and take everyone in this castle with her.

The girl was a holy mess. Bands didn't understand what was happening to her, but she could see that much.

A fourth realization struck her. Oedandus kept Medophae alive; he couldn't kill himself if he tried. The nearly destroyed god rejuvenated Medophae to look exactly as he had been when Oedandus found him. Medophae didn't need to shave because he had shaved just before Oedandus infused him. He couldn't have short hair for more than a day or two because it would regenerate to the length it had been that day. Was it really Mirolah keeping herself alive with the GodSpill? Or was her tempestuous lover forcing her body to stay alive because it wouldn't let her go? If Mirolah had *wanted* to die...could she?

You poor girl.... What happened to you?

Bands gestured, pulling threads and whispering, "Scatter." The snow on both benches blew off. She wanted to show Mirolah that she, too, was a threadweaver. "Will you sit?" Bands asked.

Mirolah's rainbow eyes regarded Bands. She didn't look at the bench.

"Why would I sit?"

In a petulant noble, Bands would have seen the comment as verbal fencing. But Mirolah's voice had no inflection. She spoke like a child. She didn't know why she would want to sit. She did not have the normal responses of a mortal woman.

She has lost her memory.

"It is a human convention when conversing," Bands said calmly. "If you prefer to stand, I am happy to stand."

Mirolah glanced at the bench, then walked to it and sat down. She was barefoot, but of course the snow didn't bother her. Her body was dead.

Sniff whined, padding over and lying down in the snow at her feet. Even lying down, the giant dog's back rose higher than Mirolah's waist. He shivered, and suddenly the snow melted away underneath him. The water raced away and, in a moment, the entire space around the dog was dry.

Mirolah watched Bands with interest. Bands approached and knelt. "Will you take my hand?"

Mirolah hesitated, then took Band's hand. Her flesh was odd, cooling and warming in the pulse of a heartbeat.

"I am here to help you," Bands said softly. "What you need...I want to make sure you get it."

"Who am I?"

"You're a threadweaver from the small town of Rith. You came here with Medophae, Stavark the quicksilver, and Sniff the dog."

"And Elekkena, the false quicksilver," Mirolah said.

Bands nodded. "Yes."

"I did not know who you *really* were when I first met you," Mirolah said.

"No."

"Are you in your normal body now?"

Bands hesitated. "No."

"So you're giving me another false face. You're lying to me." Mirolah withdrew her hand. "I don't like lies."

This wasn't getting off to the best start. Bands stood, retreated to the other bench and sat down. "It is necessary," Bands said.

"Lying to me is necessary?" Mirolah's lip curled.

"I did not want to hurt you," she said simply.

"How would truth hurt me?"

"Because I was Medophae's beloved for a thousand years. And when I returned, you and he were...together. I thought it best if I did not reveal myself."

"Medophae..." she whispered, and Bands could see that his name struck a chord. "I loved him."

"Yes."

"You would have taken him away."

"My presence would have...unbalanced things."

"You were hiding from him."

"More so than from you, yes."

"Why be around him when he could not know who you are?"

Bands drew a breath and folded her hands in her lap. She hoped that she was going to play this correctly. "Because I love him, and because I have always had a hard time staying away from what I love."

Mirolah narrowed her eyes. Bands looked down at her hands for a moment, then back up.

"You're lying again," Mirolah said.

"No," Bands said. "I've told you one of two reasons."

"What is the other?"

"The dragon god, Avakketh, told me to kill Medophae. I refused. So Avakketh tried to kill me and failed. I escaped, returned to protect Medophae. But I...chose poorly. When faced with two threats to Medophae, I saw Avakketh as the greater and fought his agent in Teni'sia. I left Medophae to face Zilok Morth alone. I underestimated Zilok, which is not something I typically do."

"Zilok Morth..." Mirolah whispered. Her head twitched, and the rainbow swirls in her eyes receded a moment, revealing the brown beneath. It happened for a flickering instant, then the rainbow colors slid over her eyes again. "He trapped me. He hurt me."

"He...stabbed you."

"No, a boy with silver hair stabbed me. I remember that. I remember his curved sword. Over and over."

"It wasn't Stavark," Bands said.

"Stavark..." Mirolah said the name slowly, like she was tasting it.

"Zilok controlled him. He fought against Zilok's control as hard as you fought Zilok's trap. Stavark is destroyed with guilt over it. He wants to die."

Mirolah's eyes narrowed. "You are saying that Zilok killed me, not Stavark. That Zilok was using his body like Stavark used the sword."

"He... Yes."

Mirolah didn't say anything for a long time.

"Mirolah," Bands said. "I want to help you. And we need your help in turn. Avakketh wanted to kill Medophae because of what he can do. Avakketh is afraid because Medophae would have stopped the dragon god from destroying Amarion."

Mirolah frowned. "Amarion is a continent."

"He wants to kill every human in Amarion."

She gave no reaction to that, and instead looked over at Sniff. The dog whined. "Sniff says I should care about this."

"You should."

"Why?"

"Because you're human."

Mirolah's head lowered, but she kept her gaze on Bands. "You're lying..." she said quietly.

123

"Mirolah, you *are* human. You're also...something else. I want to help you—"

"You keep saying that, but I don't believe you. You're afraid of me. You want to control me. And you want to use me, but I am done being used. You say you want to tell me the truth, but you stand there in a form that is not your true form. I don't think I can trust anything you say."

"Some masks are necessary to make things right. If I took my true form..."

"Humans would know you for what you really are. A dragon. And they wouldn't trust you."

"Mirolah—"

"I don't think they *should* trust you. You are full of deception."

"Please... There is more to the story than that. It is necessary for you to believe me. Time is so short. It may already be too late."

Sniff whined.

"Someone is coming." Mirolah raised her head.

Bands stood up even as Zilok Morth's burning blue eyes materialized in the garden.

Dammit! It was falling apart so quickly, and Bands had to get on top of this situation. The last thing she needed was Zilok returning. Zilok would see Mirolah as an advantage to be seized and manipulated.

In a futile gesture, Bands stepped between Zilok and Mirolah.

Zilok's burning blue eyes hovered in the air. This time, a crown with tall, fat crystals hovered where his brow would have been. The Crown of Natra.

"Back so soon?" Bands asked calmly. She tipped her chin at the crown. "Is that it?"

"You knew this would happen," Zilok said.

Her belly fluttered with butterflies. Ambition stood atop disaster perched on the edge of calamity. This moment was going to give her a stomach ache. Zilok, arguably the most powerful threadweaver in Amarion, had returned with an artifact that could destroy gods. Sitting on a bench next to an absurdly large skin dog was a bundled GodSpill catastrophe waiting to happen. And bearing down on them in a matter of days—or hours—was the dragon god, bent on genocide. This could explode at any moment, swift and horrific.

Bands did what she always did in such situations: she stayed calm.

"To what are you referring, exactly?" she asked. "The suddenly warm weather? The new royal baker who nearly burned down the kitchens, or that Mershayn is shaping up to be quite a king?"

Zilok's eyes burned brighter. "Did you cause this to happen?"

"I've never been able to control the weather. Mershayn was a hidden gem. And the baker was simply incompetent."

"Don't fence with me," Zilok hissed.

"Then get to the point."

"You know of what I speak."

Bands's heart dropped as she suddenly realized what he must be talking about. "You've been to the north," she said softly. The attack had begun.

"You knew the dragons were coming."

"I told you," she said, waiting for Zilok to look beyond her, to see Mirolah, and to have that disaster blossom. Zilok had killed Mirolah. When he noticed her, he'd likely try again. And if she remembered him, she'd save him the trouble of attacking and go for his throat. Bands kept waiting for Mirolah to surge to her feet.

She didn't. And Zilok either didn't notice who she was, or simply didn't care.

So Bands continued the charade, feeling like she was walking on a floor of thin glass laid over a chasm.

"It's war, then," Zilok said.

"What did you see?"

"Corialis Port is in flames."

Bands swallowed. "How many dragons?"

"Two."

That was a relief, if anything could be a relief when hundreds of innocent people had just died. But if only two dragons had come south, then that meant Avakketh hadn't committed all of his followers just yet.

"They flew back to the north," Zilok said. "Why? If he's invading, why send two dragons and not a hundred?"

"You know the answer," she said. "There's only one reason Avakketh would hesitate to come south. He's afraid of—"

"Save your impassioned speech. I'm not giving you Medophae."

"Then you'll watch your homeland burn, you selfish spirit. I almost died trying to protect humankind. What have you done? And what are you *willing* to do? Where does your allegiance lie?"

"I have striven for centuries only to lead humans to the place that they rightfully deserve. My plans never came to fruition because your *beloved* kept stabbing me in the back."

Still, Zilok didn't seem to care that Mirolah was right behind Bands. It made the hairs on the back of her neck stand on end. Even if he didn't recognize Mirolah, at the very least he would care that some bystander was overhearing their conversation.

Was it possible that, somehow, he didn't see her? The very thought flummoxed her. It wasn't possible. Mirolah burned like a twisted sun made of bundled threads. Surely he could see that.

Bands desperately wanted to look over her shoulder to see if the girl had vanished, but she held herself still.

"Tell me everything you know about the Crown of Natra," Zilok said.

"Give Medophae to me."

"Put Medophae from your mind. He belongs to me. But if you help me understand this crown, quickly, I will stand with you against Avakketh."

Allying herself with Zilok Morth made her skin crawl, but he followed his own code of honor, as twisted as it was. If she could leverage that, having him in the fight against Avakketh could be advantageous. Zilok had been crucial in the fight against Dervon, and he'd only been a fraction of the threadweaver he now was.

"I will help you with the crown," she said.

"Time is short."

"Time is short for all of us, not just you. But we could end this war before it begins. You and I can only annoy Avakketh. In the end, he will win. Medophae could kill him. We need him. You want to know why Avakketh only sent two dragons to attack Corialis Port? It was meant to draw Medophae out into the open. Avakketh knows he has to deal with Medophae before he can have his way with Amarion."

Zilok's eyes flared. "Amarion will burn to ashes before I let Medophae go."

"Zilok—"

"Think well, Bands. I will return soon. If you have no answers for me, then I will leave Amarion to Avakketh and find a new place to haunt. Good luck with your defense, such as it is."

Zilok vanished.

Bands stood there for a long moment. She paid close attention to the flows of GodSpill. When she was certain Zilok was really gone, she turned.

Mirolah sat on the bench, the skin dog by her side. She hadn't moved.

"He didn't see you," Bands said.

"I didn't want him to see me." Those kaleidoscope eyes watched her.

Bands opened her mouth, closed it. Finally, she managed to say the only thing she could think of. "How...?"

"I willed it."

Bands looked away so her reaction didn't show on her face. The morning light sparkled on the snow. She tried to take some semblance of calm from the beautiful scene, and she tried not to be afraid of the woman who stood behind her.

Bimeera, the seneschal's page, suddenly slid around the edge of a hedge row. Her little face was beet-red, and her little chest pumped like a bellows, as if she had run up and down every set of stairs in the castle.

"Lady..." she huffed, unable to speak she was breathing so hard, "...Bands. There...has...been..."

"Corialis Port has been attacked by dragons," Bands said calmly. "Thank you, Bimeera. I will go to the council chambers immediately." She turned to Mirolah. "Will you accompany us, Lady Mirolah? This may concern you."

Bimeera's mouth went wide at Bands's foreknowledge of the attack, and stayed open when she saw the rainbow colors dancing in Mirolah's eyes.

"Yes," Mirolah said. "I will go."

17

MERSHAYN

THEY ALL WATCHED Mershayn enter the council room. Down the hall, the great royal clock ticked on old gears, and he shut the door against the sound, trapping himself with the kingdom's influential nobility. They were out of time. Every loud click on that clock whispered to him.

Now. Now. Now... The dragons are coming now.

It was an oval room with a large oval table set in the exact center. In years and decades past, Teni'sia's nobles had gathered in this place to discuss threats to the kingdom. No doubt the famous Queen Tyndiria's parents had sat in this room discussing the final Sunrider invasion. Perhaps they, like him, wondered if this was the end of the world. But this wasn't just an invading army of savage south men headed their way. These were dragons.

Mershayn stopped where he was, surveyed the nobles, and wondered crazily what historians would write of his reign.

An embarrassing side note in Teni'sia's distinguished history was Mershayn, the Bastard King. He ruled for one week. During that time, he was reviled by most, made catastrophic mistakes, and was burned alive by dragons.

Wall-mounted lamps lit the big room, illuminating this assortment of scheming nobles, legendary figures, and monsters. The table was large enough to seat fourteen people, and it was full. Each of the important houses were represented, including most of those who didn't think well of Mershayn. Lord Framden, Lord Balis, Lord Giri'Mar, Lady Ry'lyrio, Lady Mae'lith, Lord Baerst, Lord Mekenest, Lord Bordi'lis, Lord Kuh'ter, Lady Ari'cyiane, Lord Vullieth, and, of course, Lord Sym.

Bands stood by the window, looking absently at the night sky. Mershayn and his dragon ally had spent the afternoon interviewing Lord Baerst about the dragon attack. A longer conversation followed between just himself and Bands, talking about what must now be done.

Not for the first time, he wondered who was really running this kingdom, him or her. She deferred to him in public and private alike, but what Bands suggested always came to pass. Mershayn didn't like leaning on just one person time and again, trusting her implicitly, but Bands had had been right every time. She seemed to know the future.

Silasa was here, as well. Her long, black hair flowed down her back, unbound. It was almost always fixed into a long braid, and he wondered if there was any significance to that. The vampire waited in her old-fashioned black dress with her even-legged stance, her hands hanging calmly at her sides. The corners of her mouth were turned slightly downward, as usual.

Lord Vullieth, an imposing man at six and a half feet tall, sat at the far end of the table. Apparently he'd had difficulty walking in the first few days after Sym's tortures, but he seemed to be recovered now. Orange light danced across his sharp features. His carrot-colored ponytail wound around the side of his neck and onto his shoulder. He watched Mershayn with a quiet intensity. Was that hope or hate in his eyes? It was hard to tell with Vullieth.

Lord Baerst lingered near the door, studying a coat of arms from some ancient Teni'sian royal family. Baerst's information was invaluable, and he suddenly seemed friendly to Mershayn—if obnoxious. But Mershayn trusted him less than the hostile nobles who had put Sym on the throne. Even Bands seemed suspicious.

The man was acting...oddly.

Four days ago, Baerst—under the guise of serving as an advance scout for unusual activity in the north—had been banished because of his collusion with Grendis Sym. This afternoon, he returned by ship with the tale that two dragons had destroyed his escort and the entire city of Corialis Port. Mershayn might have considered Baerst's story a ridiculous lie fabricated to gain himself passage back into the castle, but the crews of two other sailing ships, also newly returned from Corialis Port, had confirmed Baerst's story. Corialis Port was gone, burned to the ground.

Still, how Baerst himself had survived when the rest of his escort had died was a tense mystery. Baerst had given an unlikely account that involved hiding from dragons in flight, lying in a rowboat for half a day, and at least two heroic attempts to save his comrades. Only one returned with him. That woman, horribly burnt, lay unconscious in the infirmary. If she lived, they would not get her account for days.

Mershayn found the story hard to swallow, to say the least. And then there were the changes in his personality to consider. Baerst had always been a taciturn, humorless man. His servants told of how strict he was, quick to find fault and mete out punishment.

That was not the same man who had returned. This casual, swaggering fellow was quick to laugh and quicker to drink. He carried a flask on his waist constantly now, and he sipped from it when he didn't have a tankard in his hand, which he currently did. Even Mershayn could see the difference, and he wondered if the shock of seeing a dragon close-up had addled the lord's brains. The man had smiled more today than in all the months Mershayn had known him.

Baerst caught Mershayn's gaze and hooked his thumbs into his wide belt. His smile was all but hidden beneath the thick, curly blond beard which hung almost to his belly.

Stavark sat cross-legged on the floor not far from Mirolah, looking miserable. His silver gaze either looked at Mirolah or at his own shoes. The gods only knew what he was thinking. When he'd heard that Mirolah had returned this afternoon, he had rushed to the threadweaver's side and begged her to take his life. Bands said that Mirolah—with no malice on her face—had been about to oblige the quicksilver when Bands stopped her.

The monstrous skin dog lay at Mirolah's feet, apparently sleeping. The nobles were all afraid of him, and Mershayn found a comical irony in that. Of the odd characters standing by the wall, the skin dog was the least dangerous. Mershayn wouldn't want to fight the dog, but he'd certainly rather tangle with it than face Silasa's unearthly strength, Stavark's unearthly speed, Mirolah's ability to change reality, or Bands's dragon ability to, apparently, destroy entire cities with fire if she wanted.

Mirolah focused entirely on Mershayn, as though no one else in the room held any interest for her. She flicked that rainbow gaze toward Lord Baerst once, but only briefly. Then she watched Mershayn again. The sight of her sent a quick thrill through him, which he tried to ignore. Like her, his gaze kept wanting to go to her. He felt...bound to her, and he thought of those painful hooks that had turned so sweet afterward. He wanted to touch her, put his hands on her cheek, into her hair, put his lips on hers...

Mershayn shook his head and looked back at the nobles.

"I would like to call this urgent meeting to order," he said.

He received affirmative noises from the few nobles who supported him. Reluctant nods came from those who had been loyal to Sym, but the fact that they were here, now, was testament to Bands's wisdom in keeping Sym alive. They might not like Mershayn, but most of them wouldn't even be here if he had executed Sym.

Lord Framden, watching Mershayn with narrow eyes, looked like he'd eaten a lemon. Lord Bordi'lis stared incredulously at Mershayn's companions, as if Mershayn was parading Wave-altered horrors before them just for shock value. Lord Giri'Mar looked like he wanted to draw his sword, keeping an eye on the snoozing Sniff. And of course, Ari'cyiane glared daggers at him. Like Mirolah, Ari'cyiane only had eyes for Mershayn, but they were very different eyes.

Still, there were some who seemed happy to see him in charge. Lady Mae'lith gave him a warm smile and an inclination of her head. Lord Vullieth watched him with what Mershayn imagined as encouragement, though no emotions ever really crossed that man's face.

And Lord Baerst suddenly seemed friendly. He bowed at the waist. "Your Majesty," he said in his rumbling voice, without a trace of sarcasm. Stavark turned his haunted gaze up from Mirolah. Bands did not look away from the window.

"I called you all here to discuss a threat to the kingdom," Mershayn continued.

"What needs to be said?" Baerst asked. "Corialis Port is gone. And where do you think the dragons will turn next? Teni'sia, that's where. North Fort is between Corialis Port and here, and there are a handful of villages, but I doubt those monsters will even bother with them."

"I find it difficult to believe," Lord Balis said, his high-pitched voice cutting the air like swords screeching against one another.

"Perhaps you should visit poor Kye'fala in the infirmary then. Burning is believing, as they say." He winked.

Mershayn opened his mouth, but he didn't know how to respond to that crass comment. He glanced at Bands. Her brow had wrinkled at Baerst's insensitivity, but she continued to stare at the night sky.

"I am willing to concede there was a fire," Lord Giri'Mar said, his eyes glittering in the firelight. "But Lord Balis is correct. Dragons are stories,"

"Damn near burned my beard off!" Baerst protested.

"How close were the flames, I wonder?" Giri'Mar asked in a flat tone.

"And what are you implying, my lord?" Baerst growled.

"Implying? Nothing. I'll state it outright. The rest of your escort is dead or dying, my lord, but you are unhurt. The only way you could have escaped that fire is if you started the fire yourself, or if you are a coward who ran while they stood their ground."

Baerst's face went beet-red, and he spluttered.

"We aren't here to point fingers, Lord Giri'Mar," Mershayn interjected. "Lord Baerst is right. The dragons are coming. We must meet this threat, and I ask for your counsel." He focused his attention on Giri'Mar. "Many new and strange things have happened this past month. GodSpill has returned to the lands and with it, many changes. Is a dragon so hard to believe?"

"I acknowledge your Wave-altered...oddities with their strange eyes," Lord Balis said, flicking a finger at Mirolah and Silasa. "But that does not mean there are dragons in the world."

Mershayn clenched his teeth and tried not to explode at this lord who, in conjunction with Lord Balis and Lord Bordi'lis, had wanted to cage all the Wave-altered and either experiment on them or kill them outright. One of the first things Mershayn did as king was release all of the Wave-altered. Giri'Mar and Balis had hated him from that moment forward. It was said Lord Bordi'lis had foamed at the mouth.

"There are no dragons in the world," Giri'Mar growled through his bristly black beard, which seemed to stick straight out from his face. "Tales from legends. Nothing more."

"I, too, have never seen a dragon," Mershayn said, striving to stay calm. "But they exist." He glanced at Bands, who still had not joined the conversation. "This was something we surmised even before Lord Baerst went north. That he returns with stories of dragons is not unexpected."

"You sent me, knowing the beasts were up there?" Baerst blasted, stunned.

Mershayn shook his head. "I sent you north to scout possible threats. When I did, I was of the same mind as Lord Giri'Mar. I did not believe in dragons. But I believe in them now."

"I do not, Your Majesty," Giri'Mar said. "When your half brother sat the throne, there were rumors of many things. Monsters in the forests. Monsters in the deep of the Inland Ocean. Threadweavers rising like the tales from long ago. Yet all I have seen are aberrations. Ugly dogs. People with strange aspects, yes, but nothing like the legends tell. These are dangerous freaks, Your Majesty. They must be contained as such. But I refuse to believe in dragons and unicorns simply because the drunk Lord Baerst says it is so."

"I understand your reluctance," Mershayn said. "But in fact, threadweavers have returned. And if there are creatures like that," he gestured at Mirolah's monstrous skin dog, "then we might believe in dragons and unicorns as well. And threadweavers, well... There are two threadweavers in this room right now."

Giri'Mar leaned back, eyes narrowing. Bordi'lis's fat cheeks turned red as his fearful gaze flicked from Silasa to Mirolah to Bands to Stavark, then started over.

Giri'Mar was cooler about it, but his gaze came to rest on Stavark. "The boy with the silver hair?"

"No," Mershayn said. "Lady Bands and Lady Mirolah."

"Prove it to me," Giri'Mar said gruffly. "Turn Lord Baerst into a rat."

Baerst roared indignantly.

Mershayn held up a hand. "We're not turning anyone into anything." He looked to Bands for help, but she was still ignoring the lot of them, staring out the window. A little reluctantly, Mershayn turned to face Mirolah's swirling eyes, which were still focused on him.

"Lady Mirolah," he said softly. "Might I ask you for a small demonstration, simply to put this argument to rest?"

"Shall I turn Lord Baerst into a rat?" she asked without a trace of humor.

"Now wait a minute!" Lord Baerst roared.

Mershayn held up a placating hand before Mirolah could answer. "I don't believe that would be very constructive. Perhaps something else? Something to convince Lord Giri'Mar?"

Mirolah turned to Giri'Mar. He returned the gaze, and some of his cool haughtiness melted away under her unearthly stare. He squinted like he was looking into the sun.

With a groaning sound, a flagstone pulled away from the floor. It rose three feet into the air and floated toward Giri'Mar. He gripped the armrests of his chair tightly, but did not flee. Rock cracked and dust drifted to the floor. The flagstone turned lazily in the air as chunks broke and fell away. Once the bulk had been reduced, the remaining stone began to spin lazily, then spun faster and faster, shedding chips of stone.

The spin slowed and stopped. A wide, short-stemmed grail, engraved with the coat of arms Baerst had been studying, floated toward Giri'Mar. It hovered above his lap for a moment, then dropped.

Giri'Mar jumped, barely catching the grail before it tumbled to the floor. He took a long moment, staring at it in astonishment, then he flicked a glance to Mirolah. Finally, his gaze went to Mershayn. Giri'Mar swallowed. "I will concede the point," he said in a barely audible voice. His breath came fast, but otherwise, Mershayn thought he remained remarkably composed.

"There are dragons, my lord. Best believe it," Mershayn said.

The nobles all looked shaken. Mershayn felt the same way the night Silasa had pulled him out of the dungeons, like a man who had swum in the ocean his entire life and suddenly realized there were giant sharks just beneath him.

"Now that we all believe the same things are possible, I think we should listen to Lord Baerst's tale. The news he brings will occupy much of our time in the near future." Mershayn inclined his head toward Baerst, then sat in one of the fourteen chairs encircling the table.

"I wish I had more to report than I do," Baerst said, raising his hands and letting them fall at his sides. He let out a breath and tugged at his beard. "We sailed into North Fort on the first night. Everything was well there, so we continued on. The next day, we sailed into Corialis Port. Again, all was well. We stopped at a dockside inn for some rest and a tankard or two." He raised his tankard and took a drink. "That night, the city exploded."

"Please be specific," Mershayn said.

"Two dragons flew in. The beasts burned everything. We started by trying to fight. My escort drew their swords, but how do you fence with something that flies over your head? Swords are useless, and we had only four bows among us, so we pulled them. We even hit one of the bastards as it flew over..." He paused at that word, looked at Mershayn. "No offense, Your Majesty."

Mershayn had long ago learned that the more he reacted to people calling him "bastard" the worse it was for him. Best to let such things pass. "Please continue, Lord Baerst."

"Well, we might as well have thrown a pebble at it. The arrow bounced off the scales. O' course, the dragon took offense to it and turned its breath on my archers. Burned three of them to nothing. I'm not kidding. To nothing. There were no bones left or anything. The rest of us retreated to the docks, thinking that being near the water would be best when dealing with fire. Didn't matter. We fired again with our last bow, and the dragon breathed on us again. This time, I managed to save only one of my people. The rest died in fire. I knew then I had to retreat and warn the kingdom. I stole a rowboat, dumped poor Kye'fala into it, and swam next to it, submerged in the water and moving as quickly as I could. Luckily, the dragons didn't seem interested in one little rowboat heading out to open water." Baerst cleared his throat and took another drink. "Luck was with us. *Kaylan's Star* and her crew witnessed the entire horrifying slaughter, and they came for us. They are to be commended for their courage. Instead of fleeing, which would have been the sane thing to do, they sailed toward Corialis Port and took us on board. Captain Lyndyr and her men are the only reason I'm standing here now."

"And how did you escape injury?" Lord Balis inquired in his high-pitched voice.

"Thalius was looking out for me. That's all it could be," Baerst said.

Balis raised an eyebrow.

"If you could provide a little more detail, Lord Baerst," Mershayn said. "You understand. We might need to fight dragons in the very near future. I am interested as to how you remained unburnt."

"Fight 'em? Hah! I hope you've got a plan, because I'll tell you this, cold steel doesn't work. Arrows don't work. Might as well throw sticks at 'em."

Baerst paused, picked up his tankard and frowned into the empty bottom, set it back down.

"Why didn't they fly out and burn the ships that escaped?" Vullieth asked. "To something that flies, it could only have been a few moments to do so."

"How should I know? Now I think on it, I didn't see either of them fly over the ocean. Not once. They looped about the city several times, but always over the plains or mountains."

"Dragons do not fly over water." Bands spoke up for the first time, but still faced the window. "The waters of the True Ocean are deadly to them, so not only do they avoid touching those waters, but they avoid flying over them. They also avoid the Inland Ocean out of habit, though its waters are not deadly to them. Dragons have their own superstitions."

"And how would you know?" Baerst asked.

She turned around and finally looked at the assemblage with those emerald green eyes. "I know a few things about dragons," she said.

"You have studied dragons then, I take it?" Balis asked.

"For many years. Yes."

"And you've seen these creatures as well?" Giri'Mar asked.

"Many times."

"Then how do we kill them?" Giri'Mar demanded.

Bands drew a breath, keeping her calm gaze on them. "If we are to fight dragons, we will need many things. The first is weapons that can hurt them. As Lord Baerst says, normal steel is useless. Their scales are bound with threadweavings that will turn normal weapons."

"Threadweavings?" Giri'Mar said.

"Constructs fueled by GodSpill. It makes their scales supernaturally tough," she replied. "Imagine these enhanced dragon scales as three suits of plate armor. You would have to pin a dragon down and hammer a spike into their scales to get through. A slice will do nothing."

"Then how?" Baerst asked. "How do we fight them? You're saying we need new weapons?"

"No, Lord Baerst. We will need old weapons."

18

MERSHAYN

THE COUNCIL ADJOURNED after Bands talked about the need for enchanted weapons from the bygone age of threadweavers. That was the next step, to secure those weapons, and she said she would handle that part.

As Bands and Mershayn had discussed earlier, Mershayn turned to the assemblage.

"I have come to you for counsel. Does anyone have any at this moment?"

The room fell silent. Bands had predicted this would happen. Only Baerst had any experience with dragons. How could you counsel about something you didn't understand?

Giri'Mar cleared his throat. He seemed as taken aback by the information as anyone else, but his usually angry face looked thoughtful. "There are two catapults on the Northern Walk, Your Majesty. And on the western wall. I think we can repurpose them to shoot at the sky, rather than at the base of their respective walls. There are also the parts of several others in the lower levels of the castle. Queen Tyndiria had them dismantled barely a year ago, once the threat of the Sunriders was gone. We could reassemble them in locations that might best brunt an attack from the air."

Mershayn pointed at the squat, muscular lord. "That is the kind of thinking I need. Thank you, Lord Giri'Mar. If you would please lead a group to reassemble those catapults."

"Yes, Your Majesty."

"We will need more guards for the city," Lord Balis said in his high voice. "If the dragons are coming here, every man, woman, and child will need to fight. Lord Bordi'lis is excellent at training."

Balis and Bordi'lis were two of Sym's staunchest allies. Mershayn didn't like the idea of allowing Bordi'lis to create his own militia. That could go wrong in so many ways, but Balis wasn't wrong. Everyone needed to be in this battle, because they'd all be dead if they failed to repel the dragons. He turned to Bordi'lis.

"Would you be willing to assist conscription and training?"

Bordi'lis's sour face turned to Mershayn. "I won't work with any of the creatures distorted by the Wave." He flicked a gaze full of contempt at Bands.

"I wouldn't dream of saddling you with more than you could handle, my lord," Mershayn said. "Lady Mae'lith is renowned for her sword skill and training expertise. She will lead this task with you."

Bordi'lis's lips pressed together so hard they turned white. Lady Mae'lith hated Sym and his associates. There were whispers that her husband, Lord Grimbresht, had not died naturally, but rather had been assassinated because of his vocal opposition to Lord Sym and his agenda.

Checks and balances were handy.

"Of course, Your Majesty," Bordi'lis said coldly.

"It would be my pleasure," Lady Mae'lith said with genuine pleasure in her voice.

Mershayn commanded that the rest of the nobles prepare their houses for war. Battle could come in a week. It could come in a matter of hours. They should make preparations immediately.

The nobles left the room urgently, one at a time. Lady Ari'cyiane gave Mershayn a venomous scowl as she passed him, but her husband stopped and clasped Mershayn's forearm in a strong handshake. He didn't say anything, but the gesture said volumes.

"Thank you, Lord Vullieth."

The tall lord nodded and left.

Silasa followed Sym to make sure he returned to his handlers without any detours. Stavark waited for a moment, then also left quietly. Mirolah watched Mershayn, then went to the window where Bands had been standing, and jumped out.

Mershayn reflexively reached for her before he remembered that a step out a window was no more dangerous for Mirolah than walking across the floor. Sniff got to his feet and bounded after his mistress into the wide expanse of the night.

Mershayn went to the window and watched them both float gently down to the snowy slopes below, then turned away.

Bands stood by the table where the nobles had assembled, her hand on the polished wood. "That went well," she said.

"For a while, I thought you weren't going to say anything," he remarked. "You're the expert here, you know."

"Your nobles don't need to see me whispering in your ear. You're the king. They should look to you."

"But I look to you."

She paused, as though such a thing was distasteful to her. "We have been lucky to have this past week," she said, shifting the subject. "It's a gift. Avakketh doesn't know Medophae is gone, and I suspect that is the only reason we've had this precious week. If Avakketh knew Medophae was gone, he would have hammered Teni'sia already and not just made a feint at Corialis Port."

"That was a feint?" Mershayn asked, chilled. An entire city had been destroyed.

"I believe he's trying to draw Medophae out, which means Avakketh may have a plan for containing him."

"Why not just attack directly?"

"Fighting Medophae one-on-one puts Avakketh in the most danger. Avakketh suspects he could overcome Medophae—and he's probably right—but he doesn't know it for certain. There is too much chance, and all gods hate leaving things to chance except Tarithalius. The fact is that Oedandus killed Dervon through Medophae. And if he could do it once, why couldn't he do it twice?

But if Avakketh can pinpoint Medophae's location, then he can either attack elsewhere, reducing the human population without having to face Medophae, or he can set a trap for Medophae."

"Is Medophae really that important?"

"He is the only way this fight ends with us still alive. Humans fighting dragons is nearly impossible. At best, we can bloody them and buy time. But when Avakketh comes south, we will lose unless Medophae fights him. We can't beat a god. Not me. Not you. Not all the humans in Amarion. Even Tarithalius would lose against Avakketh."

"Tarithalius? The god of humans Tarithalius?" Mershayn asked breathlessly.

Bands nodded. "Avakketh is the most powerful god still alive. Tarithalius is probably the least powerful."

"But then how can Medophae kill Avakketh?"

"Oedandus was once the most powerful, save Natra. Of course, he has been bent and broken, tortured and diminished such that he barely has any wits left. But his vast power was still there when Medophae destroyed Dervon. It might be enough."

"Might be?"

"Just how much does Oedandus have left to give? If Avakketh pushes with all his strength, would Oedandus even have enough strength to brunt such an attack? No one can possibly know. I do know that Dervon died because he was overconfident and didn't think for a second that Medophae could kill him." She shook her head. "Avakketh won't make that mistake. If Avakketh comes prepared to fight, he will have the advantage. Avakketh is a full god at the height of his powers. Oedandus is broken, insane, and must squeeze himself through a mortal to affect anything."

Mershayn turned away, trying to assimilate all of this. Just when he thought he understood the gravity of the situation, Bands added a new level.

"So we can't fight him," he murmured.

"Medophae must."

Mershayn threw his hands up and looked at her. "But Medophae is gone."

"A secret that we must carefully guard," she said.

"You're missing my point," Mershayn said. "We don't have Medophae. Whether Avakketh knows or not, eventually he's going to come. And when he comes, we die. What is the point of trying to find a way to fight his dragons, then?"

"Because we have to play for time."

"To what end?"

"Medophae will return."

"Oh? Well, good," Mershayn said sarcastically. "Why didn't you say so? When?" He frowned at her.

"Soon."

"How do you know?"

"Because I know Zilok. And I know Medophae."

"Then where is he?"

"Leave Medophae to me. That will be my part of this battle. The reason I spent so much time with you is to make sure you can handle your part."

"By the gods..." Mershayn shook his head. "My part. You mean the part where I convince a kingdom that mostly hates me to mobilize so we can fight invincible dragons we can't reach with enchanted weapons we don't have?"

She smiled. "Just imagine the stories that will be written when you succeed."

"We're going to die," he murmured. "It's impossible."

"Impossible," she said, and her gaze became thoughtful. A small smile crept across her beautiful face. "I've seen mortals do the impossible over and over. Every time they do, it's because they look at the dark wall of impossibility for one small crack that shows light. I've watched Medophae do it time and again. Mirolah has done it at least twice that I know of. When almost all options vanish, we choose the one thing we can choose. Then, step by unlikely step, we achieve the impossible. That's the only way it's ever been done. I suspect that's the only way it ever can be done."

"That's...that's no comfort at all."

"It's joyous, actually."

"How?"

"Your back is against the wall, Mershayn. What will you do?"

"I don't know."

"Yes, you do. If I was Avakketh, and I attacked you right now, grabbed your throat, and put you up against he wall, what would you do?"

"Fight," he said. "And die."

"Well, let's start with the first one. There's plenty of time for dying later."

"You really think we can win?"

"We *will* win," she said.

He laughed darkly, invigorated by her optimism despite himself.

"Hold strong, Mershayn. As long as we have a chance, we will take that chance, one unlikely step at a time."

He bowed his head. "Okay." He wrapped his mind around this bizarre dueling field and forced himself to commit to it. Their foe was superior, and the only way to defeat a superior foe was take the big risk every time, just like Captain Lo'gan had said. Every strike could be their last, so every strike had to be desperate. "Okay," he repeated. He put his fears behind a thick door in his mind and locked it. "Step by step."

"Step by step." She nodded her approval as though she could see his thoughts.

"As always, I will follow your advice. I've had no cause to regret it. But I want something."

"If I can give it, I will," she said.

"We're being attacked by dragons. I want to see one. As king, I should know what we're dealing with. I want to see one up close."

Her chin lifted slightly as she realized what he was asking. "Ah..."

"I want to see what you look like."

She looked around the room, as if sizing it up. "If you wish." She stepped away from the table. "It will be cramped. Stand on the table."

"On the table?" He glanced around. The room was more than fifty feet long.

She gestured at the desk. It floated gracefully away from her, stopping when it butted up against the south wall beneath the coat of arms.

"If you please. On the table. And don't move until the

transformation is complete."

"Of-of course." He climbed onto the table.

She went to her place by the window, gave one more critical look at the oval room, then spoke a few words Mershayn could not understand.

The air around her shimmered as though a great heat had been released. Translucent waves rippled in front of her. She fell onto all fours, and her head shot upward on a scaly neck, widening and thickening. Scales appeared, overlapping each other as they rippled across her growing body like a wave. Her shoulders expanded, growing wider than Mershayn was tall. Claws burst from the tips of her fingers as her knuckles curled and widened. Her long body curved around the table, filling the room. Her front legs thickened, supporting the swelling, massive chest. Huge, thin wings sprouted from her back and tucked against her emerald body. The last to appear was her tail, probably as long as the rest of her whole body. It followed the contour of the oval walls, poised in the air.

She was bent like a wheel, nose to haunches, encircling the entire room, which suddenly seemed tiny. Mershayn felt like a mouse. Her wide, flat head ducked below a coil of her light-green banded neck, and faced him. Her head lowered and rested gently on the table, nearly as tall as he was. Her lips peeled back, showing a fortress of pearly white teeth as long as swords.

"Are you okay?" Her voice emanated from those great jaws. Her breath was hot and smelled like the bakery at the bottom of the castle.

"By the gods..." he murmured. He tried to imagine jumping on something like this and trying to kill it. It would be like trying to kill a mountain.

"Have you seen what you needed to see?" she asked. Her lips moved against those teeth, and her voice sounded precisely as it did when she was a woman. How could that be?

"Can I... Can I touch you? Your, um, your tail?"

She laughed, and it was an enchanting thing. He did not know what he expected, a booming roar or an unearthly shriek? But her laughter was like chimes in the wind: subtle, delicate and compelling.

"Of course you may."

His fingers trembled as he reached down. Her scales were cool, but as he held his hand there, he felt warmth rise underneath, as though she was burning deep inside.

"And you...breathe fire?"

"Not in here."

"I have no idea how we are going to defeat creatures like you..."

"One step at a time. We go as far as we can go. We go until we can't go anymore."

Numbly, he nodded.

The air shimmered again, and her transformation reversed itself. In a moment, Bands stood by the window as she had before: a tall and slender human with muscled arms and a brilliant emerald gown hugging feminine curves. She pushed a lock of blond hair back from her eyes.

"So what next?" he asked.

"You prepare your people for war," she said.

"And you?"

"I am going on a journey to talk with ghosts."

19

MERSHAYN

MERSHAYN LEFT his guards in the hall and closed his bedroom door. He let out a breath and leaned back against it. His felt the oak, rough beneath his fingers. Solid, real.

His mind wandered away to one year ago. One short year. He, Collus, and their father, Lord Bendeller, had visited Buravar. It was a beautiful city, old and full of history, one of the few cities still around that had stood during the Age of Ascendance. He and Collus had treated it like their own personal playing field. They would steal away to Gretienna's House, start the night there with a snifter of brandy and a bawdy story or two. What cares did a Teni'sian lord and his bastard half-brother have? The only worry was if they would run out of wine or willing women. The nights seemed to last forever.

And the days were full of diligence, sweat, and hard work. While Collus spent time at court, Mershayn had spent time with local swordmasters expanding his one talent. Mershayn had wanted to ensure that—though he would never have pure blood—he could at least best any pureblood with a blade. He had resented the station of the purebloods because they could achieve what would always be denied him.

And now he was king. He had thought the pleasures would be endless with such a high station, but it wasn't that way at all. There was no snifter of brandy awaiting him. No careless nights and bawdy stories to set his blood racing. Now his blood raced for unpleasant reasons, like Teni'sia burning by dragon fire.

He leaned his head back against the door and closed his eyes. The events of the past week had split him into two men. One man tried hard to be a king. That man directed nobles to prepare for invasion. That man stood unflinching as a woman turned into a mythical monster.

But the other man wanted to run. He was a selfish rogue. When he saw something dangerous like a dragon, he wanted to get himself out of harm's way, not put himself there to protect another, let alone an entire kingdom of others.

He glanced at his table where an array of liquors sat side-by-side, and he laughed to himself.

He thought of Bands's advice: one step at a time.

He thought of Silasa's advice: a king sleeps.

Perhaps this was a moment to think like the Mershayn of old. He had no companions, but he could still drink. There was no clever minstrel to tell him a bawdy story, but he had his imagination. He crossed to the table and poured himself a brandy. He would sit and think of things that a king should not have time for. Perhaps he would dream a little dream of Mirolah, of what this kingdom would look like if he'd never become king, and she'd arrived in this city alone. A girl from the country, come to sample the excitement of a city.

Mershayn closed his eyes and pictured it. He downed the entire glass of brandy one measured gulp at a time. Mirolah's open smile, her brown eyes. In his imagination, he reached out to take her hand and she let him. They ran up the cobblestone street of the Barnacles, laughing—

A dog yawned loudly.

Mershayn jumped, sitting up and opening his eyes.

Mirolah stood within the shadows of the far corner of the

room. Her dark hair tumbled down to her shoulders, framing her face, and her swirling eyes sent colored lights on the wall and floor. Sniff panted, then sat down next to her, his bony butt thumping on the floor. He opened his jagged mouth and yawned again, ending in a little yowl, then laid down on the stones.

Mershayn stood up. "My lady," he said. "It's... I'll make a fire." He started for the hearth.

Suddenly, he wasn't cold at all. It was as though he was standing in the summer sun. He looked at her sharply.

"The cold bothers you," she murmured. "I did not want you to be bothered."

His heart beat faster. "Well...don't do that."

"Why?"

"Mirolah..." he began. "If you want me to feel comfortable, don't threadweave so much around me."

"You don't like the way I am," she said.

He held up a finger. "That's not it. I like you. I like you a lot. But this...the threadweaving. That's not *why* I like you."

She cocked her head.

He turned to the fire. Someone had already prepared it, and all he had to do was light a stick from the wall lantern and touch it to the tinder.

"There is no difference," she said. "Between the threadweaving and me. I am the threadweaving."

"You're not."

She came to him and stood uncomfortably close. "I want to know," she whispered. "Who was I? I want to remember."

"I want that, too," he said.

"The nobles look at me and see a monster. Bands looks at me and sees disaster and opportunity. Stavark looks at me and sees a horrible vision of himself, a mortal debt that must be paid. But you look at me like you want to kiss me. In them, I see fear, duplicity, self-involvement. From you, I feel...passion."

Mershayn cleared his throat. "Yes, well. It's one of two things I have in plenty." He picked up another snifter from the table and filled it with brandy. He pressed it into her hand. "Here."

"What is this?" she asked.

"Poison that kills your better sense," he said.

"Poison?"

"It is good for those who think to much or who are too serious." He raised his glass. She watched the movement, but didn't join him. "You raise your glass," he clarified. "It's a toast."

"Ah." She raised her glass, and he clinked his against hers.

"Now we drink."

He downed his in one gulp. She did the same, then frowned. "It hurts," she said in a raspy tone.

"At first. It feels better later."

She set the glass down, and Mershayn kept thinking about his recent thoughts. There wasn't any time to equivocate.

"Let's get your memory back," he said.

"Yes. How?"

"We're going to talk. All night if we need to. We're going to go through everything you recall and everything I recall. We'll put your memories back one at a time if we have to." He held out his hand.

She took it, holding it on top of the table.

"I'm going to just start talking about myself," he said. "You're going to listen, and when you feel like speaking, you interrupt me and tell your story."

"Okay."

"I'm a bastard," he said. "I was born to Lord Bendeller, who owns lands far to the south of Teni'sia. My mother was a prostitute who died giving birth to me. My father was a good man who cared for me when he could have left me on the street. He raised me with his pureblood heir, Collus, whose mother also died giving birth to him. While my father treated me decently, none of his peers did. In their eyes, I wasn't the son of a lord. I was the son of a whore."

Mirolah's eyes began to change. The rainbow colors retreated, sliding back to the edges of her brown eyes. Mershayn took that as a good sign. It seemed that whenever the Mirolah he knew came to the forefront of Mirolah's personality, her eyes returned to normal.

"That's sad, isn't it?" she asked.

"Yes." He waited for more, but she didn't continue. "It was for me, but my sadness didn't last long. I changed it to anger, I suppose. But luckily for me, my brother didn't care about my parentage. He always saw me as his brother, despite how others saw me. He wasn't swayed by my mother's low station or the opinions of his peers. He often fought with the other pure-born children to defend me. So from a young age, the only things I cared about were my father, my brother, and learning how to beat the pureblood nobles, to prove to them they weren't better than me. They seemed to prize swordplay and other tests of arms highly, so I took that from them first. My father let me train, even paid for a master to tutor me, and I worked myself to exhaustion until I was better than every single one of those snotty jackasses."

"What do you mean you 'took it away from them'?"

"Country folk don't use swords. It's a way for the nobles to lord their superiority over everyone else. If they tell you that they're better than you, and you stand up to them, they stick you with a sword. Then it seems like they're right, because who is going to argue with them? But when they try to stick you with a sword, if you parry and stick them instead, well... They learn to respect you, even if they hate you. So yes, I took that advantage away from them and looked for any other advantage I could steal. I learned to out-fence them, then I learned to out-talk them. Then I learned how to take away their women..." He trailed off.

"What did you do?"

"I don't usually talk about this with...well...other women." He scratched the back of his head. "In fact, I never talk about this with anyone except Collus."

"You're embarrassed," she said.

"Well, let's just say I learned a lot about what idle noblewomen dream about. I got very good at spotting the types who not only dreamed about some handsome rogue sneaking into their room, but those who might...actually enjoy it if they got the chance. I became that rogue. I gave that adventure to them. And it allowed me to take something else from the nobles."

"You took their women?"

"I took the attention of their women. I could never actually steal a pureborn lady, because no matter what happened behind closed doors, when the sun rose, I was still a bastard. No lands. No station. None of them would ever run away with me," he said, and he couldn't help thinking—with a pang of regret—that Ari'cyiane had offered to run away with him. Ari'cyiane, who now hated him with more passion than any of the nobles he'd originally tried to steal from. "But yes, I stole the attention of the women they were courting. In some cases, the women they were married to."

He felt the blush in his cheeks, poured himself another glass of brandy, and downed half of it, telling himself the flush was from the liquor. He expected Mirolah to give him a sneer of derision, but she spoke in the same emotionless tone.

"Did it make you less sad?" she asked. "Stealing these things from the nobles?"

"Well..." He held his hands up. "Yes and no. It felt good, knowing I could do it. It felt better, knowing that *they* knew I could do it. But it didn't really change anything. I was still a bastard to them. I still wasn't going to inherit any lands or hold any high stations within the kingdom of Teni'sia. Then my father died, and Collus asked me to help run the Bendeller estate."

"Did that hurt? Your father dying?" A bit more of the rainbow colors had receded. There was only a fringe around the edges of her brown eyes now.

He cleared his throat. "Yes. It did. He took sick and there was nothing we could do for him. But Collus stepped up, just as he had been trained to do. Our father had prepared him for that. Unfortunately, father hadn't prepared Collus for what came after. Queen Tyndiria was murdered, and the nobles called for Collus, her nearest relative, to take the throne." He sighed. "So we came here, and they killed him...."

His voice broke, and he tried get himself under control, but he wanted to cry. He'd never really had a moment to mourn Collus, and there were times Mershayn kept looking for him, expecting Collus to simply walk through the door. "This nest of snakes killed my brother...." he said again. "So I took their country away from them." He smiled mirthlessly, lifted the decanter, and poured himself another drink. Mirolah watched the gesture, then pushed her empty glass at him. He refilled it, too. "How about that?"

Together, they lifted the glasses. "I took swordsmanship. I took their women. Now I've taken their highest title. I win." They drank.

"I had a brother, too," she said. "He was small. He was a threadweaver like me. And they killed him, too."

Mershayn set his glass down, pulling himself out of his self-absorbed reverie. "I'm so sorry...."

"I loved him more than anyone else, like you loved your brother. And I couldn't stop them from killing him, just like you. Dorn. His name was Dorn. He was innocent. He didn't know...didn't realize how dangerous they were. He was trying to impress them. He was trying to delight them. But he didn't know...that they were so scared of him. So they killed him." She looked up, and the only color in her eyes was her natural deep brown. He squeezed her hand. "That's when I told myself I wasn't going to show anyone that I was a threadweaver. No one would ever know what I could do."

"And your parents? Where were they?"

"They had already been killed by the Sunriders."

He swallowed, and squeezed her hand. A tear appeared at the corner of Mirolah's eye.

"Did you live on your own, then?" Mershayn asked softly.

"I lived with another family...with many sisters. Casra. Locke. Mi'Gan. Lawdon and Tiffienne. In a city called Rith. I stayed there, quiet. I wrote letters. I didn't let anyone know what I could do. But then a man came.... He was frightening at first, but then... then...he... Orem. His name was Orem." She gripped his fingers tighter. "Orem taught me. He helped me. He led me to an incredibly powerful place called Daylan's Fountain. And there I fought a woman, a spirit called the Red Weaver. She tried to kill me, led me into the center of the fountain. She led me... She meant it to kill me.... It was supposed to kill me.... And I... And I..."

Mirolah screamed. Spikes drove into Mershayn's mind, into his arms and legs and heart. He seized up. It hit so fast, he didn't even have time to yell. His body spasmed, throwing him backward.

He remembered falling. He remembered the monstrous skin dog leaping to his feet and barking. Then he remembered nothing....

MERSHAYN AWOKE to the sound of sobbing. He was sprawled on the floor, a shattered glass of brandy near his head. He was groggy, could barely remember where he was. His whole body hurt, like someone had taken a rake to his insides. He tasted blood in his mouth. For a moment, he thought he was in Buravar with Collus. He had the wisp of a memory that he and Collus had spent the night at Gretienna's, and he was flat on his back, drunk.

But he was in Teni'sia. Collus was dead.

He shook his head and sat up, looking for who was sobbing. Mirolah knelt before the arched window. Her brown hair shimmered in the half-light, cascading down to cover her face like a veil. She clung to the windowsill with hands like claws. The skin dog towered over her protectively, his head low.

Mershayn's mind cleared, and he took a sharp breath. Everything came back to him. Mirolah! He blinked, a memory of her leaning toward him, her eyes wild with colors, strands of multi-colored lightning lashing out at him.

She raised her head at his movement, and her gaze found his.

He leapt to his feet, started toward her.

"Stop," she breathed. An invisible force held him. "Don't touch me. I'm not safe. I don't know... I can't..."

The force released him. He remained where he was, but he ached to go to her. "Mirolah, I want to help."

"I know," she said with effort. "You did. You...made me remember. I remembered everything, and I almost killed you because of it."

The detached monotone of her voice was gone. She sounded like the woman he had met in the caves when she healed him.

"You didn't almost kill me, I was—"

"The GodSpill tried to rip you apart because you brought me back to myself. I barely stopped it." Her hand still clutched the windowsill like she needed it to ground her. "It wants me, Mershayn. It doesn't want me to remember Mirolah. It wants me to join with it, to become one with it. And when I'm Mirolah, I separate from it. It fought me, and I almost vanished completely."

She watched him warily as he approached and knelt next to her.

"I'm dangerous to you," she said. "I don't have control of this

TODD FAHNESTOCK

thing."

"I don't care."

She began to cry again. "I hurt you. Oh gods, I hurt you. It wanted to kill you. I'm so sorry."

"I'm okay."

"You shouldn't do this. You shouldn't try to help me. It could kill you. Why are you helping me?"

"Because you need help," he said. He didn't tell her that he needed to be near her, that he could barely control the compulsion..

"I think...I died." She sounded scared. "I think I'm supposed to be dead. I've been telling myself that I brought myself back to life, but I don't think I did. I think I'm just...holding this body together..."

He put his arms around her. She let go of the windowsill and clung to him. "I cannot be this thing the GodSpill wants me to be," she murmured into his shoulder. "It wants Mirolah gone. Erased. The only reason it hasn't taken me is because of Sniff. And..." She looked up at him. "And now you." Flickers of multicolored light slipped into her eyes.

"Stay with me, Mirolah," he said. "Stay here with me."

"No," she whispered. "It's going to take me."

"It's not. We're not going to let it."

"Please," she whispered. "I don't want to go."

"You're staying right here. Just hold onto me."

20

MEDOPHAE

"HE LOOKS DEAD." The voice was a woman's, and the tone suggested she didn't care whether he was dead or not.

"If he's not, then maybe I'll finish him." A man's voice this time, enraged.

Medophae coughed, and he heard the angry man draw in a hissing breath. His back and shoulders were on fire, dozens of cuts packed with sand. His stump throbbed, and his head felt two times too big.

"I might thank you for it," Medophae mumbled. He blinked his eyes, and looked at the assemblage gathered around him. There had to be two dozen people there, villagers from the little bay town.

How had he gotten to shore?

"Don't touch him," a third person said, and this time Medophae turned his head to track the voice. A man with weathered skin, blue eyes, and a ponytail as long as his waist—tied in three places—looked at Medophae with narrowed eyes. "He's touched by the goddess. Give him space."

"Don't start your preaching, Sanoen. He's not touched by the goddess. He stole my boat, sailed it over the reef, and She smashed it to pieces. My ship! He wasn't on her ocean for two seconds before she tried to kill him."

"If she wanted to kill him, Dumaelin, he'd be dead," Sanoen said.

"That's ridiculous."

"Don't ignore the signs, Dumaelin. The water carried him to the shore."

"Others have washed up on shore—"

"You ever seen a man get tumbled in the reef like that and survive? She lifted him up over it. She delivered him to shore. Mark my words. You kill this man, and you'll incur her wrath. A dozen years of ill favor, my friend."

Medophae sat up. Dumaelin drew a short sword from his side, leveled it at Medophae. "Maybe she delivered him to me to answer for his crimes."

"Saraphazia doesn't care about the crimes of humankind," Sanoen said sagely.

"Put that sword away, Dumaelin," the woman said, and Medophae recognized her as the one who had seen him steal the boat. "You're no killer."

"If that thief doesn't stay where he is, you'll see different. He just destroyed my livelihood."

"You have another boat."

"By Oedandus, Londa, why are you taking his side?"

"Maybe we should ask him why he did what he did," she said.

Medophae couldn't wait for these people to decide whether or not to kill him. He needed to get away from here, bind his wounds, and figure out what he was going to do next. Saraphazia had spurned him, then attacked him, and his anger burned almost as bad as his wounds.

No arrogant goddess is going to dictate where I stop.

He made a move to stand up, and his back flared in protest. It was as though his entire body was a raw nerve. He gritted his teeth and pushed through it.

The sword tip tickled his chin next to his ear. "Stay where you are, thief," Dumaelin growled.

"I am sorry about your boat," Medophae said. "But it was necessary. If I had time to explain, you would understand. Much is at stake, and I cannot remain here."

"Sit down!" Dumaelin insisted.

"Point your sword elsewhere, friend."

"You're going to answer for your—"

Medophae lunged, leaning sideways just enough that the blade whispered past his ear. His fist arced high overhead, and he drove his knuckles into the back of Dumaelin's hand. The sailor gasped and dropped the sword. Medophae spun in the sand and crouched low, hitting Dumaelin in the back of the knees with his heel. Dumaelin went down. Medophae snatched up the blade and stood. There were a few gasps, and most of the crowd stepped back warily.

Dumaelin was suddenly wide-eyed and fearful, sprawled below Medophae, who now had his weapon. The man seemed unable to find his tongue.

Medophae's attack had been clumsy and slow, his injuries making him feel like a ninety-year-old man. Each move had hurt. But the woman had been right about Dumaelin. That sailor wasn't a killer, and he certainly wasn't a swordsman. This blade might as well have been for show.

Dumaelin's incompetence allowed Medophae to look more fearsome than he currently was, and he desperately needed that advantage with such a large crowd. He couldn't fight even one half-decent swordsman in his condition. He'd never be able to fight a mob if they suddenly decided to take him down.

Using his momentary advantage, he walked between them, and they parted. He started up the beach, and nobody tried to follow him. In a few minutes, they might find their courage, might organize and go hunting for him. He had to be as far away as possible by the time that happened.

But each step was a trial, sending flares of pain through his back and legs, and Medophae wasn't sure how long he'd last. He had to get the wounds washed out. Coral wounds could easily fester. Some stretches of coral were even poisonous to humans. If he didn't wash these cuts, and soon, his situation could go from bad to worse.

He headed back toward the hut Zilok had initially brought him to. He couldn't think of anything better to do. There was no other haven for him.

He stumped up the beach, pushing through the agony. One thing living with Oedandus had taught him was how to handle pain far beyond a normal mortal's capacity. While the god had always healed even the most grievous wounds, he never quelled the pain. Pain that would cause a normal man to pass out only made Medophae grit his teeth.

Still, he was nearly at his limit. His hunger, his exhaustion, his wounds, it was all adding up. And now he'd frightened a flock of villagers. He kept checking over his shoulder, looking for pursuit, but so far he was lucky. Perhaps they'd all decided the prudent course was to leave this one-handed madman alone.

Finally, Medophae reached the stretch of beach with the burnt-out campfire where he'd met the strange blue-haired girl and the ruffians who'd tried to rob him. He turned up the beach and stumbled into the forest.

Uphill was even harder than walking through sand, and his vision began to swim.

Keep going....

After walking between the trees for a few minutes, Medophae thought he had gotten lost. The trees began to blur, and everything looked the same. His back burned like someone had rubbed pepper in his wounds. The coral... It was the coral. Poison... He was poisoned. A memory from his childhood returned in a flash. A single cut from the poisoned coral around the isle of Dandere could make you sick as if you had the flu. And Medophae had dozens of lacerations.

His vision continued to blur. It was getting worse, and his muscles were weakening.

Miraculously, he stumbled into the clearing with the hut. He tripped, lost his balance and almost fell, but he managed to stagger forward and reach the steps.

But that was as far as he could go. He put one foot on the first step and fell to his knees on the second step.

Get up....

But he didn't have the energy to stand up again. He tried once and almost fell off the steps.

Come on. Focus....

He forced his trembling muscles to work and pushed up onto all fours. One limb at a time, he got up the remaining stairs and crawled into the hut, pushing the door open with his head.

The waterbox seemed a mile away. He held his stump against his chest so he wouldn't be tempted to use it, and crawled like a turtle to the basin. He managed to get upright, leaning against it. With his hand shaking, he stripped out of his bloody clothes and filled the bowl.

The poison is in me.

He could feel it like slimy water in his veins. Meticulously, he poured water over his back, shoulders, and legs until the groove in the stone floor carried pink water toward the door. He turned back to the waterbox, but now there were two of them. He shook his head to clear his vision, and the basin resolved into one again for a moment, then doubled again and started to tip sideways.

No. The basin isn't falling sideways. I am.

The bowl clattered to the stones, and his head hit the floor.

Get up....

But his muscles wouldn't respond this time. All he managed to do was lift his good hand, then he passed out.

THE FEVER DREAM took him instantly. Colors raced past him, roaring like lions. Then he was falling through misty white clouds. He waited to hit the ground, but it never came. Instead, the clouds resolved into the shape of a dragon.

Medophae clenched his teeth, thinking that Avakketh was sending him another dream, but then the clouds formed into a whale.

Am I doing this? Am I cataloging the gods who have attacked me?

But then the clouds formed into a horse next, and he definitely hadn't thought of that. Next, the mist became a squat tree. The base of the trunk had to be ten feet around, and the thing only stood twice as tall as Medophae, with long, meandering limbs that looked like spindly, multi-jointed arms with curling leaves fanning out like hands.

Finally, the clouds formed into a female human, with large breasts and wide hips. Cloud became flesh and a flowing gown of many colors. Golds, blues, reds, purples, greens, and oranges all mixed together like paints thrown into a swirling pool. Her face became clear, with bronze skin and rainbow hair that mixed with the gown. She had a beak nose and deep-set eyes as black as the night between the stars. It gave her a predatory look, like she was a giant bird about to swoop down upon Medophae and rip his limbs off.

Then she smiled, and it was gentle. Suddenly, the hawk nose and intense eyes seemed like those of a mother who would stop at nothing to protect her children, and her smile told him that he was one of them. He felt safer than he'd ever felt in his long life.

"Medophae," she said.

The clouds continued to rush past him; it still felt like they were both falling through the sky, but it didn't bother him anymore. The blur of clouds was just the way it was, the way it had always been, it seemed.

"Who are you?"

"You have endured so much suffering," she said. "More years of suffering than a short-lived human was meant to endure."

He felt her compassion like a hand pressing against his chest, and he knew instantly she was a goddess. She exuded power like the sun exudes light, like Saraphazia exuded disdain and Avakketh exuded fear.

Being in the presence of a god made everything else seem small, as though you'd never encountered anything important until that moment. This woman felt like that, but he didn't recognize her. Medophae had met every god there was except Zetu the Ancient. He would bet his life that this wasn't Zetu, even in disguise, but she certainly wasn't any of the other gods, either. She didn't talk like Saraphazia or Avakketh. No matter what form White Tuana took, she always had milky eyes. He supposed this could be Tarithalius. He loved to hide behind a myriad of masks, but this woman seemed serious and compassionate. Thalius was a trickster.

"I..." Medophae said. "Are you a goddess?"

The woman's gentle smile became a wry smirk, but she didn't answer. "You have lived so long, for a human, and yet you still strive for more. Despite the suffering. Despite your own despair."

"I have to."

Her eyes narrowed, as though she was looking for the truth written on his soul. "I see that you do. Why?"

The question thrummed inside him. Half a year ago, he would have thrown his life away if he could. He had been so beaten down by his failure to save Bands that he couldn't see worth anywhere he looked, least of all within himself. But Mirolah had revitalized him. She'd reminded him that every moment was precious, even if you failed. Especially when you failed. She had reawakened his love of life and of humanity. She had loved him.

And then Zilok had killed her. She'd died, and he refused to let her gift die with her. Medophae wasn't going to quit this time. He wasn't going to quit ever again.

Amarion needed him. Humankind needed him, and he would do everything he could to help them. He would wield Oedandus for the benefit of people like Mirolah.

"Why?" he repeated her question. "Why live? Because I'm the shield," he said, seeing Mirolah in that tiny room in Gnedrin's Post, shouting at him, breaking through his self-absorption and making him re-engage with his own life, re-engage with the purpose that had been given to him. He had the power to change history, and that meant he was obligated to use it.

In a different memory flash, Medophae saw Bands standing calmly next to him. She gave him that slight nod and that quiet smile, like she used to do, like she had done a thousand times when he made a decision she liked.

"Because humans are an experiment to Tarithalius, an affront to Avakketh, and an annoyance to Saraphazia," he continued. "But not to me."

The goddess watched him carefully, but didn't say anything.

White clouds continued to rush by them.

"Because the gods act like selfish children. If I don't protect humans, no one will."

"Do you see yourself as a god?"

"No. But I can fight them. The gods are responsible to those they look after. They're responsible for their actions, even if they don't think they are."

She narrowed her eyes again, and he saw anger in that hawkish face, but her smile never faded. "So you wish for more life to fight the gods?"

"No. To protect humankind. I have no wish to fight, but I will."

That wry smile returned, as if she didn't believe that he didn't like to fight. Medophae held her gaze.

"Your body is dying of coral poisoning on the floor of a hut that no one will find," she said. "You say you want to help humankind, but you can barely help yourself."

"Then I push until I drop."

"If you survive, how will you help them all? There are so many."

"One person at a time."

"And the gods?"

"I will fight them if I need to."

"I meant will you help them, too, if they need you?"

"Help the gods?"

"Yes."

"They don't need my help."

"Are you certain?"

The question caught him off balance, and the thought confused him. Why would the gods need help? They could do whatever they wished. Nothing governed them except their own wild emotions. They were like raging rivers or rampant fires. They would crush or drown or burn without a care as to who was killed. He'd spent his life fighting with Oedandus inside himself and fighting the other gods outside himself. It had never occurred to Medophae to try to help them. With the exception of Tarithalius's random bursts of benevolence and Saraphazia's self-serving assistance in killing Dervon, Medophae had never once approved of anything a god

162

had done.

"What do you think of love?" the goddess asked.

"Love? What do you mean?"

"Did you know that the gods don't love?"

"What?"

"Love isn't natural. Tarithalius created it as an experiment for humans, and in the beginning, it only existed in humans, but it leaked out into the greater world. Little Thalius is the weakest of the gods, but in a way, he may also be the strongest, to make such a subtle thing. That spark he created changed the world, the other races—even the gods—forever. It transformed Oedandus. His love of his human woman was the beginning of his fall."

"Love didn't kill Oedandus," Medophae said, feeling the old rage rise inside him, which was curious. That rage belonged to Oedandus, or at least Medophae had thought. "Dervon, White Tuana, and Zetu the Ancient ganged up on Oedandus to destroy him."

"A human. And a god," she continued, seemingly talking to herself now. "It was the most unlikely thing."

"Which goddess are you?"

She ignored the question. Instead, she said, "I believe in you, Medophae Roloiron, son of Jarissa Chandura and King Jarod Madis Roloiron, great-grandson of Oedandus the Binder. I believe in what you say, and in what you want to do."

"Who are you?" he repeated.

"There will always be those who need your help; it pleases me that you see this. I will give you two gifts, Medophae. One is the vitality you crave to continue your crusade. The other is knowledge, and that you must put to work yourself. Take my gifts and wield your power for those in need. Gods and mortals alike."

He looked at her hands, but she held nothing there.

"What gifts?"

"Remember your stories."

"I know a thousand stories!"

She smiled like a mother smiles at an impatient child. "Go back to the beginning. Oedandus was the first god ever to fall in love, and love was why he brought your people to this island. Remember that story. Remember the stories that followed."

"How is that going to help me?"

"Go back, Medophae...."

The rainbow colors of her gown trailed away into the rushing clouds like paint in a river. She went with them, the wind stretching her body. Her colors mixed with the white clouds, then she was gone.

Medophae continued to fall. The rushing white whipped past him, and yellow sunlight suddenly ripped open the clouds and revealed the ocean and the tiny island of Dandere far below. He rushed toward it.

He clenched his fist as he plunged into the canopy of trees. The roof of his little hut was right below him. He struck it and—

The dream ended.

Medophae gasped, opening his eyes to the flagstone floor of the hut. He was facedown, and the bowl was overturned next to him just where he had dropped it. The sun was high in the sky outside. He was weak from hunger, and his cheek felt bruised from where it had lain against the stone. He suspected he had slept the rest of the day and night since he had fallen. But his wounds no longer burned. His vision was no longer blurry, and his muscles worked the way they should. His fever was gone. He had survived the poison.

He sat up and groaned. The rainbow woman's words rang in his head. She'd said to remember the old stories about Oedandus forming this island kingdom.

The first stories he'd heard about Oedandus were from the island's holy men, doctrine that had been handed down through the generations and were as dry as a bone. Most of those stories had faded in his memory.

But Bands had told different stories about Oedandus, not tales twisted to themes of morality, but simple stories. He remembered Bands's first counsel to him, the exact words she had used:

The artifacts of the gods are best left for the gods....

She had said that right after she had saved his life on the top of Dandere's volcano. Then she had told him the story of how Oedandus had colonized this island out in the middle of the True

Ocean, far away from Amarion. Saraphazia tried to stop him. She didn't want any other creatures traveling over her ocean; she didn't want them filling up the islands on her waters. So Oedandus made an artifact that allowed him to control her whales. He brought his colonists to Dandere on the backs of those enthralled whales as Saraphazia raged around him.

Medophae levered himself to his feet. He was weak with hunger, but not crippled by poison any more. He limped to the door and, by the time he got to it, his stiff muscles started to loosen up. He went outside and climbed on top of the tiled roof, using his good hand and his right elbow. When he stood atop it, he could see that volcano. In the distance, above the trees, rose Mount Thengir, the dormant volcano that had formed the entire island of Dandere. Religious leaders said Oedandus had gone into the volcano when he left his people and rumbled there still, deep beneath the earth. Well, that wasn't true, but Oedandus had gone to the top of the volcano at least once...

Because that was where he had left the artifact that could control Saraphazia's whales.

21

MEDOPHAE

FROM THE TOP of the hut, Medophae spied the short sword he'd taken yesterday from the sailor. It lay discarded on the meandering path to the hut. He hadn't even remembered carrying it this far, let alone dropping it. He climbed down, retrieved it, and went back into the hut.

First, he drank from the waterbox until he had filled his belly. He also found strips of dried goat meat and stale bread in the box beneath the cot, weeks' worth of food stored for the coming winter. Everything was either in wax-treated bags or wax-sealed pots. Medophae ate his fill, then packed one of the bags with as much food as it could carry.

He pulled the waterskins from the wall and filled them at the waterbox, then slung them over his shoulder.

When he'd first awoken here, he'd thought Zilok had created this hut, but the more he looked around, the more he was certain the spirit had found this place...or killed the previous inhabitants. There were too many incidentals of everyday living for it to have been spawned from a quick threadweaving. There were stains on the walls, used pots hanging by the stove. This place had been lived-in.

Medophae shook the thought out of his mind. He couldn't worry about Zilok's atrocities right now. Time was short, and if he couldn't get off this island soon, there would be no more Wildmane and, worse still, no more need for a Wildmane.

He smirked, realizing he'd just thought of himself as Wildmane. He had always hated the dramatic moniker created by Thedore Stok, the famous bard from the Age of Awakening. But in this moment when he was truly just Medophae again, the name suddenly felt right. Oedandus was a god who had been nearly destroyed. Medophae was a mortal man. Wildmane was the union of them both, a mortal who *wanted* to protect humanity, combined with a god who actually *could*.

An aberration. A mistake...

And hopefully exactly what was needed.

He slipped the short sword crudely into his belt, left the hut, and started uphill.

Mount Thengir was in the center of the island, and that was where Medophae was going. He set a swift pace, remembering the days of his youth when he ran all over this island with his mother.

He followed an animal track south, walking swiftly for more than an hour before he came to the ocean on the southern side of the island, where there were more cliffs than beaches. The smells and sights evoked memories he'd nearly forgotten, memories from a childhood lost a millennium and a half ago.

He came upon an outcropping where the forest pulled back. There was a half circle of trees bordering a rocky shelf, and Medophae felt a chill. Was this just random chance? Or had his feet unerringly guided him to this place? The trees were different, closer to the shore than they had been so long ago, but the shelf was the same. No. This was definitely the spot.

The water pulled back, then the waves curled forward and smashed underneath the rock shelf upon which he stood.

"Huskpincers," he murmured.

A huskpincer was a shelled creature about the size of his forearm, with a long, lashing tail tipped with a pincer. They didn't exist on the Inland Ocean; he had only ever seen them around the island of Dandere.

A huskpincer fed by floating in the water, gripping a rock face with its pincer, and waiting for food to come in on the tide. Catching a huskpincer was tricky, but relatively easy once you knew the trick. It required levering a piece of wood into the pincer. The huskpincer would squeeze the wood, and you could coil the tail around your arm while it did, then pluck the thing out of the water. His mother had taught him and his brother how to catch them.

Medophae watched the water and soon saw the shadows of the creatures floating just below the surface, waiting as the next wave to roll in. Medophae adjusted his pack, and looked to the west. That's where his father's city, the capital city Oedan, had been. It had been Medophae's city, too, until he was eight years old. That was where his father, brother, and sister had died.

He paused there, looking at the waves and the huskpincers. He hadn't thought about his mother or father, his brother or sister, in centuries. They were from another life, one so long ago that it had faded.

His father, King Jarod Madis Roloiron, had been a calm man. Medophae remembered his father as a good king and a good man. There was no question his father couldn't answer. The king spent time in his throne room with the Dandenes who came to him with problems, and no matter what they brought him, he always sent them away with answers. Sometimes they were direct answers: Do this. Do that. But most of the time they were not.

Medophae remembered the day he understood that his father didn't actually give answers to his supplicants, not most of the time. He pushed them to come up with their own answers. Father would ask questions. Sometimes it was just one question, sometimes it was a series, and the supplicants would give him answers. By the time they were done talking, they had answered their own question. They would leave, bearing their own wisdom and a deep satisfaction. Medophae had been seven when he'd understood what was happening there. He'd never forgotten that lesson.

Medophae's father was steady like bedrock, but Medophae's

mother... She was full of fire and passion. The people saw her as a holy woman, sent by Oedandus himself. They said she hadn't been born on Dandere which, as a child, Medophae thought was silly. Back then, he'd thought Dandere was the entire world; he couldn't conceive of people coming from anywhere else. He thought they meant she had come from the far east of the island.

But Mother had come from Amarion. She hadn't told him that story when he was little, when the island was still safe. Only after the disaster did she tell him everything. Mother had flown to Dandere on the back of a great green dragon, fell in love with Medophae's father, and decided to stay.

While Father had striven to give his people the confidence to solve their own problems, Mother wanted to experience everything. Medophae grew up following Mother and his older brother everywhere while she carried his little sister on her back. She took them around the island, through the woods to her favorite places, which were also often dangerous. Mother and Father had arguments about that. There were places Father said weren't safe for children.

Mother scoffed at his fears, ignored him, and prevailed on every single argument save one. Father forbid her to go to the top of Mount Thengir. For some reason, she listened to him on that point, never taking the children to the top of the volcano. The volcano was sacred to Father and the people of Dandere. He wasn't afraid of it, but rather reverent, and while Mother didn't respect fear, she did respect reverence.

He watched the huskpincer shadows beneath the shimmering water, floating at the end of their tail tethers. Getting them was dangerous work, so Mother had enjoyed it.

He thought back to that day, the last fateful day they had been here, and it returned as clear as if he was living it again.

MEDOPHAE HAD JUST SNAGGED his third huskpincer when he surfaced to find Mother watching the sky. A greasy cloud hovered over the capital city of Oedan.

"That's not normal," she whispered.

"It's just a cloud," Medophae said, but even as he said it, he wasn't sure. He'd never seen a cloud that dark, that oily. It was like the clouds that brought the ice storms, except those clouds covered the entire sky, horizon to horizon. This was so small, almost like...a creature.

He tossed the huskpincer back into the water and pulled himself onto the rock shelf next to her. "Let's go. We need to get back home."

"No," she said, blocking him with an arm. She was more serious than Medophae had ever seen her. "Wait."

A tentacled monster fell from the greasy cloud. It looked like a ball of giant maggots and wormlike tentacles.

"Mother!"

"By Thalius..." she murmured. Everyone else swore by Oedandus, but not Mother.

Strangely, she looked away from the palace toward the volcano.

"We have to go help!" he insisted.

He'd never seen such indecision in his mother before. She didn't answer him, just kept that one arm on him, as if to keep him still, or maybe to steady herself. Her brow furrowed in thought.

"Mother—"

"Quiet, Medin."

"You always say to overcome our fears. We have to—"

"I also tell you to use your brain. We can't fight that thing. But there is someone who can."

"Who?"

"Come. We must run faster than we've ever run before. And we must hope that we are lucky today." Unbelievably, she turned away from the city and ran into the forest.

He leapt to follow her and called out. "Mother! We're running away from it!" He had become a strong runner during the many days of trying to keep up with Mother on these daily jaunts, and he prided himself that he could match her stride for stride now.

But as Mother's fear drove her, he realized she had been holding back on their runs. She leapt over fallen limbs and dodged trees like some hero from the legends she told him. His eight-year-old legs couldn't keep up, and she slowly left him behind.

He pushed, striving to make himself stronger, to make his legs longer. He growled and leapt over a fallen tree, rolled underneath the low branches and sprinted forward. His legs burned, and his saliva tasted like copper.

He barely had her in sight, and he was about to call out to her when she vanished into the foliage. His heart hammered, and he grunted, suddenly realizing he had no breath to call out. He plunged after her into the same dense thatch.

The thatch gave way to a wide meadow that stopped at a cliff face, and his mother skidded to a halt. They had run all the way to the side of the volcano.

"Randorus!" Mother shouted.

Medophae gasped for breath, his chest heaving. He put his hands on his knees.

"Randorus!" Mother ran to the mouth of the tall cave, then vanished into the darkness.

"Wait," he gasped, forcing his wobbling legs to work again. He limped across the meadow and followed her. Inside the cave was like a house. It had a flagstone floor, a bed, a wardrobe, a waterbox, and polished walls. He'd never seen a cave like this before.

"Rand?" Mother called softly.

"Who is Randorus?" he gasped.

Mother bit her lip, turning around. The cave-house was obviously empty, and there was a thin layer of dust on everything. The only possessions were two old blankets on the bed at the back, folded neatly. Medophae opened a wooden wardrobe that leaned against the miraculously straight and polished wall of the cave. The wardrobe was empty.

"Dammit!" Mother shouted, and it spooked him.

"Mother, who is supposed to be here?"

She looked down at him, an angry frown on her face. "A friend," she said. "I had hoped that..." She shook her head. "It doesn't matter. She's not here. She told me she was going back to the mainland, but I had hoped..." Jarissa smacked her palm against the smooth stone wall and shouted her frustration.

"Mother!"

"It was stupid of me," she said to herself. "She can't save us."

He wasn't sure what scared him more, thinking about that monster that had fallen on to Oedan, or his mother shouting at nothing. He spoke the first thing that came to his mind. "The mainland? What do you mean the mainland?"

"Amarion."

"What's Amarion?"

"The land beyond the True Ocean. A different place with its own kingdoms."

It was like she was speaking gibberish. Everybody knew there was nothing beyond the True Ocean. Dandere was the only place humans lived. Saraphazia saw to that. The goddess of the ocean killed any sailors who sailed too far onto the water. Dandenes were permitted to sail the perimeter of the island, never into open ocean.

"Who is Randorus?" he asked.

"We need to get back to Oedan," Mother said suddenly. *"This was a mistake. She can't help us."* She turned and ran out of the cave.

"Mother!" he shouted, limping after her on his tired legs.

She didn't answer, so he shut his mouth and worked to keep up with her again. The cramps in his legs began to ease as he moved. Mother did not slow her pace, but Medophae somehow managed to stay with her. He jumped over fallen logs, scrambled down slopes, pounded his feet against the soft loam of the forest floor. He made his sole purpose to keep her retreating back in view, always in view.

He was so exhausted and so focused on running that he didn't even realize when they reached the city. Mother had to catch him and pull him back. She whispered softly in his ear. *"Stop running. We're here, Medin..."* Her voice was sick. *"The gods help us, we're here."*

Medophae blinked, looking at the smoking ruins of his city. Buildings were cracked like they had been hit by some giant mallet. Some were collapsed, some burned, and there were bodies everywhere.

He panted, horrorstruck.

"Quiet now, my Medin," she whispered, drawing him back into the cover of the trees. *"We are in great danger. Whatever attacked did so with purpose. That purpose might include us."*

"Father..." he gasped. *"Daen and Laeyena—"*

"I know," she whispered, her voice trembling with emotion. *"We must be strong, my Medin. Fear and grief will breed mistakes if we let them. We must keep our wits about us and push emotion away for now. Just for now. There will be a time to give way to our hurt, but not now."*

"But Father—"

She got down on her knees which, because he was such a tall boy, actually brought her lower than eye-level with him. "Listen to me, Medin. We must be heroes now, you and I. We must find our strength, and it must be greater than the villain who did this. We must be hard."

He wanted to cry.

"Can you be that? Can you become granite for me?"

"Mother..." he began. He wanted to ask her what she thought had happened to their family, but her intense gaze caught him, and he realized she didn't know. She was asking him for strength, maybe not just for himself, but also for her, to help her be strong, too.

"I can be granite," he said in a quavering voice, and he clenched his teeth to stop them from chattering.

She smiled grimly. "That's my Medin. We are heroes now, you and I. We will face whatever dangers there are, and we will overcome them."

"Yes, Mother." His voice was steady this time.

She paused one more moment, still holding him with that gaze as though she would look into his soul and see if he was lying. He raised his chin, giving her his bravest face.

"That's my Medin," she whispered. "Now, this is the plan...."

They waited until nightfall, then went straight to a shop that sold winter cloaks. Its roof had been broken, and one whole wall cracked off and demolished, but all of the cloaks were still inside. They took two of them.

In cloaks with deep cowls, they snuck into the ruined palace. As he had feared, they found the bodies of his brother, Daen, and his sister, Laeyena, horribly lacerated and left where they had fallen. They did not find Father.

A part of Medophae wanted to fall to his knees and cry, but he remembered what Mother had said. He thought of himself as granite. He looked at the horror with flat eyes. When Mother asked him to lift Laeyena and carry her away from the palace into the woods, he did. Mother carried Daen.

Together, they took the bodies away from Oedan, and they buried them in the forest a stone's throw from the ocean. Only when they were finished with the graves did Mother finally lead him away. His arms and legs were numb. His back ached, but he went with her step by step. After they were far away from the graves, Mother laid her cloak down, then took his off and made a pillow of it.

Again, she got on her knees and looked him in the eyes. "You did amazing," she said. A tear welled in her eye and streaked down her dirt-smeared face. "I could not have imagined such strength within you until you showed me."

Her tear broke him, and he began to cry. "Daen..." he sobbed. "Laeyena..." She hugged him, and they cried together. Finally, she laid him down on the cloak and snuggled up behind him, arms around him. She held tight to him until he fell asleep.

22

MEDOPHAE

THE SMELL of the ocean spray, the leaves of the forest rustling in the autumn breeze, and the shadows of the huskpincers—it all brought back that pivotal moment in his life. That was when Medophae had stopped being a child. At eight years old, he had transformed from a child into an adult.

He let the memory flow through him, and he let it go.

He had to do that again, now. He had to transform from who he had become, this lost and damaged demigod, into a hero. His mother's words echoed in his mind.

We must be heroes now, you and I. We must find our strength, and it must be greater than the villain who did this.

He couldn't save his father, his brother, or his sister. He hadn't been able to save his mother, either, years later. But there was still a chance he could save humankind from Avakketh. And the truth was, he might be the only one who could.

He broke into a jog, following that same course his mother had taken to the cave, straight through the wild forest. The journey seemed to take much less time now than when he was eight, and he stopped in the clearing. The forest had crowded almost up to the face of the cliff. Vines had grown over the cave's entrance, but he could still see the darkness beyond.

Mother had come here looking for Randorus. Medophae had not known at the time, but that was only part of the name of her friend. Randorus Ak-nin Ackli Forckandor was her full name, and Medophae would later nickname her Bands.

Bands had known Medophae's mother long before he'd been born. Jarissa and Bands had adventured for a decade before they had dared to cross the True Ocean looking for whatever they might find.

They had found Dandere, and Mother had found Jarod Madis Roloiron. And so Mother's adventures with Bands ended and her adventures as a wife and mother began. Bands had stayed on the island for another decade before going back to Amarion. As it turned out, she had left one year before the maggot monster ripped Medophae's life apart.

Much later in life, Medophae had put it all together. After the battle where Dervon destroyed Oedandus, the evil god took steps to exterminate his rival's mortal progeny. He knew that the royal line of Dandere had Oedandus's blood in their veins, and he had sent that monstrous maggot ball expressly to murder Medophae's family.

Medophae turned away from the overgrown glade and covered cave. He circled the slope until he found the old path that went to the top. The Path of Oedandus was not for just anyone to use. It was sacred, and it was said horrors beyond imagining would befall any who used it without the permission of the holy men of Oedandus. But Medophae knew what was up there. There were no horrors. At least, not anymore.

After the maggot monster destroyed Oedan and what it thought was all of the royal line, it took up residence as the new god of the Dandenes. It installed a new king, and it lived atop the volcano.

Medophae had spent the next ten years in the forest with his mother, hiding, staying cautious about the civilized areas of Dandere. After a year of hunting and gathering, he and Mother visited the markets of a local village to trade for supplies. They always went cloaked, never to the same market twice in a month, and they never made friends. But even with all that, their luck ran out after a decade.

When Medophae was eighteen, a tax collector of the new king, a man who had been a minor official in the palace of King Jarod, saw Mother at the market. He got a good look at her face, and he recognized her. That was the beginning of the end.

The new king, King Haerolk, captured Mother and took her to the new capital city of Dervos. They killed her there in front of King Haerolk's court before Medophae had even known she was gone. He had been in the forest hunting. It was a routine he and Mother had done many times. She went to shop; he went to hunt. Medophae hadn't even thought to worry. He'd finished his hunting, returned home and sat there, waiting for his mother. He'd been waiting just like that, oblivious, while they tortured and killed her in front of everyone.

He had never forgiven himself for that mistake, and it changed his life forever. For the first time, he didn't care if he died, and that recklessness led him to the improbable assassination of King Haerolk. After, it led him to face off with Dandere's false god—the maggot monster. And finally, that recklessness led him to his lost god.

And it started here, on the Path of Oedandus.

He drew a breath and began hiking up the volcano.

It took half the day of hard hiking, wending through trees until he broke above the tree line. The warm fall temperature dropped steadily as he ascended. By the time he began to struggle with the thin air, he could feel the chill of winter nearby. The brief autumn of Dandere was about to turn. The ice storms would come quickly after that.

Medophae stopped, breathing hard. He unslung a waterskin and drank sparingly, looking over the western side of the island. A half dozen large cities dotted the coast, breaking through the forest. Things had changed. Oedan had been the only city of that size when he had lived here.

Medophae now wished he had thought to bring a cloak. His exertions had kept the cold air at bay, but now that he had stopped, the chill set in. The skies overhead were deep blue, with a white cloud here and there, but winter could strike tonight, for all he knew.

Slinging the waterskin over his neck, he began the last part of the climb. In less than an hour, he crested the ridge, jutting up like spikes on a crown that ringed the summit. The top of the volcano was a flat rock floor with deep cracks in it. Between those ominous fissures, orange fire glowed. The volcano hadn't erupted the entire time Medophae had been here, but it always seemed ready to.

His heart beat faster, despite himself. He had fought the monster here, right here, and, unlike the rest of the island, this place looked exactly the same.

Bands had followed him the whole way. At the time, she had been disguised as a tall, blond-haired girl from a nearby village, and he had no idea she was really Randorus Ak-nin Ackli Forckandor, the dragon who had flown his mother across the ocean from a mythical land called Amarion. He had told her to go back to her village. He told her he was going to die, and if she was with him, she would die, too. But she had stubbornly refused to listen to him.

Medophae took a deep breath and stepped down onto that flat, cracked floor of the volcano's top.

Back then, the maggot monster had dropped onto him from its greasy cloud just like it had dropped onto the city of Oedan. Medophae had wielded an ordinary longsword, backed by plenty of training from his mother...and he'd stood absolutely no chance of stopping that supernatural horror.

A dragon, however, was more than a match for it.

When Bands at last transformed into a giant green-scaled dragon, Medophae didn't know who was more surprised, him or the maggot monster.

The fight had been short and brutal. The maggot monster had about as much chance against Bands as Medophae had had against it. It took two swipes at her with its mucous tentacles, missed, and then she blew a hole in it with dragon fire. It fell down the mountain, a burning wreck, and Bands resumed her village girl form. Slack-jawed, Medophae had stared at her as she tried to calm him and explain.

Medophae crossed the hot, flat rock to the far side of the platform. The short, rock pedestal still held the pearlescent horn. It was shaped like a long trumpet, thin at the mouth and flaring at the end. It swirled, as if it had once been a shell that had been twisted into a horn. There were no pictures carved onto the surface, no filigree or any other decoration that Medophae had seen on numerous other arcane artifacts made by threadweavers. But then, this wasn't a horn made by a mortal. It was a horn made by a force of nature, a god. It wasn't for ceremony or for intimidation, but for a specific purpose.

"The artifacts of the gods are best left for the gods," Bands had said to him so long ago. In the aftermath of the maggot monster's death, he had gone to pick up the horn, thinking correctly that it was some enchanted weapon. Bands had told to leave it alone.

"What does that mean?" he had asked.

"That this was created by Oedandus himself."

He had listened to her and left the horn alone.

But that was then. He picked up the horn, and could feel the potency of it in his hand, a thrumming vibration, a deep warmth. This horn had been made to thwart a goddess.

He took his prize and climbed back up the ridge. Far away to the east, the horizon was a thin line of black. A storm. It could be here soon if a fierce wind pushed it. He had a matter of hours to reach the shore and call the whales.

Shrugging the waterskins higher onto his shoulders, he tucked the horn under his arm and began the descent.

23

MEDOPHAE

MEDOPHAE HAD BEEN BEATEN, sliced, poisoned and disfigured. He was exhausted, but he pushed himself down the slope as fast as he could. The storm on the horizon was moving fast—the storm that would begin winter on Dandere—and he needed to be off the island before that happened.

So he hiked strong, running when he could. He thought about what he must do once he reached the shore. The story Bands told him was that the horn controlled whales, and he thought about how to best use that power. He skipped down some loose scree to solid dirt again and thought about his options.

Saraphazia always appeared as a whale. Would the horn control her? He had to assume it would not. The real question was whether it would summon her along with her whales. If it summoned Saraphazia, Medophae wouldn't make it any farther than he had in the boat.

But even if Saraphazia wasn't summoned by the horn, she would sooner or later discover he was controlling her whales. He had to plan for that.

He dodged around a boulder and continued running down the slope. The trip up the mountain had taken hours. The trip down took only half that time, and Medophae soon descended out of the cooler air into the warm forest of the island. He turned south, heading straight for the coast, and eventually came again to that isolated little cove where he had once hunted for huskpincers.

He took a deep breath. To his left, the storm had grown, climbing up the horizon with iron-gray billows. That monster of a storm was an hour away, maybe less.

"Okay..." he murmured. He lifted the horn in his hand, braced the middle of the horn on his right forearm, and blew.

A high-pitched keen filled the air and seemed to shake the rock underneath him. Golden fire crackled around the horn, wrapping around both his arms. It filled him, and he gasped. It felt just like Oedandus!

The god had put a piece of himself into the horn, and it was so familiar that Medophae felt suddenly invincible. He blew the horn again, long and loud, and the horn wreathed him in golden flame. It also drew the breath out of him, pulling as though the horn expected him to blast on the thing forever.

He yanked it away from his lips, and only then did it stop sucking the air from his lungs. He gasped, coughing, and he wobbled on his feet.

The horn had also pulled life from him. Perhaps it would have done the same to Oedandus, seeking fuel for its purpose from the never-ending GodSpill of an actual god.

Medophae blew on the horn a third time for as long as he could. The golden energy crackled around him, drew the air from him again, and yanked at his very soul. He crashed to his knees, barely keeping himself from tumbling into the water. The horn clattered to the rock, sliding right up to the edge

One more, he thought, but it took him a second to gather his wits, and even longer to pick up the horn and push himself to his feet. He wobbled, raised the horn...

And stopped.

A swell rose from the ocean, just like it had when Saraphazia had come at his summons, but this swell was smaller. A jet of water burst into the air, and a huge whale surfaced. The little eyes glistened, focusing on him.

Another swell rose beside the first whale, and in the distance a whale breached and fell heavily onto the water. A third swell, then a fourth and fifth and...

They just kept coming. In moments, the water just off the southern coast of Dandere was filled with whale heads and backs, pushing above the waterline and ejecting water from their blowholes. Spray filled the air and reached all the way to the shore, blotting out the sun and coming down like rain.

"By the gods," he murmured. There had to be a hundred of them out there.

The horn vibrated in his hand, and the golden fire leapt from hand to stump and back again. Streaks of yellow lightning shot out, one jagged fork at a time, into each whale, connecting them to the horn. Then the horn shot a hundred little bolts of golden lightning into Medophae.

He gasped, and the energy lifted him off the ground like he was a leaf on the wind. Each streak of lightning lodged into his vital organs. He shouted and clenched his teeth, gripping the horn. He felt the struggles of the whales, resisting the call. They yanked at him, trying to rip him down from the sky.

This was the battle of wills. This was the fight he had to win.

He growled. This was a tool for a god, and no doubt Oedandus had more than enough will to quickly bring these whales to heel. But this wasn't a tool for a mortal. Already, Medophae felt his body slowly being torn apart.

But Medophae wasn't just any mortal. He had wielded power like this before; he had housed it for hundreds of years. The crackles of Oedandus were familiar to him, and he harnessed them. He let the power soak into him, let it make him stronger. With a grunt, he used that power to hold his body together.

He yanked on those lightning threads. The pain was excruciating, like every hair on his body had been lit on fire, burning deep under his skin one needle-thin point at a time.

He could not budge them. Pulling on the lightning was like pulling on iron handles bolted into a cliff face. His mortal vitality wasn't enough to compel these huge creatures. He needed overwhelming strength, a presence larger than a hundred whales, and he was just one human. He didn't have the endless GodSpill that comprised Oedandus. He needed more GodSpill. He needed to be filled with it just like Oedandus.

"No..." he growled. His body began to come apart again. He could feel the bones separating from the ligaments under the pressure of his failing will, and the whales sensed his weakness. They pulled harder.

But there was something...

The lightning had connected Medophae's meager reservoir of GodSpill, the tiny bit that every living creature possessed, with the vast ocean of GodSpill within a hundred whales.

The lightning connected him to the whales like a river connected a lake to the ocean, and all of his personal GodSpill was running to them. But if he could reverse the flow of the river, rather than fighting the strength of their combined wills, he could pull their GodSpill into him.

Medophae had swelled with Oedandus's power, swelled with GodSpill beyond a mortal's capacity, before. When he had destroyed Dervon, or brought the Deitrus Shelf tumbling down, he'd housed enough to make him shine like the sun.

He stopped trying to dominate the minds of the whales with his little reservoir of GodSpill. Instead, he commanded the flow of the golden lightning to reverse, to fill him.

Golden energy flowed into him, and he swelled like he had with all of Oedandus at his command. The life force of each whale flowed into him until their combined GodSpill became his.

"Yes," he breathed, gathering that immense power and turning it into a single command for the hundred whales.

"You...are...mine!" he shouted.

He grabbed the lightning cords with his one remaining hand. Golden fire crackled around his fist, but he clenched them all. He yanked them, and every whale in the ocean shuddered, sending waves of water toward the shore. Some actually thrashed, trying to get closer to him.

This is how he did it. Oedandus could have used his own personal power to dominate them, but it would have exhausted him. Why do that when he could simply pull the GodSpill he needed from the whales? With every whale added, it added more power to the horn. It used their own strength against them.

The whales stopped thrashing. They stopped shooting water into the air, and each became docile, floating just beneath the surface of the water.

Medophae looked down at himself. He glowed like a sun, floating a dozen feet above the coast. He imagined himself floating toward the whales and it happened, taking him over the water. He landed on the back of the nearest whale, one of the largest of the frightening gathering.

The whales waited patiently for his command, and he obliged them.

He sent three whales to the north and three to the south, telling them to swim for a day in that direction. The rest, save the one upon which he stood, he told to swim west toward the continent of Amarion. He told them to spread out, commanding the southernmost whale to swim for Calsinac and the northernmost whale to swim for Irgakth, the land of the dragons. He commanded each subsequent whale to spread out, each hitting the coast somewhere between those two points.

Go now, he thought to them. Go as fast as you can swim.

He commanded the final whale, the one upon which he stood, to wait.

If Saraphazia came upon the first whales headed for the Amarion coast, he wanted her to spend her time jumping from decoy to decoy. That might keep her busy long enough for him to punch through to the coast and rejoin Oedandus.

Medophae waited an excruciating half an hour. He worried that with each passing second, Saraphazia would emerge with a vengeance, and this time she'd make sure he died.

But she didn't come, and when Medophae could stand still no longer, he spoke to his whale. "Take me to Amarion," he said, feeling his will flow into the whale on a river of GodSpill given to him by the other ninety-nine whales. He gave it a picture of the coast north of Teni'sia and, after a moment, the whale began to move.

It kicked its tail and surged forward. The lightning connections kept Medophae upright like they were lines harpooned into the whale's flesh. He could no longer see the other whales moving away on their various missions, but there were still invisible connections to him. If he had a different command for them, they would hear him.

At Medophae's behest, the whale he rode stayed above the surface of the ocean. Medophae used the overwhelming flow of GodSpill to refresh himself, and it held his fatigue at bay. He stayed awake, standing, for hours as the water rushed by. When he had flown on Bands, this journey had taken an entire day and night. He could only assume that it would take twice as long on a whale. He stood the entire first day, munching contemplatively on dried goat meat. As night fell and the whale still continued at the same strong pace, he lay down and rested. He didn't fall asleep, worried that his connection to all the other whales might break if he stopped concentrating.

He forced himself to stay awake through that entire first night.

The next day passed much as the first. Salt spray soaked him, the lightning connections kept him attached to the whale, and the whale continued forward, unflagging.

He found himself wondering how long it would take for Saraphazia to notice that her whales were being controlled.

That night, an hour after the sun went down, the connection to Medophae's southernmost whale, the one he'd sent to Calsinac, suddenly winked out. He hadn't released it. It was as if someone had simply cut the cord.

Saraphazia had found his first whale.

24

BANDS

BANDS STOPPED on the road about a mile from the walls of Teni'sia. The thin moon gave some illumination, but clouds sailed the skies tonight.

Stavark stopped beside her and watched her carefully. She'd hesitated in bringing him, but she was going to need an extra pair of hands tonight, and the boy needed something to take his mind off his troubles. She marveled at his depth and strength. He carried the weight of two peoples on his shoulders, and yet he had managed to bear it with grace all the way through the Wave and the journey to Teni'sia.

But slaying Mirolah might have been too much for him. He had wanted to die, but Bands had blocked his request by telling Mirolah not to kill him. Now, he just seemed miserable in his own skin. He did what was asked of him. He went where he was requested to go, but he seemed to take no joy in anything.

"We leave the path here," she murmured. He nodded, and they walked into the woods. Bands led him through the trees for another ten minutes until she found the clearing she sought. It was a dark enough night, and this glade was far enough from the city that no one would see her in the night's sky. Stavark stood waiting, hands at his sides.

"From here, we fly."

"You will change," he said.

"Yes." She walked to the center of the glade. "Stand back."

He moved silently to stand beside the tree. Bands reached within herself and focused on her true form. The trigger was an easy one, well-used. She'd done the transformation so many times, she did not need words to focus her threadweaving, but she said them anyway out of habit.

Bring me out.

The air warped around her, and her form expanded. Wearing the body of a human woman had become comfortable, but whenever she took her true form, it was like she was being released. There was a pressure, being in another form. There was no pressure in her true form.

Stavark's silver eyes widened and his jaw went slack, but only for a moment. The stunned expression changed to reverence.

"Kaarksyvihrk. Maerstek dumir Kaarksyvihrk," he murmured.

She smiled. "You are too kind, young Stavark. Shapeshifting is not so impressive as it may appear." She looked to the sky and flexed her wings. "Come, my friend." With her teeth, she picked up the two bags that held the fishing nets they had brought, and secured them on a pair of spine spikes along her back.

His pack bobbing, Stavark ran forward and leapt as high as he could. He scrambled atop her, settling himself between the bags.

"Hang on tight. The beginning is the roughest." She rocked back on her powerful legs and launched them into the air. They soared above the treetops as if shot from a crossbow. Just as their momentum ebbed and they began to fall, Bands unfolded her wings and caught the air. She pumped twice fiercely, evened them out, and began a steady rhythm, taking them high into the sky.

She glanced back at him. Stavark narrowed his eyes and pointed his serious face into the wind, his hair flying behind him like a silver banner. His fingers were white-knuckled where they gripped the spike before him.

They soared away from Teni'sia.

She kept the castle behind them and pushed southward. Only the most intent would be able to see a dark green dragon against this cloudy sky.

To their right, the Inland Ocean glimmered like a dark sheet of glass. Below, the jumbled landscape of young mountains and tenacious alpine trees rushed by. The Corialis Mountains could not compare to the overpowering size of the Spine Mountains, but they were powerful and beautiful in their own right.

Bands banked left and drove upward toward the summit. They said goodbye to the Inland Ocean, and she bucked the turbulence at the ridge as the eastern wind rushed at her. She used it to climb higher, then ducked her head and shot downward. They swooped along the eastern slope and skimmed the edge of the True Ocean. Black and fathomless, the True Ocean stretched on from here to the horizon. So far as the humans of Amarion were concerned, nothing existed beyond the True Ocean. The malicious waves churned and rolled all the way to the end of eternity. No human had ventured more than a mile out onto those waters since before human history was recorded, except for Medophae. And no dragon had even flown over them since the War of the Behemoths, except for her.

Bands often wondered how much of that adventure had been fated. If she had not bucked the superstitions of her kind and discovered that dragons didn't die when they flew over the waters of the True Ocean, if she hadn't traveled far out over those deadly waters with her partner-in-adventure, Jarissa Chandura, she would never have found the Isle of Dandere. Jarissa's heart would never have been stolen by Jarod Madis Roloiron. And then there would never have been a Medophae Roloiron, prince of Dandere and heir to the rage of Oedandus. The great god would have remained imprisoned under the thumb of Dervon the Diseased forever.

The Corialis range pushed them closer and closer to those dark waters, curving inexorably to the place Bands sought. What would have been a day-long gallop by horse took less than an hour by dragon flight.

Bands's keen eyes scoured the cliffs, and she found the spot she was looking for: a sheltered cove, almost invisible from the ground. The cliffs ended abruptly, bracing the persistent crashing of the waves, forming a broken "C" around the hidden beach. She wheeled about and dove to land on the sandy bank.

Stavark jumped from her back, landing on the patchy grass and sand. He rubbed his hands together vigorously. The poor thing looked frozen through and through.

"I am sorry, my friend," Bands said. "It has been long since I had a mortal rider upon my back. I forgot to ask if you were cold. Here." She turned and sent a jet of her breath onto the beach. A riot of flames exploded, creating a bonfire.

"Warm yourself. I will return."

Bands transformed back to her human form. She left Stavark by the enchanted blaze and walked through the sand to the edge of the jagged cliffs.

Through tangled vines and undergrowth, stone steps meandered up the slope and through an archway covered with moss and eaten by time. Beyond that archway lay the Tombs of the Lost, a monument erected to the dead of the Battle of the Deitrus Shelf. The tombs sprawled across a flat shelf that clung to the cliff overlooking the bay. Short-branched trees thick with leaves rooted at the edge of the bay and even along the sides of the path, reaching for the night sky like spears. Clusters of sea vine meandered up from the water and twisted about the stone walls and archways of the tombs. The trees and vines were everywhere, obscuring the somber tombs, the archways, the flagstone walkways. The Deitrus Shelf hadn't seen the touch of humans for generations.

The bay below the Deitrus Shelf was almost perfectly round, creating an inlet that was cut off from the True Ocean by long strands of rock reaching around it like arms. Where the "hands" would have been, the rock wall disappeared into the water. Rock spires rose up from the bay at random places, mirroring the tall, thin trees that clustered near the shore.

A light touch on her arm caused her to jump. Stavark looked up at her. "These are the tombs," he said. The boy made no sound when he walked. She'd forgotten how quiet quicksilvers could be.

"You are familiar with the Deitrus Shelf?" she asked.

"Orem told me the stories."

"Ah." She gave him a sidelong smile. "I think I'd like to meet this Orem. Everyone seems to think very highly of him."

"He said the dead are restless here," Stavark said. "I can feel it."

"Yes."

"The weapons are in the tomb?"

She pointed at the bay. "In the water."

He watched the gently lapping shore for a moment, then turned his attention back to the hill. "This is a sad place. The dead refuse to rest. Why?"

"I don't think they know they are dead yet. What do you see?"

"Nothing," he said, as his gaze fell on the archway that led up and onto the shelf. "But I hear them. They howl."

She reached the flagstone and took the steps slowly toward the first arch that led to the platform of tombs. Stavark resolutely followed her. Eerie silence settled about them as they approached the tall, sturdy arch. They stepped through, and Bands heard the voices Stavark had already heard.

The noise of battle rang in the air, but quietly, as though echoing around the corners of the mountains. The muted screams of the dying and the distant roars of victors surrounded them. Stavark walked with his head high and his silver eyes wide. His hands clenched into fists.

"They cannot touch us," she said to him.

He nodded once, but there was no relief in his eyes.

Bands navigated her way through the ivy-choked cobblestone paths, past the spear trees that cracked the flagstones in their violent desire to rise. She found herself looking for blood on the rocks. They'd found so many bloodied stones as they built this place, so few bodies.

It was difficult to keep the memories from overwhelming her. These ghosts lived only one moment over and over: the Battle of Deitrus Shelf. They desperately sought a resolution that would never come.

After wandering past the stone tombs and archways, images flickered about them and joined the noises. Every now and then, a transparent figure ran between tombs, welding sword or spear. Hundreds of ghostly figures fought as though Bands and Stavark stood in the middle of a battlefield. Stavark's face had become rigid, and he walked closer to her. His gaze darted back and forth, following the ghostly violence.

"We're almost there," she murmured.

Again, that single nod, but he kept his eyes on the ghosts near them.

They crossed the grand courtyard, more green than stone now, and headed toward the tallest tomb, covered in sea vines that had climbed up the steep cliff from the bay. Those thick walls housed the ghosts of the two dead kings who had met here with their armies. Massive granite pillars held up the façade. Medophae had constructed that tomb by himself, a somber penance for his horrible mistake.

She and Stavark ascended the steps slowly and entered the dark tomb. Two ghosts within glowed in the darkness: Seldon Tyflor and Matro Den. Swords flickered in the darkness as they struck at one another. Thrust and parry. Hack and deflect.

It was always the same, and Bands remained where she was until the fight ended. Stavark's breaths came quickly, but he remained steady, watching the battle play out.

Finally, the ghost of Seldon Tyflor made his fated error. His sword swung wide, allowing Matro Den the opening he needed. Despite the cataclysm that would follow, Matro made the strike as he always did and always would until the end of days. The tyrant's sword ripped into Seldon's side. The young, self-made King of Tyflor staggered back with a roar that was half agony and half frustration. He held his side as his life's blood leaked through his fingers. His sword clattered to the ground.

Matro Den lunged forward, thrusting his sword straight through Seldon's chest. It cut through armor and bone like paper. Seldon's roar ended abruptly. Slowly, he slid off the ghostly blade and collapsed at Matro Den's feet.

With a wicked grin, Matro raised his head and howled his victory.

Silence fell over the Tombs of the Lost. The muted battle, the distant cries, everything ceased. The war was over, because as Matro Den slew Medophae's friend Seldon Tyflor, Medophae lost control. He exploded into a berserker rage, releasing Oedandus upon Matro Den and his army. Even Bands could not remember exactly what happened, only the golden energy that shot from Medophae like a tunnel of fire. It knocked everyone on their backs. It incinerated Matro Den...

...and the shockwave brought down the Deitrus Shelf, killing everyone below.

This cove was created on that day, and miles of coastline to the north and south crumbled into the ocean.

But that was then.

At the silence, Matro turned and looked at the visitors. His lip curled in a sneer.

"The dragon bitch returns," he said. "What army have you brought with you this time?"

"No army, Matro Den."

He appraised Stavark. "A quicksilver boy? You're more in need of a man, I think." He leered at her. He stuck his sword into the chest of Seldon's corpse and left it there, quivering, while he strode forward. "Have you come to beg for mercy? Do you think I will play nicely with you if you beg?" He shook his head. "You should have given yourself to me the first moment you knew I was coming. You should have knelt before me and honored me. Perhaps then, I would have honored you."

Bands watched him, unmoved. Stavark tensed, his hand going to his sword. Matro noticed the movement and showed his teeth. "Come then, quicksilver." He opened his hands. "I know the secrets of dealing with your kind. Come for me, and you will see what the son of Buravar Den is famous for."

Bands shook her head. "You're a ghost, Matro. You have been for centuries."

Matro slowed at that, his eyes narrowing as though she had said something he should remember. He looked down at his ghostly hands. "What threadweaver trickery is this?"

"No tricks. You are dead."

Cold realization dawned on his pale, glowing face. "How? The day is mine. I have won!"

"You lost," she said. "You picked the wrong enemy. Seldon Tyflor was Medophae's friend."

"Who?"

"Wildmane."

Matro's eyes narrowed, and his fury grew. "What?"

"He brought down the Deitrus Shelf. It took both armies into the True Ocean."

Shaking with rage, Matro leaned forward as though he would launch himself at Bands. She watched him carefully, but did not move.

Then, a transformation took Matro Den. His rage vanished, and bitterness settled in its place. His bright eyes clouded over, and his shoulders stooped. He looked around himself, noticing the walls of the tomb as if for the first time. He glanced over his shoulder at the ghostly corpse of Seldon Tyflor. It had vanished.

"Yes..." he said through tight lips. "I remember now. I remember dying. Stone, so heavy..."

"Yes," Bands said.

"Then why have you come, woman?"

"To see if you still haunt these halls."

"Haunt them? Before you came, I was in glorious combat..." His eyes narrowed to slits. "What did Tyflor call you? Anciella?"

"Yes, but that is not my name. You may call me Bands."

He spat at the ground. "Wildmane's love. So you lured us to our deaths here."

"Medophae did not mean to bring down the shelf. He did not expect you to slay Seldon."

He sneered. "Then Wildmane is a fool."

"Perhaps," she said.

"I should have won this battle. In my mind, I am winning still, but this..." He waved a hand at the tomb. "This is a burial house. Centuries, you say? I have been dead so long?"

"Longer than you can imagine. The world has changed."

"And my country?"

"It survives, though very differently than when you left it."

"My sons?"

"Long dead, though only one by violence. Your third son, Candon, went on to become a great ruler. Buravar still survives because of him."

"Buren was my heir."

"He continued your war."

"And?"

"He died under mysterious circumstances. It is my belief that Candon had him killed."

"Little Candon..." Matro mused. The barest hint of a smile showed at the corner of his mouth. "A brave move for a boy."

"He was a brave boy."

"And Matender?"

"Fled when he heard the news of Buren's death."

Matro spat. "I always knew him for a coward. He was his mother's son." He paused. "And yet..." He looked up at Bands and watched her for a long moment. "I have heard this story before. How?"

"You and I have spoken before."

"You have told me this entire story..."

"Yes."

He growled. "Then have you returned to mock me? Is that it?"

"No. I returned in grief, as did Medophae. We found you this way. We built these tombs for you and your soldiers. For Seldon and his soldiers."

"How many times have we spoken?"

"This will be the fourth."

"You built these tombs the first time. Why did you come a second time?"

"To see if you had found peace."

"And the third?"

"The same. Medophae bears the guilt of this battle like a scar across his heart."

"And why do you come this time, love of Wildmane?"

"I may be able to free you."

He said nothing for a long time. "Free me from...what?"

"This existence. I have recently been freed from imprisonment. I had much time to think...about many things. The Tombs of the

Lost was one of them. I think I know why you remain here."

"And why is that?"

"Great amounts of GodSpill were used in this place, GodSpill that was connected to each and every one of your soldiers through your weapons. They were the most powerful of the age, and there were so many of them. I have had long years to ponder this, and I believe that a bond develops between enchanted items and their users. It may be they hold you to this place. I have come to remove them, to give you rest at last."

He frowned. "Then, at best, I may look forward to no life at all. Not even a ghostly one?"

"Is this life for you? There is more beyond the Godgate, it is said."

"And how would you know?" he asked, some of his original fire coming back into his speech. "You lie, dragon bitch. I have no time for your lies. I have a war to win."

"Matro," Bands said, her voice charged with command. He ignored her, turned and walked deeper into the tomb, back to where he had slain the ghost Seldon Tyflor.

"Matro!" she called, her voice echoing off of the walls.

He waved a dismissive hand over his shoulder. "Go! I will see you on the battlefield. When I have taken the upstart's head and destroyed his army, I will defile you on the battlefield for all my loyal subjects to see. You will not speak so brazenly then." Seldon's body reappeared in a flicker. Matro grabbed his sword and pulled it out, then continued walking as if he had not even seen the dead body of his foe.

He vanished into the back wall. Bands let out a long breath and stared after him for a moment. In the distance, a single sword rang out as it came down on some hapless soldier. Another muted clang sounded, and then another. Soon, the tombs were filled once more with the noise of a battle that had ended centuries ago.

"Come, Stavark," Bands said. "We tried. It appears as though the ghosts will not help us."

He nodded, obviously relieved at Matro Den's absence. "What do we do next?"

Bands turned and left the tomb of Matro Den and Seldon

Tyflor. "We go with my guess. We take what we need and hope it is enough."

25

BANDS

BANDS STARED down at the waters of the bay. The surf lapped softly at the rocky beach, stopping inches from her boots.

"Do we swim to get them?" he asked.

"We threadweave, which I wanted to avoid. I had hoped we might entice the ghosts to bring the weapons up from the depths, but it was a thin hope to start. It hinged on Matro Den. He's the only one I could ever get to acknowledge me at all. The rest simply continue their fight as if I am not there. I thought if I could get Matro to help us, he might command the others to help as well. Unfortunately, we must do it the other way."

"Why not threadweave first?"

"Tampering with Saraphazia's ocean is dangerous. She doesn't like those who meddle in her realm."

"And we cannot swim because...?"

"I cannot touch this water. It connects directly to the True Ocean, and those waters would eat me alive."

He raised his eyebrows.

"Saraphazia destroys all human vessels she catches in her

waters, but oftentimes those sailors may swim to shore, if they are lucky. Not so for a dragon. To you, this water is just water. To me, it is like acid."

"Why?"

"It is a powerful spell set in place by Saraphazia, the goddess of the true ocean, spawned from an ancient argument between her and Avakketh. Her whales do not venture onto land. Dragons do not touch her waters. It is the same for the children of Dervon. Dramaths, darklings, and the others. They burn also because of her hatred for Dervon."

Bands cleared her mind and reached into the threads of the great tapestry. Deep down, past the water, past the silt and muck of the bay floor, she sensed the concentrated GodSpill. Each weapon glowed in her threadweaver's sight, powerful weapons from the Age of Ascendance.

Yes. These will do. These weapons will cut a dragon's scales.

She whispered words in her own tongue, a fallback from when she pulled GodSpill directly from Avakketh. Dragon threadweavers manipulated the threads by whispering litanies of praise to Avakketh. She no longer whispered prayers to him, but when she manipulated the threads, she still whispered. Often, it was simply whispering what she wanted to happen over and over, but it was always in the tongue of dragons.

Bring the weapons up. Bring them up. Bring them to me.

It focused her mind, and she felt the threads of the steel beneath the water, beneath the fish in the water, beneath the kelp on the bottom of the bay, beneath the muck of hundreds of years. There were so many of them, so many threads to pull, so much weight to overcome. Thousands of weapons, hundreds of thousands of threads.

Bands bowed her head, her arms trembling as she exerted her will on the those steel threads.

Come.

She turned her hands palms up, curling them into claws.

The bay churned as thick mud was dislodged far below and bubbles fled to the surface. The water became more agitated until the first sword broke the surface. Covered in muck, the curved blade glinted in the moonlight where one spot had been washed clean. Then the surface of the water erupted. Old spears, swords, shields, axes, maces, halberds, practically every weapon imaginable hovered above the waters of the bay.

She heard Stavark's slow intake of breath.

Come to me....

Slowly, the weapons began to float toward the shore—

Bands hissed as the threads were suddenly jerked out of her grasp and a dozen threads of air rippled at her, smacking her backward. The weapons fell, splashing back into the water. Bands staggered away. Droplets of the deadly water splashed near her boots.

Her mind still ringing from the harsh slap, Bands looked to her left. The outer rocks separating the bay from the True Ocean had been obliterated by the bulk of a gigantic whale.

"Saraphazia!"

The front of the whale's huge mouth curled upward, showing a fortress of tall, white strands that were Saraphazia's teeth.

"How dare you...?" Saraphazia boomed at her. "I show you kindness. I rescue you from certain death, and you repay me by stealing from my waters?"

"Saraphazia, my apologies," Bands said. She spared a sideways glance, looking for Stavark. With the goddess, in all her majesty, having risen before her, Bands suddenly became concerned for the quicksilver's welfare. Gods were unpredictable, and Saraphazia was already angry. If this went badly, Bands's life might be worth very little to the goddess, and Stavark could be killed just for being Bands's. But the quicksilver was nowhere to be seen.

Thank the gods, Stavark. You are a clever boy.

He must have hidden the moment the goddess rose, as quickly as only a quicksilver could.

"I know you care nothing about the affairs of humans," Bands continued. "I simply thought to pull these human weapons from the bay. I didn't think you would care about—"

"When you use threadweaving on my ocean, you use it on me."

"That was not my intention. I didn't want to disturb you, and my need is great. A war has begun. Avakketh invades Amarion. He intends to destroy humanity. Every kingdom. Every village—"

"I know of Avakketh's plans."

"You do?" Bands murmured. She wanted to ask how Saraphazia knew, but didn't. Saraphazia had been generous to Bands a handful of times in the past, but she didn't seem in the generous mood at the moment. "Then you... Certainly you don't want Avakketh to succeed."

"I care nothing for Avakketh. I likewise care nothing for humankind."

"I simply...I came to help—"

"You came to steal."

"Only to keep from disturbing you."

"Do not lie to me, Randorus. Or what little respect I have for you will die."

"We're desperate. Will you not help us?"

"Let Tarithalius protect his own," she said, then in a lower tone, "he is swift to make messes. Let him clean it up."

"I do not know where Tarithalius is."

"He is probably hiding as a squirrel or a dog or an ant. Anything that ill-befits his station, I expect. Or look to the battlefield. He loves to fight." The goddess's voice echoed across the bay.

"That will be too late. The dragons come for Amarion now."

"And?"

Bands swallowed. "The next kingdom they will attack is beloved of Medophae. All will be ashes and fire in a matter of days. Maybe even a matter of hours. Please, I beg you to grant me this favor."

"Another favor, dragonkind? When Medophae cast your gem into my ocean, I ensured my waters did not destroy you. I even gave you counsel, which you chose to ignore. Just days ago, I gave Medophae similar counsel. He flung it into my teeth just as you did. After all I have done for both of you, you spurn me. You have nothing but contempt for the rules I cherish and for the advice I give freely."

"Wait... You know where Medophae is?" Bands asked. If Saraphazia could free Medophae, that would solve so many problems in one stroke. "If you know where he is, then I...I would ask you to tell me."

"Another favor? How many would you like?" Her huge eyes narrowed. "You think your needs are special, that because you crave something, it ought to be yours. Your need does not give you the right to take whatever you wish from whomever you wish. I have no more favors left for you, Randorus dragonkind. You have exhausted my goodwill."

"Please..." Bands said. "It's not for me. It is for all of Amarion."

"Perhaps you should have started with begging, rather than trying to steal from my waters. If Amarion sinks into the ocean, then it will be under my protection."

Bands tried to think of what to say to convince the goddess. The weapons didn't really belong to Saraphazia, but she wouldn't see it that way.

"Avakketh wants everything," Bands said. "With Natra gone, with Oedandus insensate, Avakketh believes he is the ruler of all creation. He has told his dragons that he created the world."

"Let him lie to his scaled lackeys. What is that to me?" Saraphazia asked.

"But with Natra gone and Oedandus neutralized, who can stop him from taking the entire world?"

Saraphazia's giant lip curled upward. "That is the same argument Medophae made. It did not move me."

Medophae could be anywhere from Irgakth all the way to the endless plains of the Sunriders, so long as it touched the True Ocean. Bands needed a location. How could she make the goddess tell her?

Perhaps if Bands painted a picture of Saraphazia as the ruling goddess over not only the True Ocean, but also of Amarion, that might hold her interest. "What if Avakketh were removed for good?"

"Bribery, Randorus? Despite your desperate hopes, Medophae cannot overcome Avakketh. You cannot deliver your vain promises. There is nothing you have that I want."

"Then I would ask you to do what's right," Bands said.

"Right?" Saraphazia's great head rose, and her eyes flashed. "Humans talk incessantly about what is 'right' while breaking every law they can break. You do not get to tell me what is right, dragonkind. *I* tell *you* what is right. I made a law that others were not to take from my waters, and you have broken that law. The penalty is death."

Bands braced herself to flee.

Saraphazia shifted, grinding rocks beneath her. "But I will spare you. This is my one favor, and it shall be my last. You and Medophae helped me destroy Dervon, and for that I bore you goodwill. Today, you have spent the last of it. Go now. I give you your life. Take it and leave. It will be the only thing you take from this place—"

The enormous goddess stopped speaking in mid-sentence. Her head rose, and her great body crushed boulders to sand as she turned toward the sea. The rock wall that outlined the bay crumbled into the water.

"What have you done?" Saraphazia whispered to the horizon, then she thrashed back, facing Bands. Bands backed away, wary of the deadly water Saraphazia threw about her.

"Did you know about this?" Saraphazia hissed. "Did you distract me here while he committed this atrocity?" Her voice blasted at Bands like a hurricane, and she staggered backward.

"What are you talking about?" she shouted into the wind.

"The horn," Saraphazia boomed. "Your paramour has used the accursed horn!"

The goddess had lost her mind. Bands turned, scrambling over the uneven ground to get away.

"He will pay for this atrocity with *your* life!"

The wind from her booming words was so strong, it threw Bands to the ground. She tumbled and rolled to her feet. She tried to bring her focus to bear in the blast, sending her awareness into the threads.

Saraphazia thrashed, spinning her vast bulk and destroying the rest of the wall between the Deitrus Bay and the True Ocean. She whipped her tail down hard, and a fifty-foot wave rose behind her, arcing toward Bands.

26

BANDS

THE WAVE HIT FASTER than Bands could threadweave, faster than she could transform into a dragon. She barely had time to turn when the water smacked into her shoulder. It hit her like a claw, tearing at her skin, ripping deeper—

Then Stavark was there.

Silver lightning flashed around her as a thousand hands pushed back the water, lifted her, and shoved her away out from under the wave that fell all around. The terrain whipped by so quickly, Bands couldn't breathe.

When the silver lightning stopped, Bands tumbled to the rocky ground of a thin deer path high on the ridge. Saraphazia's deadly wave smashed into the side of the cliff below her.

The splash that had hit her shoulder burned, raking deeper, eating through her skin, through her muscle, trying to get through her shoulder blade to reach her ribs and her heart.

More lightning flashed around her back, and with her peripheral vision, she saw Stavark's face in a thousand different positions as his hands worked at her shoulder. She felt little stabs like pinpricks, and she realized Stavark was *picking the water* out of the wound!

Unbelievably, the aggressive burning stopped, though the sear of the wound it left behind was abominable. Gritting her teeth against the pain, she turned. Stavark stood before her, his slender fingers covered with her blood.

"You are safe," he huffed, then his eyes rolled up into his head, and he collapsed.

"Stavark!" She scrambled to her knees and cradled him. She felt for his pulse and found it. He wasn't dead, just spent after lifting her up the side of an entire cliff, holding a wave away from her, and somehow cleaning her wound of every speck of the horrific water. She'd never seen a quicksilver do so much while using their flashpowers, not during the Age of Awakening, not even during the Age of Ascendance. Stavark had exceeded the normal bounds of his abilities, and he had paid the price.

She glared back at the endless True Ocean below. Saraphazia was nowhere to be seen. Something had happened to provoke her, something far away. And from the sound of the goddess's accusations, Medophae was behind it. Something about a horn.

Bands fashioned bandages and a makeshift sling for her left arm out of strips from her tunic. She could still use the arm, but every time she did, it felt like someone was jamming a knife under her shoulder blade. She should heal it, but healing herself was exhausting, and she still had work to do here. She couldn't heal herself and lift the weapons out of the water. She couldn't summon enough GodSpill to do both. The arm would have to wait. She put a gentle hand on Stavark's unconscious forehead. "Noble *syvihrk*. Rest," she said. "I shall return."

The deadly wave had crushed the scrub brush flat and cracked the spear-like trees in half. They lay like fallen soldiers everywhere. Careful not to touch the wet rocks with her bare hands, Bands made her way down the cliff. She spotted the bag in which she'd kept the fishing nets. She removed them—they were blessedly dry—and spread the nets out on dry ground. Afterward, she wound her way through the shrub and tree wreckage and stopped at the shore of the bay.

If Saraphazia was nearby, she'd return with a murderous

vengeance the moment she felt Bands's touch on the threads of her water. But Bands was betting her life that the goddess was now preoccupied with Medophae's attack, whatever it was.

Bands made a habit of keeping her temper with others who failed to keep theirs, but she'd had enough of the crazy goddess. The weapons in that bay didn't belong to her. There was no reason for Saraphazia to keep them from the people who needed them. If Medophae was distracting her with some horn that drove her crazy, then Bands wasn't going to waste the opportunity. In fact, thinking about Medophae going toe-to-toe with the goddess gave her a warm feeling. Medophae was relentless when provoked.

Kick her in the teeth, my love. And stay alive. I'm coming for you.

Bands was going to take the moment Medophae was giving her. She would ensure Teni'sia had a fighting chance. She reached into the threads once more, holding her good arm toward the water, and whispered.

Bring them up. Bring them to me.

The bay churned as the weapons rose from the depths again. They weren't buried in mud this time, but Bands had to fight the agony of her wound while still concentrating on thousands of threads.

Come on....

Sweat broke out on her forehead.

Every threadweaver had personal limits based on the might of their own body. A threadweaver could pull GodSpill—nearly infinite power—from the lands all around to affect things, but the concentration to reach into those threads came from the finite GodSpill within Bands's own body. Trying to lift ten swords was easy. Manipulating fifty threads, no more than five per sword, was a fine exercise for a moderately talented threadweaver.

Raising two thousand weapons was a challenge even for Bands.

If she had all the time in the world, taking them out a dozen at a time might have been preferable. But every moment she waited was a moment she didn't have. Avakketh could already have sent his dragons against Teni'sia. If even a pair of dragons attacked the city before she returned, Teni'sia would burn just like Corialis Port.

Bands's bad arm drooped as she sucked the GodSpill from

herself to maintain her concentration. Thousands of little fingers of her attention wriggled into the steel of the weapons. They rose, dripping, above the waterline for a second time and hovered over the bay. The weapons were clustered together in a line that mimicked the ragged coast, and she made them float toward her, a twisting, spiky steel river. They moved past her and piled together near the giant fishing nets.

When the last weapon fell, Bands swayed and barely managed to keep her balance. On unsteady feet, she went to the pile. She was going to have to burn that water away before she could touch them. She put her good hand on her knee and rested.

"You got them," Stavark said right next to her.

Bands turned and almost fell. "Gods," she said. "You're okay." She took his hand.

He nodded somberly.

"I can't touch those weapons," she said. "Not until I get rid of that water."

"I brought rope," Stavark said, unshouldering his pack and pulling out a twenty-foot length of rope.

Bands laughed. "You brought rope?"

"I thought we would tie the nets to your back."

"I think you're my favorite person in the world, Stavark."

He bowed his head. "You honor me, *kaarksyvihrk*."

"I am the one who is honored."

She took a deep breath, thinking of the journey ahead. "Let's get moving." She moved beyond the wet area where the wave had struck, then let go of her human form, letting herself flow into her dragon form.

The pain in her shoulder exploded like her arm was being pulled off. Bands screamed into a roar as she became a dragon. Fire shot from her mouth, hitting the side of the cliff and melting rock, and she staggered to the side.

She craned her long neck to look back at her shoulder...

Her left wing was melted and ruined.

"Kaarksyvihrk!" Stavark shouted, running to her side.

"My wing..." she said. Fear thundered in her heart. She had been wounded before, but she had never been maimed. Bands could heal flesh and mend broken bone, but could she reconstruct an entire wing? The thought of being forever grounded was a lance to her heart.

She stared at it, stunned, and Stavark remained silent, waiting.

Shake it off, Randorus. You have work to do. The people of Teni'sia need you.

"It doesn't matter," she said, her voice coming out calm. "I wasn't going to fly with tons of weapons anyway. I...I always intended to carry them overland." But she had intended to fly them over the snowy mountain range one trip at a time. That wasn't going to work now. "We're going to have to cart them up the coast of the True Ocean, then take what we can over the summit."

"Yes, *kaarksyvihrk*," Stavark said.

"Let's..." Her voice faltered, and she spoke again with more force. "Let's get these weapons dried off and strapped to me."

27

MEDOPHAE

THE RACE against time had begun. Saraphazia had discovered what he was up to. Medophae didn't know how far he was from the coast. A day, maybe two. Medophae had never sailed the True Ocean—no human ever had.

Another hour passed, and a second connection winked out. This time, the goddess's thoughts tried to follow the connection back. Medophae dropped it immediately, hoping he was quick enough. Another thirty minutes passed, and a third whale was discovered. He severed that connection, too.

They came quickly then, one after the another, roughly twenty minutes apart as he imagined Saraphazia speeding through the ocean, seeking her whales. Every time another connection was cut, he sensed her overwhelming fury. And so it went, whale after whale as Saraphazia raced south to north, freeing them, raging that no whale seemed to hold Medophae as a rider.

Night ended and day began again, and still Medophae couldn't see the coast. If Saraphazia caught him in open water, that would be the end of it. For Medophae to have a chance of fighting her, he had to make it to Amarion. Otherwise he was, just as she said, a mere mortal.

The whale itself did not seem to tire, but Medophae's fatigue dragged at him. He hadn't slept in two days now since he'd passed out in the hut, and the horn's power seemed to be at its limit. He struggled to keep his eyes open, and sometimes he found himself slipping from the whale before the golden lightning caught him and returned him to the top of the whale's back.

By noon, all but a couple dozen of the ninety whales he'd sent as decoys had been released by Saraphazia. She'd been faster today, every fifteen minutes or so, like clockwork. She had discovered his pattern and was methodically tracking down her whales. Then, however, she stopped. She didn't free any more whales. The northernmost whales continued along the path he'd commanded them.

Medophae shook his head to keep himself alert. He had found a barnacled area of the whale's back and stayed close to it. It was the best area to hang on. The golden lightning failed intermittently, and the last thing he could afford was to pitch headlong off the whale. It still surged forward with as much power as it had at the beginning of the journey, and Medophae revered the stamina of these creatures.

The sun sank steadily down the sky, and there were still no attempts to free the northernmost whales he'd sent. Each of them were heading for the Corialis Mountains or higher.

She's figured it out. She knows I'm not on any of them. She's questioning why I would I go so far north, almost into Irgakth.

Medophae clutched the horn and forced his flagging will to send a new directive to the northern whales.

Come south, he thought to them, and gave them a picture of the southern Corialis Mountains. Medophae gave new direction to his own whale, told it to head there as well.

The whale shot water up through its blowhole, then changed course.

Saraphazia was now trying to outthink him, and she would go to the area around Teni'sia, south of the Corialis Mountains. He had called to her from that kingdom during his time with Tyndiria. She knew he had spent time there, and it would be a reasonable guess for her to think that was where he was going. And, indeed, it had been.

But Medophae didn't need to land near Teni'sia. He simply needed to get his feet on land. After that, he would regain Oedandus, and possibilities would open up again. If Medophae veered north, perhaps he could pass Saraphazia without her knowing. She would seek him to the south while he would go where all the other whales converged. If, for some reason, she came to that spot, he would use the rest of the whales to fight her, giving himself that one chance to...

In the distance, he saw land.

He levered himself to his feet. There was a thin line on the horizon, not just the black line where water met sky, but something else. Thicker, bumpier. A coastline.

"Ha!" he laughed, and his voice was horse. He drank the last of the water from his final waterskin. He was going to make it. He was—

His gaze caught another anomaly along the horizon to the south. A bump marred the perfect flatness of the ocean, heading directly toward him.

No....

Saraphazia had found him. She had indeed gone south. He had gotten past her, but she'd doubled back.

"Go!" he commanded the whale, but it didn't increase its speed. The feeling he got from it was that it was already moving as fast as it could.

Medophae watched the coast. It was getting closer, but the swell of Saraphazia was coming much faster. He wasn't going to make it.

"Dammit!" he cursed. He was so close. There had to be something. He looked down at the horn. The hum of its power had diminished almost to nothing. The intermittent flashes of golden lightning no longer raced along its surface. But maybe there was enough left. Maybe...

He released the other whales. They were too far away to get here in time to make a difference. And he wasn't sure he could get them to fight her, anyway. For all he knew, the moment she touched them, it would destroy his tenuous hold.

The power in the horn surged with that release. A few tendrils of golden lightning raced over its pearlescent surface. Again, he glanced at the shore. He could make out the peaks of mountains now, but it was still terribly far off.

"Fine," he said, turning to face the swell that was almost upon him. He tried to form the godsword. Golden fire gathered around his fist, and it grew into a shape that was vaguely dagger-like. It flickered, and for a moment he thought it would die, but it stayed.

This is what I have. A flickering fire dagger against one of the original seven gods.

The giant head of Saraphazia's whale form cut the surface, glowing blue with rage. Medophae spared one quick glance at the approaching coastline, then yelled at the goddess of the ocean.

"Turn away, Saraphazia! Just let me reach the shore and there is no need for us to fight!" He waved the golden dagger.

She didn't slow. Her great form rose up, jumping over the whale upon which he stood. He ducked, but her massive fin smacked him. The lightning threads connecting him to the whale snapped. If Medophae hadn't been charged with the GodSpill of the horn, he would have been crushed by the blow. He gasped, drawing in a breath as he hit the water and plunged beneath. He was spun about in the current created by Saraphazia's attack, and before he could get his bearings, he saw the flat face of Saraphazia's enormous form bearing down on him. She hit him, pushed him like a wall. He tried to spin, to get out of the way, but her enormous flat face went fifty feet in every direction. She hit him and dove. The pressure of the water mashed him flat against her. She shoved him into the depths, straight down.

He held desperately to his breath as the pressure increased. He wanted to shout at her, try to talk sense to her, but he didn't dare open his mouth.

Then, she stopped pushing, and he floated free. She lashed away from him, and the current battered him, spun him around again. The water pressed in on him from all sides, and his lungs felt like they would explode. He tried to find out which way was up, but it was pitch-black everywhere he turned. Saraphazia spun to face him, as large as a mountain range, blotting out everything. Only the blue light emanating from her allowed him to even see her. It was like a nightmare where the only thing in the world was an angry goddess. Her eyes flashed, and a bubble of air formed over his mouth. Medophae gasped and breathed desperately.

"Let me go," he said. "What do you care if I help the humans? They're nothing to you! Give me the chance to stop Avakketh. You hate him!"

"I despise him. I have suffered affronts and attacks from my vicious uncle, but he has the right to make those attacks. We are family. You are nothing! How *dare* you use Oedandus's horn against me, against the creatures under my protection?"

"Saraphazia—"

"How *dare* you!"

"I didn't hurt them—"

"You think you are a god, but you are nothing but a broken vessel, a cracked imperfection created by my idiot brother."

The water constricted around him.

Her eyes flashed, and that blue glow crackled in agitation. "You have lived centuries past your time," she said. "It is time for you to die."

She spun again, her massive bulk creating a surge in the ocean. It hit him, throwing him backward, ripping away the bubble of oxygen. Saraphazia sped upward, swimming through the heavy water faster than a dragon could fly. Her blue glow grew smaller and smaller until it was gone and he floated in the dark.

She'd taken him so far down he couldn't reach the surface before he drowned, and she'd left him here. He clenched his teeth and swam after her, but it was like swimming through sand. It was utterly black, and water crushed him from all sides. The tiny flicker of GodSpill from the horn was leaking away. He knew, once it left him, the water *would* crush him.

He kept swimming, hoping for a glimpse of light, some sign that he was close to the surface.

There was nothing.

The golden fire flickered across his arms, faded, and his body went cold. His arms and legs suddenly felt like they were full of wet clay.

He kept swimming, though his lungs wanted to explode.

One more stroke. One more....

His focus wavered, and he realized he wasn't kicking.

One more kick....

But he couldn't make his legs work. They were feeble.

Try harder.

The darkness around him filled his head. He tried to make his arms cup the water, tried to make his legs kick, but he could barely move his finger. His mouth opened.

That's bad. I can't open my mouth. That's...

His lungs spasmed, and he sucked in a lungful of water. The cold coursed into him, through him, and his whole body shuddered.

I can't...

He felt a rush of warmth in his chest then, insidious and wrong, like his panicked brain couldn't tell the difference between cold water and warm air anymore. It simply wanted to stop feeling pain. The cold and the crush of the water faded, replaced by a seductive warmth. He saw Bands in his mind, the side of her face as she turned, her face lighting up with a smile for him. Just for him. Finally, he was going to see her. And they'd be together again.

Bands...

28

MIROLAH

MIROLAH STOOD on the ramparts of the Northern Walk in the dark hours of early morning, staring at the horizon, fighting herself, and feeling an impending doom.

She had regained herself last night, finally. Up until this moment, it was as though Mirolah had been a tiny voice screaming at the bottom of a dark well, alone and helpless. Mirolah remembered what it was to be human again. She had crawled up, out of that darkness, and remembered who she was, the moments that comprised her, the pains and the pleasures of her life.

She clung to those memories, hanging onto the edge of that deep well by her fingernails. She didn't want to go back into the darkness again. The GodSpill hummed inside her, angry, trying to bury her little voice. She realized now that the GodSpill had its own agenda, its own desires. It wanted to absorb her. The insistent power sustained this body at her demand, but it didn't like it. It wanted her to cut free from her mortal self and become one with it: the vast GodSpill that permeated everything in Amarion. That sentience, that...craving of the lands, had almost gotten what it wanted when Zilok made Stavark stab Mirolah to death, but she had forced herself back into her body and healed it.

But somehow she'd done it wrong. She didn't feel the same as she once had. Before she'd been stabbed, the GodSpill sentience whispered to her, beseeched her to leave her body, but she had been—for the most part—in control.

Now, she had to concentrate just to stay in her body, as if she didn't really belong here.

Sniff sat next to her on the Northern Walk, eternally patient. Winter winds whipped around the walls, across the flagstones under their feet. Two guards plodded past them, their cowls drawn tightly against the cold. They didn't see her or Sniff because Mirolah didn't want them to.

Dawn peeked over the Corialis Mountains like a glimmer along the edge of a frosty knife, and the doom Mirolah had been feeling finally appeared.

The first dragon was a flash of purple against the blanket of white, barely a dot at this distance. An iridescent blue dragon followed close behind. None of the guards could even see them yet. But they would. The rest of the flight appeared over the ridge and dove, a tumble of jewels over a white tablecloth.

She'd felt them coming for hours now. Since her...death, the lands of Amarion felt like her body. She was connected to the Spine Mountains, to the shores of the True Ocean south of Calsinac, to the north where Irgakth and that hazy red wall began. The threads of Amarion thrummed at the presence of the dragon invaders. She could feel each of them like ants on her arm.

They stayed close to the ridge line, disappearing behind a nearer mountain, then rising over the next crest. The two guards, suddenly seeing the dragons, shouted and sprinted past her, naked fear on their faces.

Mirolah glanced down at her feet. She'd forgotten her boots. She'd have to remember her boots if she wanted to look normal around everyone else.

And was that what she wanted? To be just like everyone else?

Sniff whined. "They come, mistress."

Mirolah looked up. The dragons were nearly upon them, six of them, moving at an incredible speed toward the castle.

That's what I want, isn't it?

The lead dragon, the purple, burst into view, soaring over her head. Its shadow darkened half the palace, then it was gone. The iridescent blue dragon followed, whipping overhead, here and gone. Then a black dragon, whose scales looked like they had each been dipped in gold, soared overhead. The following three came side-by-side: a huge gray with dark blue spines down its back, another that was pure shimmering silver, and the final dragon had diamond patterns of copper and black. Screams rose from the city. Sniff whined again.

"Is that what I want?" Mirolah asked him, feeling the connections to her memories—to herself—slipping away.

"Serve the pack," Sniff barked.

"Yes."

"The pack of scaled others comes to kill," he said. "To kill your pack."

"No," Mirolah murmured to him.

"No," Sniff growled.

"We won't let them."

Sniff barked his approval.

29

MERSHAYN

MERSHAYN HAD JUST CLOSED the conference door and sat down opposite Giri'Mar who, for all his unhelpful blustering, was a genius when it came to military tactics. He and Mershayn had been drawing up a plan for the defense of the city when the knock came.

"Enter," said Mershayn.

The door swung open, almost banged into the wall before Deni'tri caught it. Casur stood just behind her. His blond hair was disheveled, and his eyes were wild. Mershayn leapt to his feet.

"They've come," Casur said. "The dragons are here."

"No..." Mershayn said. It slipped out before he could stop it, and he inwardly cursed himself.

He needed to project calm and confidence, like Bands always did. That's what the people of Teni'sia needed right now. But Bands had left last night, and she hadn't returned. They had no enchanted weapons. Teni'sia was going to burn.

He glanced at Deni'tri. The bald guard watched Mershayn with solemn confidence, waiting for the command that would save them. He wanted to scream at her that he didn't know what to do.

217

Instead, he leapt across the room and grabbed his sword belt from the peg on the wall. He slung it around his waist and buckled it in one swift motion.

"Archers to the ramparts, as we discussed," he said to Giri'Mar in a voice that came out steadier than he had any right to expect. The lord, already on his feet, left the room swiftly.

"Deni'tri," he said. "With me. Casur, spread the word. Nobles first, officers of the castle next. After that, whoever you can find. We had hoped to implement our plan when Bands returned. We will have to go ahead without her."

Mershayn sprinted into the hallway, and Deni'tri followed him. They reached the end of the hall, turned left, banged through the door into the main hallway.

"Are you ready to die?" Mershayn asked between breaths as they ran side-by-side.

"Yes, Your Majesty," she returned. After a slight pause for breath, she said, "Are you?"

He grinned, and a sort of madness came over him. No more waiting in fear. No more doubts. It was time to fight, live or die. This, he understood. "If the Godgate claims us today, we will give it a spectacle," he said.

"Yes, Your Majesty." The fear left her eyes, replaced by determination, and for a flickering moment, Mershayn felt like a good king.

They raced down the hallway together, reached the entrance to the Northern Walk. Two wide-eyed guards stood aside as Mershayn shouldered his way through the door.

"You two, come with us!" he yelled, not even pausing. They ran to catch up.

The king and his three guards pulled up short just outside the door as the shadows flashed overhead. Purple, green, then an explosion of colors. Every single one of them was as enormous as Bands in her true form, and there had to be a dozen of them.

"By the gods..." Mershayn said, the wind going out of his sails. The dragons wheeled around and roared. His heart thundered in his chest.

"Don't just stand there!" he shouted, as much for himself as those who stood around him. "Archers at the ready!"

Thankfully, Mershayn saw a handful of archers already on the walk. He ran to one of them and took the man's bow. He couldn't shoot an arrow as well as he could fence, but right now, everyone needed to reminded what to do. They needed to fight for their lives. He nocked an arrow, then saw that the other archers watched, slack-jawed, as the dragons wheeled in the sky.

Holding the bow and arrow tightly in one fist, he stepped up and slapped one of the stunned archers across the face.

"Listen to me!" They all turned their attention on him. "Calm your hearts or they will distract you. Today, you die. We all die so that our countrymen may live. Accept that and purge your fear. If you falter, your deaths will be in vain. If you stand fast, then we die to save others. So stand fast! Stare down these beasts. Aim for the eyes. Take your time. Don't miss."

"Yes," Deni'tri said with heartfelt conviction. The others stood transfixed.

"Do you hear me?" Mershayn shouted.

"Yes!" they said, shocked from their speechlessness.

"Then follow me!"

He sprinted up the Northern Walk toward the approaching dragons, and they followed.

Behold my tiny army. Seven guards and a bastard king.

Bands's words returned to him from the previous night: If the dragons defeat us, they will burn Amarion down to the soil. We stop them here or there is no tomorrow.

Mershayn ran like he had never run before toward the wheeling dragons. He skidded to a stop on the parapet, dropped to one knee, and readied his bow. The rest of his small band arrived, and the other three archers nocked their arrows. The dragons approached again, low, skimming the snowy slopes.

Mershayn looked quickly over his shoulder. "They will appear suddenly, moving faster than anything you've seen before," he said. "Be ready. Choose, aim, and fire." Mustering a smile, he winked at them. "Steady, Teni'sians. Make them remember us."

He was rewarded with nervous looks.

Somewhere to the south, fire exploded against the castle.

"Steady," he murmured.

Flames licked over the roof of the West Hall, and the iridescent blue dragon shot into view, drawing another breath. It spied them and dove toward them.

"Hold," Mershayn said, steadying his nerves. "Aim for the eye..." he murmured, stretching the string to his ear. He wanted to see the eye. Bands said no normal weapon could pierce those scales, but she said their protective spells were weaker around the eyes to enable the dragon to see clearly.

Mershayn released, and each of the archers behind him released at the same time. Four arrows flew at the fanged blue face. One sailed over the head. Two shattered against the iridescent blue scales of the dragon's jaw.

The fourth hit home, striking the eye. The dragon shrieked, and its wings jerked, sending its body sideways toward the castle.

"Cover!" Mershayn shouted. The dragon slammed into the rampart, scattering stones like leaves. Mershayn leapt to one side, but the monster's massive neck struck him. He saw one of the archers go over the edge. Deni'tri was thrown against the castle wall.

He crashed to the stones. The air whooshed from his lungs, and his head cracked against the ground....

30

MIROLAH

NEITHER THE GUARDS nor the king saw Mirolah and Sniff as they rushed past to shoot the dragon. She watched them draw their bows, watched the king lead his impossible attack, and watched it—miraculously—succeed. The arrow blinded the dragon in one eye. Now the beast thrashed, cracking the stones of the castle as it keened its rage. The entire walkway shuddered.

Not "the king," a little voice said inside her. His name is Mershayn.

We are one.... the voice of the GodSpill trampled over the smaller voice. It washed through her, tried to pull her from this body, and Mirolah resisted. She looked down at herself, and the arms and legs of this human body suddenly seemed foreign. A moment ago, she'd...been thinking of something.

Mershayn slid across the stones toward her, limp, unconscious.

"Serve the pack," Sniff barked urgently.

Mirolah looked at her hand. Rainbow colors passed across her fingers. Those colors came from her eyes, and it gave her a foreboding feeling.

"Mistress," Sniff whined again. "Will you help him?"

221

"Why is it so hard, Sniff? I knew who I was. But it fades so quickly...."

"Mistress!"

She felt Sniff's urgency, so she reached through the threads, let the vastness of herself flow into Mershayn and repair his wound. A memory fluttered to her then, of when she had healed him before. It had exhausted her, but it didn't now. Her body was so vast, she couldn't be exhausted.

Mershayn came awake, shaking his head, groggy. Fear came from him in waves, but he staggered to his feet and ran toward the thrashing blue monster.

"That one," Sniff yipped. "He is important. Your scent, his scent... They change when you are together."

The memories she'd held only moments ago, of Mershayn helping her recall her childhood, flashed through her again. She remembered why she was here, and what she must do.

She stopped her fears and focused on what needed doing. Teni'sia was under attack, and she could do something. So she must do something.

Serve the pack. This is my pack.

Mirolah reached out to stop the blue dragon's heart from beating. Sparks exploded in her threadweaver vision, and Mirolah jerked her head back. The dragons scales were tightly knit with strong threads, swelling with red GodSpill. She had never seen anything like that before. It was stronger than anything she had encountered. She could not reach through it.

The dragon struggled to its feet and reared up, sensing her attack. Mershayn roared, drawing his sword and charging toward his own death. Mirolah studied the makeup of the threads that went into the dragon's enchanted protection. It was powerful beyond her comprehension. Her body was vast, her power vast, but whatever had created this was also vast.

"Mistress!" Sniff whined.

"It is protected," she said.

"This one goes!" Sniff launched from his sitting position as if shot from a catapult. His lean body streaked toward the dragon, each strand of muscle rippling under his nearly translucent skin.

The dragon drew in a great breath even as Mirolah watched Sniff leap onto the dragon's flank, chewing viciously at the scales. The dragon spat fire over the entire walkway. Roiling flames consumed them all, but Mirolah pushed air at the fire, creating a tube that shielded Sniff, Mershayn and the others.

The dragon flung itself into the air with Sniff still clinging to it, tearing at the scales without success. The dragon shrugged, rippling its body, and dislodging the dog. Mirolah reached into the threads of the air and caught Sniff, lowered him to the walkway.

The dragon glanced down and, obviously shocked, realized that its prey was still alive. It seemed to sniff the air, and Mirolah felt its touch on the threads around her. With rage in its eyes, it peered around and spotted her.

It can see me with threadweaver sight just as I can see that magnificent spell that protects it.

The dragon dove at her. Given time, Mirolah might be able to unravel the protection that had been woven into those scales, but she did not have time. She had to fight this dragon, and those scales were too strong for a direct attack.

But the air was a different matter. The air was a part of Amarion, a part of her own body.

You are an invader. You are not wanted here.

She reached out, moving the threads of the air surrounding the dragon. She stole its wind.

The dragon fell like a stone. It beat its wings frantically, but they cut the air like a scythe. It crashed into the Northern Walk again. Mershayn, Deni'tri, Sniff, and the others leapt upon it.

Mirolah watched the battle. When the dragon whipped its head around to bite Mershayn, she turned the air as hard as stone and held the dragon's jaws open.

The powerful scales pushed against her will, and Mirolah pushed back. It was all she could do to keep those jaws open even for a few seconds. They snapped shut, but Mershayn had leapt clear.

Mershayn leapt forward again, sword flashing. At the last instant, Mirolah sent her will into the metal of his blade, filling it with GodSpill.

Mershayn thrust the blade deep into the dragon's good eye. Mirolah went in with the blade, through that narrow slice in the creature's defenses. The sword drove into the beast's brain. It should have killed the dragon, but somehow that powerful threadweaving in its scales also imbued the dragon with unbelievable fortitude. The dragon was insane with the pain, but not dead.

But now Mirolah's "fingers" were past the barrier of the scales. The sword had made the opening, and that was all she needed to see and feel the threads inside the creature.

She dug deep and unraveled its heart.

The dragon thrashed mightily, screaming, then went limp.

Mershayn yanked his sword out of the dragon's eye and stumbled backward.

"Mirolah," he shouted. "I know you're here. I felt you. Show yourself!"

She let go of the threads of air she had bent around herself, and made herself visible to him.

He ran, skidding to a stop in front of her and dropping his sword. Impulsively, he threw his arms around her and kissed her on the lips.

"You beautiful woman. You did it! I felt you in my fist, in my blade. By the gods, do it again!"

The kiss crackled through her, lighting up her memories with bright clarity. That little voice, smothered in the darkness, became *her* voice. Stunned, she didn't even hear Mershayn's next words, she just felt his hands pressing into her shoulders as he shouted.

She reached up and touched her lips with her fingers.

"You brought the dragon down," Mershayn continued. "You took away its power of flight. Do it again. Do it with the rest!"

Her heart beat faster. People needed her. She had to think clearly now, move quickly. She turned her gaze on the dragons circling Teni'sia. They filled the sky, diving and rising on the far side of the castle, burning.

The orange and red lights of fire painted the sky beyond the slopes of the castle's roof. Screams rose. The city beyond was in flames. Dragons wheeled all about. One climbed into the sky, bearing the prize of a screaming Teni'sian in its claws, and dropped her.

Mirolah caught the woman, then pulled the air away from the dragon's wings. It plummeted out of sight behind the castle.

"Yes! Come on! We have to get to the city," Mershayn said. "We have to get to the other side of the castle."

"Yes," she said. *Kiss me again...*

"Let's go!"

31

BANDS

BANDS SAW the flames as she scrambled over the ridge line of the Corialis mountains. Teni'sia was burning.

"We're too late," she whispered to Stavark, who clung to her back. When she'd seen the dragons, she'd dumped half the weapons on the slope and doubled her efforts.

"No," Stavark said. "They fight. The dragons have come to the ground and the humans are fighting them."

Bands looked again and realized Stavark was right. There were no dragons in the sky.

"They wouldn't do that...." she said slowly. No dragon would crawl on the ground when they could fight from the sky.

"The *Maehka vik Kalik*," Stavark said softly. "The *Maehka vik Kalik* is fighting."

Bands stared, stunned. "She couldn't. Not that many...." By the gods... Could Mirolah really ground a whole flight of dragons?

"Then there's still time." She snapped out of her awe. "We have to join the fight. Hang on."

She leapt down he ridge, ignoring the flaring pain in her

shoulder. She bounced like a goat from ledge to ledge, throwing snow and crunching stone with her claws as she raced down the slope. Poor Stavark clung like a barnacle to her back. The great net full of weapons bounced about, doing its best to take her balance away. She fought it and kept her blistering pace.

All too slowly, they neared the base of the slope. Every minute seemed like an hour. When they reached flat ground, she sprinted like a great cat, her long body contracting and stretching. She sped straight toward the wall to the Southern Walk and leapt atop the rampart, landing heavily on the stones.

Grendis Sym was there on top of the wall. He yelled and fell over himself trying to get away from her. Stavark slid from her back, and she transformed into her human form.

The pain receded in her shoulder. The huge net of weapons clanked to the flagstones in an amorphous, spiny heap. Sym had almost rounded the corner when she called out.

"Sym!"

At her voice, he spun around, stopped when he saw the dragon was gone. He blinked and staggered toward them a pace, eyes squinting.

"Bands?" he said incredulously. "Were you... Did you..." He looked around, trying to find the green dragon that had been on the wall mere moments ago. "Did you kill it?"

"Yes," she lied. She didn't have time for this. "Where is Mershayn? Where are the dragons?"

"They're everywhere," he said in a too-loud voice. "They're in the city!"

"Where is Mershayn?"

"When I left him, he was running for the Northern Walk. The dragons attacked. They—"

"Calm yourself, Sym." She turned to the young quicksilver. "Stavark, can you run?"

He nodded.

"I need you to find Mershayn. Give him one of these swords. Tell him we are distributing the rest. Go now, my friend. Be swift."

Stavark snatched a pair of swords from the pile, a curved sword that fit his own hand and a straight longsword. In a flash of silver lightning, he vanished.

Bands turned back to Sym.

"Find Lo'gan. Distribute these to the defenders of Teni'sia. They are the only weapons that can penetrate a dragon's armor."

"Where are you going?"

"To the center of the fray," she said. Bands could barely stand, but she braced herself for the transformation. She bit back her scream and became a dragon again.

Sym shouted and staggered back. "You're one of them!"

"Go find Lo'gan!" she boomed.

Sym fled.

Bands launched herself over the edge of the parapet and landed heavily between the buildings. People ran screaming from her as she galloped through the city, following the swath of fire and destruction left behind by her fellow dragons.

By the gods...

There were only five of her fellows, but they seemed to be everywhere, smashing through buildings with their tails, burning with their breath, flinging people away with their threadweaving. She knew they would be panicked because they'd been grounded. It trapped them here in the city, and they wouldn't know how Mirolah had grounded them any more than Bands did; it made them desperate and brutal. And humans were a pitiful match for an enraged dragon. They were all going to be slaughtered if she didn't step in.

Well, Medophae, my love, here we are again. You battle a goddess and I shall brace six of my kind. If we get through this, we must raise a glass to ridiculous odds....

She charged the nearest dragon, an arrogant purple male named Dyrfalikazyn. She'd never liked him. Bands reached into the threads and calmed the noise made by her claws, using the GodSpill and the raucous noise the dragons were creating to mask her run.

Dyrfa turned at the last second, his eyes going wide.

Burn this...

32

MERSHAYN

"WE HAVE TO GET DOWN THERE," Mershayn said to Mirolah.

She stared at him with those multicolored eyes, then said, "I can take us." Sniff, who had tried to take on that blue dragon single-handedly before Mirolah had brought it down, stood once again at her side. He sat down with a *thump* and began panting, looking satisfied.

"Then let's—"

Silver light burst around the corner of the Northern Walk, flashed up to them and became the little quicksilver.

"Stavark!"

He breathed as though he'd run for miles, but grinned and held out an archaic-looking longsword for Mershayn.

"From Bands," he huffed.

Mershayn grabbed the sword. "This is...?"

"Yes," Stavark said.

Mershayn whooped. He held it over his head triumphantly, then looked at Deni'tri and the other Teni'sian archers.

"Now we have a chance," he said, testing the balance of the

blade.

"There are more on the Southern Walk. Captain Lo'gan is handing them out," Stavark said.

"Then all that remains is for us to join the battle," Mershayn said, and he turned to Mirolah. "My lady?"

A few startled cries went up from the Teni'sian archers as the entire group floated into the air. They flew over the pinnacles of the buttresses, over the royal gardens and the roof of the great hall, past the northern courtyard and down to the southern wall. They landed next to Lo'gan and Sym, who were handing out weapons to the defenders of Teni'sia, an army of maybe fifty.

"There're so few," Deni'tri said.

"One dragon at a time," Mershayn said. "We take down one dragon, then move on to the next."

The assembled guards watched as Mershayn and his ragtag half dozen guards floated down to the flagstone walk.

"Well met, Your Majesty," Lo'gan said.

"Well met, Lo'gan. It's good to see you. I worried the dragons were already chewing on you."

"No, Your Majesty."

"Maybe they tried and just spit you out again?"

"As you say, Your Majesty."

One of these days, Lo'gan, I'm going to beat a sense of humor into you.

"Report," Mershayn said.

"One dragon has broken from the main battle and is trying to reach the castle. I sent Lord Baerst east with fifty guards and enchanted weapons to stop it."

"And where is the main battle?"

"Surrounding a rogue dragon, apparently. One of the green dragons turned on them. It's the only reason all the dragons haven't reached the castle."

"She," Mershayn corrected.

"Your Majesty?"

"The green dragon with the light green bands around her neck. That is our ally, the Lady Bands."

Lo'gan's mouth hung open.

"Treat her as you would treat me," he said, then raised his voice so that it would carry to the entire assemblage. "The green dragon is on our side. Do not hurt her. She is the reason we have these weapons."

After a stunned moment, Lo'gan said, "Yes, Your Majesty."

Mershayn turned to Stavark. "Find Lord Baerst. Help him stop that one dragon. With your abilities, you're worth all fifty of us with that blade in your hand."

Stavark nodded. In an explosion of silver light, he vanished into the city.

Mershayn turned to the rest of the guards and raised his voice. "Are you ready to give back some of what the dragons gave to us?"

"Yes, Your Majesty!" they shouted back.

Mershayn slashed his sword left and right, loving the balance of it, and he grinned. The fifty or so guardsmen looked amongst themselves, as though they thought their king had gone crazy.

By the gods. Maybe I have gone crazy.

This whole battle was surreal, but he was giddy. He'd spent the last week feeling like there were reins attached to his arms, his legs, his head, tugging him this way and that. Now there was only one objective: kill the dragons. It was an impossible goal, but it was focused and unambiguous. What better way for man to die than throwing himself against a horde of dragons? *That* was legendary.

A light finger touched his shoulder, and Mershayn turned to face Mirolah. She looked solemnly at him, her kaleidoscope eyes swirling. "I will watch over you," she said.

Impulsively, he took her in his arms and kissed her. She was as hard as ice at first, then slowly melted, put her arms around his neck, and she kissed him back.

The guards cheered.

Mershayn broke the kiss and winked at her, still holding her hand. "My last kiss ought to be stolen. Farewell, my lady."

A small smile curved the edges of her lips.

Mershayn let go of her hand and faced his small army. He raised his sword over his head. "If you have life left to give," he said, "spend it for those you love. Spend it for Teni'sia!"

"For Teni'sia!" they chorused back at him.

He turned and ran down the stairway into the city. The roar of fifty voices rose behind him as they followed. Mershayn headed straight toward the loudest screams. Fire and plumes of rock dust rose from the merchant district, which was only a short distance below the castle walls.

He and his army ran for about five minutes before they rounded the corner to a nightmare battle. The center of the merchant district had once been a wide courtyard with a circular fountain. Brightly painted shops with hanging wooden signs had bordered the circle, once creating a festive, exciting air. Now it was destroyed. The fountain had been crushed, the buildings burned, and stone rubble was scattered everywhere. In the center, where the fountain had been, Bands spun, lashing out and keeping three dragons at bay. The air smelled like brimstone and sour milk, and a smoky haze slithered about the giant creatures.

The dead body of a giant purple dragon lay to the side, great rents in its neck and chest. Three other dragons—a pure silver dragon, a black-and-gold, and a huge gray dragon with blue spikes from head to tail—surrounded Bands.

Mershayn's rage boiled. It looked as though Bands had dealt with the purple dragon, but her left wing had been melted to a nub. A deep cut gashed her leg, and a dozen claw marks raked her neck and sides. Each of the remaining dragons was larger than her, but they all seemed to have a healthy respect for her. Still, it was obvious they were readying to rush her.

A low growl came from behind Mershayn, and he jumped, thinking a dragon was behind them.

But Sniff crept forward, his narrowed eyes on the scaled monsters converging on Bands.

Mershayn felt a rush of relief. Sniff was here. That meant Mirolah was here, too, doing her threadweaving.

"That's Lady Bands?" Lo'gan whispered, prudently keeping his voice low.

Mershayn nodded.

The silver dragon crouched low, about to lunge, while the large gray-and-blue dragon shifted behind Bands, blocking any attempt to escape down the sloped street.

The silver leapt.

"Now!" Mershayn roared. His little army charged out from the alley, and Sniff bounded ahead of them.

The thick-bodied black-and-gold dragon spun to face Mershayn's group. The big gray hesitated, looking angrily at Mershayn's group, but unwilling to take his gaze completely off Bands. The black-and-gold snorted as though disgusted. He drew a breath and blew fire at them.

Mershayn dove to the ground, hoping to get beneath the spray, but it engulfed him. He clenched up, expecting to feel the searing pain—

But there was nothing. He rolled to his feet in the midst of the raging orange and yellow fire. He could feel the wind, could see the spray of some kind of mist in the midst of the fire, but he felt no heat.

The fire cut off abruptly, and Mershayn looked down at himself. He was completely unharmed. The other guardsmen behind him were similarly unharmed and just as stunned.

It's Mirolah. She's blocking their fire!

By the gods, he wasn't going to waste *that* chance.

"Don't stand there," he shouted. "Chop this lizard into dog food!"

Sniff responded first, bounding onto the dragon's back. His bramble of teeth tore at the black-and-gold scales. The dragon coiled back in surprise, obviously surprised they had survived the fire.

Mershayn ran at the creature, which just got larger the closer he came. The thing's front leg was taller than Mershayn's whole body. The claws curled down, cracking cobblestones. Seeing Bands in the castle, coiled and docile, had been breathtakingly intimidating. Seeing this beast standing at full height and ready to destroy was nearly paralyzing.

Mershayn ran through his fear. The guards would take their cue from him. If he showed even the slightest hesitation, they would do worse, perhaps even flee. He barreled at the dragon like he was readying to jump off a cliff.

He reached that enormous leg, locked his stance, and swung his enchanted blade. He put all of his momentum into the strike like

233

he was trying to chop down a tree. The weapon sparked as it hit the scales and bit deep into the dragon's leg.

The dragon roared, rearing away from the pain and yanking Mershayn up in the air before he could pull the blade free. He went up, jerked his sword free, did a neat flip and landed on his feet.

"Try again," he growled at the beast. The gold-and-black dragon's eyes had gone wide. It retreated, limping, blood streaming from the deep cut in its leg, and bumped into the silver dragon that was attacking Bands. The silver hesitated, flicking a glance at the black-and-gold, and Bands went low, her frightening teeth crunching into the silver's foreleg. The silver screamed, then tried to snap at Bands's neck, but wasn't fast enough. Bands scrambled back, up and over a crumbling building. Roaring, the silver shot fire and scrambled over the rubble in pursuit.

The gold-and-black dragon said something to the big gray in an indecipherable language that included a great deal of hissing. Mershayn couldn't understand the slithery words, but he knew desperation when he heard it.

Mershayn's little army swarmed the black-and-gold, stabbing and slicing. It whirled around, throwing a half-dozen of the guards to the cobblestones, but still more hung on. The big gray whirled and ran uphill toward the castle, away from the battle.

The sight of the monster fleeing made him giddy. They'd scared the dragons! In fact, they actually had the upper hand. The black-and-gold dragon was desperately trying to escape his tenacious attackers. The Teni'sians' strikes rained down, splitting scales and leaving gashes.

Fifty people with enchanted swords can take down a dragon. We can win this war!

Mershayn was about to leap into the fray and do what he had told Deni'tri before—focus on one dragon at a time—but he forced himself to calm his jubilance and think.

You're the king. It's your job to think of the war, not just this one battle.

Mershayn's little army was beating the black-and-gold, but only because the monolithic monster had been surprised. Now that the dragons knew about these enchanted weapons, they would adjust their attacks. Now that they knew their dragon fire had been somehow evaded, they would go straight to claws and teeth.

Which meant not even one dragon could escape to tell the tale to Avakketh's army.

"Sniff," Mershayn cried as he ran after the huge gray dragon, who was only still in sight because it was taking its time to slither between the buildings.

The monstrous dog howled and leapt off the back of the black-and-gold dragon. In five short bounds, Sniff reached Mershayn's side.

"We go after that one," Mershayn huffed as he sprinted. "Get it. Slow it down if you can. I'll be right behind you."

Sniff whined, barely trotting as he easily kept pace with Mershayn.

"Go!" Mershayn commanded. "Catch the thing. Distract it. Make it pause, and I'll be right behind you."

Sniff barked, but still didn't speed up.

"No. Dammit!" Mirolah seemed able to communicate with the dog, so he knew Sniff was capable of understanding, but the dog wasn't listening to him. "I want you to—"

Sniff snorted as if impatient, then opened his jaws and went for Mershayn.

Mershayn threw himself away from those snapping jaws, but he wasn't fast enough. Sniff's teeth closed on Mershayn's tunic and belt, and with a twitch of its mighty head, the dog tossed Mershayn in the air. As with the dragon, Mershayn flipped, looking for the ground.

He landed on Sniff's skinny back.

Now Sniff ran after the dragon at top speed. The dog didn't have hair or spines or anything. Just skin and bone and muscle. Mershayn hastily sheathed his sword and wrapped his arms around the dog's neck.

"Oh, well, yes," Mershayn said into the one of the ear holes in the side of the dog's long, flat head. "That's a better idea. Well done."

Sniff snorted, his great muscles bunching and releasing as he fairly flew over the cobblestones and leapt over rubble. In moments, the dragon was in sight, but so was the castle. The great gray scrambled up the wall, sending stone and mortar crumbling to the street below.

Sniff barked, accelerating. He reached the wall and launched himself at the dragon like a spear. As mighty a jump as it was, it wasn't enough to reach the dragon. Mershayn pushed on the dog's neck to throw himself upward and deftly placed his boots on the giant dog's shoulders. At the height of Sniff's jump, Mershayn launched himself with all his might.

Sniff barked his approval, falling away below. Mershayn drew his sword as he came level with the thick end of the dragon's tail, just below its scrambling legs.

Right...there!

Mershayn stabbed his sword deep into the dragon, and the beast howled. It scrambled to the top of the wall, lashing its tail and sending Mershayn flying down the walkway. He prepared for the impact, for the breaking bones, but the air slowed him gently and turned him upright.

Landing deftly, he heard laughter and realized it was his own. He sprinted back at the dragon, sword flashing.

The giant gray looked confused. It drew a breath, and flame shot from its jaws, engulfing the entire walkway.

Again, Mershayn could see the flames and the spray, which he realized, as it ate into the stones on either side, was some kind of acid.

The wind of the attack pushed at him, but the acid and deadly fire passed around him. This time, Mershayn didn't stand amazed; he sprinted forward under the cover of the fire.

When the big gray stopped and turned away, Mershayn had almost reached it. It didn't watch him, didn't expect him to survive the fire, which seemed strange as it had witnessed Mershayn's entire army come through the black-and-gold dragon's fire unscathed. Why?

Because it doesn't know about Mirolah. It doesn't know we have a secret threadweaver.

That had to be it. The dragons didn't know about their human threadweaver. They thought it had to be Bands who had somehow protected Mershayn and his group. Now that she'd been left behind, the big gray thought Mershayn would again be vulnerable to the fire.

The dragon leapt across the courtyard, a hundred and fifty foot span. Mershayn leapt after it, trying to catch that tail again before it got out of range, but he missed. The tail lashed out of his reach, and his sword whistled through the air.

He pitched headfirst toward the cobblestones far below, but that same wind caught him, lifted him up. The dragon crunched into the side of the castle wall. Stones crumbled and fell, and it scrambled up. The wind threw Mershayn at the dragon's back.

Mershayn's laughter and sword hit the dragon at the same time, this time high on its back. The blade sank deep right next to the spine. The thing screamed and jumped sideways in its agony, pitching them both off the castle and over the city's outer wall. Beyond was only a steep, snowy slope and a deep ravine.

Mershayn sawed at the dragon's back as they fell. The fall was going to kill him, but he was determined to at least paralyze the dragon before they hit.

The dragon twisted, screaming in pain and rage, trying to get to him. Its jaws opened, as tall as a house, and descended on Mershayn as he yanked his sword out and pointed it straight upward.

Mershayn and the dragon struck the mountain. Something shoved him forward into the dragon's mouth. The jaws snapped shut behind him. His sword sank deep into the soft flesh.

Mershayn spun in sloshy wetness. The dragon's tongue was like a giant worm, slithering around him as he spun, over and over and over, hanging tight to his sword. Finally, the spinning stopped. The dragon was still moving, but not tumbling, like it was sliding down the slope instead of rolling. Mershayn yanked his sword out, bringing a gout of ichor down on himself, but the tongue wasn't quivering anymore. The jaws weren't trying to chew him. The dragon wasn't moving.

The squishy, wet mouth reeked of dragon breath and blood. He turned, blinking, and saw light between the clenched teeth. He sheathed his sword and, scrambling on hands and knees across the sloppy tongue, he reached the teeth. He could smell fresh air beyond, and he longed to get out.

Bracing his feet between two lower teeth and his shoulders against the slimy upper palate of the dragon, he pushed with all his might.

The jaws levered open, and Mershayn gasped and sucked in the fresh air.

Time it well or you lose your legs...

With one might surge, he pushed the jaws up and leapt into the snow. The teeth snapped shut behind him.

Mershayn rolled down the snowy slope and finally came to a stop. Inhaling the glorious air, he looked up at the gray dragon. The thing was as big as four houses in a row, but it was dead. The mark of Mershayn's last strike was a barely discernible blood spot on the top of its head, but it was a true strike. Straight through the brain. He heard Master Debarc's voice in his head.

Masterful strike, swordsman....

His legs went wobbly then, and he fell onto his knees, let his sword fall in the snow as he breathed hard. He knelt there for a long time, trying to catch his breath and calm his heart.

After a moment, he heard a noise, like a low roar. Frantically, he fumbled in the snow for the hilt of his sword and raised it. He stumbled to his feet, looking for the next dragon, but the noise wasn't coming from a dragon.

The wall the dragon had leapt from, high above on the top of the mountains slope, was filled with Teni'sians.

And they were cheering.

33

MERSHAYN

MERSHAYN WALKED SLOWLY through the burning streets of Teni'sia. He hurt everywhere, from his skin to his muscles to the marrow of his bones. He couldn't say what kept him on his feet, but he refused to fall. He had to see the damage.

The danger was done for the moment, the dragons slain, but the devastation was staggering. Flames rose to his right, consuming a sign that said THE WEAVER'S ART. He stared at it as it burned. The gold paint peeled and bubbled, and soon the words were unreadable. Lo'gan was organizing fire crews to haul water up from the Inland Ocean. Mershayn could only hope they would be here soon.

"We should take you to the palace, Your Majesty," Deni'tri, who followed close behind him, said.

Dead bodies lay in the street, horribly burnt or chewed in half. The battle had barely lasted an hour, but the carnage was unspeakable. And these dragons had been grounded. He could only imagine how quickly they would have destroyed the city if they'd been flying.

"He means to kill us all. Every single human," Mershayn murmured.

"Who, Your Majesty?"

He wished she would stop calling him that. She had known him before all the craziness of his kingship. But everything had changed now. Mershayn wasn't that man anymore. Deni'tri wasn't that same guard. They didn't live in a safe little kingdom where the worst enemy was a snake pit of backbiting lords vying for power. This death, this devastation... This was a war unlike anything this kingdom had ever seen. Every single person would become a soldier in this war, because there was no other choice.

"Avakketh," Mershayn said, answering her question.

"Who?"

"The god of dragons." Of course, to Avakketh, this was merely a skirmish, not nearly the end of the world, and certainly not the bulk of his forces. This may have been only to test how formidable humans would be. How many dragons would come south when the war really began? Hundreds? Thousands? Tens of thousands?

If Mirolah hadn't brought these dragons to earth, if Bands hadn't provided the weapons to fight them, they would have killed every last Teni'sian. Six dragons. They would have reduced Teni'sia to rubble and its population to zero. This beautiful city with its centuries of culture, with its lively, determined people, would have been no more. They would have been erased from history.

And we stopped them. Barely. This was a victory.

He stopped, staring at the burned body of a child in its mother's arms, half buried in crumbled stones. A badly turned stone caught his toe and he stumbled, went down to one knee next to the corpses.

Victory looks like this....

"Your Majesty?" Deni'tri knelt next to him, took his arm.

"They came to slaughter us. And they almost succeeded.... Look." He pointed. "How can we call this a victory?"

"We beat them back, Your Majesty. We did what we had to do."

"Barely...."

"You're tired, Your Majesty. You need rest."

"Yes." He could hear the concern in her voice, and she was

right. He was rambling. A guard shouldn't have to hear her king ramble.

Stand up. She needs to see you standing.

But he stayed on his knees. He gazed at the snow mixed with ash, blood, and bits of smoldering wood. His own fist was black with drying dragon blood from that terrifying moment inside the dragon's mouth. Bits of scale clung to the sticky ooze.

He placed his sticky hand flat on the black stones and stared at the corpses of the woman and her child.

You brought this, Avakketh. You brought death to my city.

"Never again," he said aloud.

"Your Majesty?"

"They're not getting a second chance to do this."

"We will stop them, Your Majesty," she said with conviction.

"No. Next time, they're going to have to stop us. Next time, we're taking the battle to them."

34

GRENDIS SYM

GRENDIS SYM FOLLOWED Mershayn and Deni'tri at a quiet distance, stopped when they stopped, and hid behind the stairstep of a broken wall. In the panic and confusion, not only was Mershayn practically alone, but everyone had forgotten about Sym. This was his moment, his only moment.

It was time for Mershayn to die.

After today, there would be no opportunity to strip the Bastard King of his political power. He was the hero of the dragon attack. Dozens of Teni'sians had seen him kill a dragon in one-on-one combat. Not only that, but it had been the largest dragon, the leader. Even Sym's staunchest supporters would swing to Mershayn's banner after that ridiculous display of courage, after such an impossible victory.

Sym had to grudgingly admire the man's unexpected success. Who had that kind of courage, anyway? It was madness or idiocy, and as a result, it would soon become a legend. The story was already sweeping through the city. It was the only thing anyone was talking about. The entire city would have carried Mershayn through the broken and burning streets on their shoulders if he'd let them. Instead, he put them to work putting out fires and tending to the many dead, which only built his legend further.

Mershayn, the Bastard King whose only concern was the people and the city.

No, there would never be a better time to put an end to the Bastard King.

Mershayn's lone guard, the bald bitch named Deni'tri, knelt next to him, conveniently offering her back to Sym as well.

Well, that suited Sym just fine. He had two crossbows, cocked and loaded only moments ago. During the battle, dead guards lay everywhere, their weapons discarded. He'd had his pick.

It would be a quick bolt in the back for the guardswoman. Then, before the obviously dazed Mershayn knew what was happening, Sym would raise the second crossbow and fire. One last bolt for Mershayn. This close, only twenty paces away, Sym couldn't miss. Afterward, he could pull the bolts out and kick the bodies into the burning building.

No one could trace the death to Sym, and Mershayn would make a much more useful martyr than he would a living king. Sym could use those stories.

The great Bastard King. Not only did he die fighting the leader of the dragons, but he vanished afterward like some hero of old. And Sym would weave himself into the tale, embellishing his own role in the dragon attack, that he had been by Mershayn's side, that he believed in Mershayn's mission. Sym could swing the overflow of goodwill toward himself.

And then he would take the reins of the kingdom once more.

Sym raised the crossbow and aimed at the base of Deni'tri's neck.

"Never again," Mershayn said.

Sym paused, caught by what would be Mershayn's last words. Perhaps they could be woven into the legend Sym planned to weave.

"Your Majesty?" Deni'tri said.

"They're not getting a second chance to do this."

"We will stop them, Your Majesty," she said with conviction.

"No. Next time, they're going to have to stop us. Next time, we're taking the battle to them."

The conviction in Mershayn's voice seemed to paralyze Sym. It was honest passion. There was no jockeying for power in his tone, no goal he could possibly have in mind by saying such a thing in this desolate street, side-by-side with a guardswoman who already belonged to him, who would jump off the castle wall if he asked her.

Sym's finger trembled on the trigger. He curled his lip in self-derision. What was he doing? The moment was now. He had to strike.

But Mershayn's courageous fight against the dragon flashed through his mind. Like everyone else who had watched, Sym had been awed when the bastard stabbed his way up that monstrous dragon. Sym had even felt, for an absurd moment, that the dragon was overmatched by Mershayn's relentless fury. Sym had faced that fury himself when Mershayn had toyed with him in the king's chambers, giving him a sword like it would make a difference, bashing aside Sym's strikes like he was a child.

For the first time, Sym glanced around at the utter devastation those six dragons had left behind, and he realized that he couldn't have stood in Mershayn's boots today. Certainly he wouldn't have attacked a dragon by himself. The very notion was ridiculous.

But Mershayn had.

If Sym had been king, he would have died today. Every other person in Teni'sia would have died today. Sym wasn't a religious man, but he was suddenly struck by a sense of destiny. What if Mershayn was the right person in the right place at the right time? Who else could have done what Mershayn had done? What kind of fool grabbed a dragon by the tail and survived?

What if Mershayn could actually lead them to a victory over the dragons? What if he was destined to do so? What if he wasn't simply a lout who knew how to swing a sword? What if he was more?

The suddenly realization staggered Sym. Up until this moment, he had known he was the best person to lead Teni'sia. He had known he was the only one with the will and capability to truly do it. An outcast son of an executed father, Sym had made his own opportunities. He had created his own network of supporters. He had dared go beyond the boundaries where other nobles stopped. He'd made his own roads. He'd taken this kingdom. He would have made it what it needed to be....

But even Sym didn't have the will or capability to do what Mershayn had done here today. Where Sym would have run, Mershayn attacked. And not only had he attacked, he had won.

Sym clenched the haft of the crossbow. He wanted the bastard's death so much he could taste it. Mershayn had humiliated him, cast him from his rightful place, torn apart his network. He wanted the bastard's ruin.

But he wanted Teni'sia to endure even more.

Once, Sym had envisioned a long and glorious rule with him as king. But now, after this dragon attack, all he could see was Teni'sia in ruins if he took the throne. When the dragons came back, what could Sym do to stop them?

His elbow ached as he lowered the crossbow, and he felt a sudden foreboding that he would regret this decision for the rest of his life.

Instead, he quietly drew a breath and steadied himself, looking down at the wall. He set the crossbow next to its fellow. When he looked up, Deni'tri was watching him. Her hand was close to her hatchet.

"My lord," she said.

"Deni'tri," Sym said. "They're looking for him. It is time for him to return to the castle."

Deni'tri nodded and, without taking her gaze off Sym, helped Mershayn to his feet. The king seemed dazed. "It's time to go, Your Majesty," she said.

"Yes."

"We're going to escort you back to the castle."

"We?"

"Sym and me. He stands behind you, ready to...protect you."

"But the fire..."

"The fires are being tended to, Your Majesty." Even as she said it, a half dozen people with buckets rounded the corner, pointing.

"See there?" Deni'tri gestured. "They've come. They'll put out the fire."

"There are...other fires...." he said, and his speech slurred this time.

"We've lost much today," Deni'tri said. "If not for you, we would have lost all. We must get you to safety and rest."

"The dragons will return...." he said wearily.

"Not today. Come." She led him up the sloped street.

Mershayn took one step, then slumped against her. His head fell limply against her neck. Deni'tri held him up and motioned to Sym. "Come, my lord. Let's get our king to the castle."

Sym hesitated. With her hands full, he could raise the crossbow. He could finish this job. He'd have to deal with the firefighters who even now threw water upon the burning building, but Sym had handled worse messes.

She saw his hesitation. Her left hand slipped to rest on her hatchet, and the moment passed. Her hard glance told him that she knew exactly what he was thinking. If he pulled that crossbow, her hatchet would find his skull before he could aim.

He took his hand off the hidden crossbow and came out from behind the wall. At Deni'tri's gesture, he picked Mershayn up underneath the shoulders. Deni'tri took the king's feet.

They started up the steep cobblestone street. Sym looked at Deni'tri and caught her glance. She looked at his place of concealment, saw the two crossbows he had left by the wall as they passed.

"You lead, Lord Sym. I'll be right behind you," she said. "Every step of the way."

35

BANDS

NIGHT HAD FALLEN IN TENI'SIA—A night of slaughter, but also of hope—and Bands wanted nothing more than to fall over and sleep for a week. She had used as much of her own personal GodSpill as she dared to heal her wounds. It hadn't been much. The great gashes Dyrfa had given her were barely scabbed over. She couldn't walk without a limp, and she did her best not to move her left arm.

She hadn't even tried healing her wing yet. Fighting the damage done by Saraphazia's spell would take more energy than she had right now. It might even be impossible, which meant Bands may have flown the winds for the last time. She tried not to think of that. She had enough to deal with.

Stavark stood gravely beside the bed where Mirolah lay, ashen, unmoving and unbreathing.

In the battle against Dyrfa's flight of dragons, the little quicksilver had once again proven himself indispensable. He had joined Lord Baerst's army against Sytherlakyleriun, the dragon who broke away from the fight with Bands at the very beginning. Syther had tried to reach the castle. Bands wasn't exactly sure why the castle had been her goal. Perhaps she'd been ordered to find the king and kill him. Knowing Dyrfa, he had probably ordered her to pull the castle down stone by stone, a grand statement that castles were no protection against dragons. That type of fear attack was exactly the kind of thing Avakketh would order his followers to do.

And Stavark had come through the battle without a scratch, at least on the outside. Inside, Stavark was horribly wounded every time one of his companions fell. He worried over everyone, felt it was his personal mission to keep all of his companions alive. Bands could never repay him for saving her from the waters of the True Ocean, yet he had done it as though it was expected. He'd asked for no thanks and hadn't mentioned it since.

And now the concerned quicksilver watched Mirolah, who looked as dead as a three-day-old fish.

To any normal eyes, Mirolah was a corpse. She had collapsed just after Mershayn fell with the dragon and had been like this since. In addition, Sniff had vanished after the battle. Bands had expected the fearsome skin dog to be right by Mirolah's side, growling at anyone who tried to touch her. The dog's absence worried Bands. Mirolah was connected to it, and if Mirolah's spirit roamed free from this body, Bands suspected the skin dog had tried to follow.

Bands adjusted her left arm in its sling, wincing. Stavark laid a hand on Mirolah's forehead, pressed a finger into her neck. "She is dead," he said.

Bands hesitated, then said, "No."

He glanced up at her, his brow furrowed. "She is cold."

"I do not...fully understand it. But she's not dead. Not like we think of people as dead."

"How?"

"Because Mirolah is something I have never seen before." In Bands's threadweaver sight, Mirolah's body glowed with GodSpill, like a foot-thick shell of light surrounded her. Dead bodies did not do that, no matter how enchanted they had been in life. "For now, I think we must simply wait."

Stavark's brow wrinkled. "Leave her here?"

The quicksilvers had complicated burial rituals. Life was sacred above all else, and the death of a loved one had to be treated with the utmost respect. To leave a body unconsecrated after death was a heinous crime.

"She is not dead, Stavark."

He frowned. "You said you did not know this thing."

"It's...complicated." She tried to find the words, but she was so tired her mind was swimming, and there was still much to do before she could rest. "It would be a mistake to do anything at this moment."

He was not happy about it, but he nodded. Frowning, he stepped away and walked to the window on the west side of Mirolah's room.

"And no one else can know she is here. She must be left alone."

"Even Mershayn?" Stavark asked with his normal acuity. So he had seen how Mershayn and Mirolah had become closer. Or he'd heard the story. Apparently, they had kissed before Mershayn went running headlong at the flight of dragons.

"I will tell Mershayn," Bands said.

After a time, she moved around the bed and came to stand behind Stavark. His words and deeds were so noble, his demeanor so serious, that it was easy to forget how young he was. Everyone treated him—and relied on him—like an adult. Certainly he must feel something of the boy he was. Surely this boy must still get frightened. Surely he must still long for the comfort of a mother or father.

Bands put a gentle hand on his shoulder. His head moved a little, but otherwise he remained still.

He reached up and closed his pale fingers over hers.

"Too many." His usually musical voice was hoarse, on the verge of tears. "The deaths cry out to me, and I cannot stop them all."

"No one can," she whispered. "Not you. Not me. Not even Medophae."

"My companions have been taken or killed. Orem first, now Mirolah. Even the *Rabasyvihrk*. They die, and yet I am still here."

"None are lost. Not yet. I will soon turn my full attention upon finding Medophae. When I do, Zilok will try to stop me, and then we will see who is the better threadweaver at last."

Stavark's hand tightened on her own.

"That *saavenvakihrk* will twist your mind. He robbed the *Rabasyvihrk* of his powers once. No doubt he has done this again. How can the *Rabasyvihrk* possibly best him without his god?"

"Do not be so quick to give up on Medophae. Before he was a demigod, he was a resourceful, courageous young man. And relentless." Bands paused, then said, "Much like you, actually. He also always thought first of his friends and his family."

Gently, she turned the quicksilver to face her. With a finger, she lifted his pointed ivory chin so that his silver eyes looked into her own.

"Take heart, noble Stavark. Those around you are lifted up by your goodness. It shines brightly in every action you make. Do not let despair dim that light. We need you."

The muscles in his jaw flickered, and his eyes glistened. But he held her gaze. "I also lost Elekkena," he said softly.

Bands wanted to break gazes with the earnest quicksilver, but she forced herself to keep looking at him. "I am sorry," she murmured. "That I deceived you."

"Why?"

"I needed to."

"And the real Elekkena is dead?"

"I do not know. I like to think she is somewhere in the woods with her parents, still alive. I waited in Sylikkayrn for many weeks after I was released from my prison. With Avakketh determined to come south, I needed a way to get close to Medophae without him knowing. Posing as a quicksilver was ideal. Your kind's inherent flashpowers could camouflage my threadweaving from Mirolah. And I knew that Medophae and Mirolah would come looking for you. If I attached myself to you, then I could naturally be a part of your reunion. So I came to Sylikkayrn. I changed forms many times, listening for a plausible back story. When I heard your father speak of Elekkena and her parents, I made my decision. She seemed a good companion for you, so I imagined what she would look like and I made myself into her."

The muscles in his jaw worked again, and he broke eye contact at last, taking her hand from his chin and holding it.

"She was a good companion," he said. "I...will miss her."

"Stavark—"

"But she wasn't real." He delicately put her hand at her side and let go. He looked up into her eyes again. "You did what was most important, and I, too, must focus on what is most important. You say we cannot fight the dragon god without the *Rabasyvihrk*, then we must find him."

"Yes," she said softly. "We must find him."

He smiled up at her, that sadness haunting his face.

"Stavark..." She reached out to touch his smooth cheek again.

He became a silent explosion of silver lightning and streaked to the door. He opened it, then looked back at her.

"I will see if Mershayn is awake," he said.

She almost called out to him again, but didn't. Instead, she did what she often did when there was no right action. She stayed still and let the world move past her. It was important to know when to do that.

But sometimes it hurt.

Stavark shut the door quietly.

36

MERSHAYN

MERSHAYN AWOKE SLOWLY. He felt injured in half a dozen places, but someone had bathed him and dressed his wounds. Gingerly propping himself up, he leaned against the headboard and drew deep breaths as the tendrils of sleep pulled away. Gods... How long had he been out?

He blinked, and the memories hit him like a cup of ale to the face. Fire. Death and fire. Burning buildings. Burning bodies. Screams...

For a moment, he thought he would be sick, but he held his bile. They were at war. This was a victory. The dragons were dead. Teni'sia had endured.

Frost gathered against the lead molding of the window, turning diamond panes into round. In another life, this was the type of day he would liked to have spent at a tavern, drinking spiced wine with friends and throwing daggers at a target.

"They are singing your praises in the city below," Bands said.

He jumped. He'd thought he was alone.

In the shadows beyond the low-flickering fire sat Bands. She was clothed in a green gown as always, but it was different from the high-necked dress she had worn before. Her shoulders were bare, but the gown also had long, dagged sleeves. Thin green laces held the bodice together, offering a modest glimpse of cleavage. The laces continued upward, finally looping around her throat in a cloth choker. The long dress hung down over her crossed knees, revealing a flash of ankles between the hem and the elegant slippers she wore.

The attire was the current style that many ladies of the Teni'sian court wore. Ari'cyiane had worn gowns like this, but to see it on Bands startled him. On Ari'cyiane, it had seemed normal. On Bands, it seemed risqué. For the first time, it called attention to the slenderness of her neck, the curve of her clavicle, the perfect proportions of her body.

"I see you have been to a dressmaker." He cleared his throat.

"Come now, Mershayn. I make my clothing when I make up my face in the morning. You know that."

He gave her a quick point with his finger. "Funny," he said. "In that way that makes a chill run up my spine."

She smiled.

He suddenly noticed the long white cloth over the arm of the chair in which she sat. That was a sling; she just wasn't wearing it in the chair. He also saw a bit of white peeking out of the upper edge of her sleeve by her bare shoulder. That was a bandage. That was even more shocking than the dress. Bands had always seemed invincible. To see her bandaged up reinforced just how devastating the battle had been.

"How are you?" he asked.

"Glad that Teni'sia is still standing. Glad that Silasa was right about you. I have heard the stories. All tell that you were magnificent, a hero-king to rival the legends of old."

"It was Mirolah. She made me...well...invincible, I think. The dragons couldn't burn me. Instead of falling to my death, I flew. I'm pretty sure she even shoved me into the mouth of that dragon so I didn't get chomped in half, and I'd be willing to bet she made sure my sword hit exactly the right mark to kill it with one strike. I would have been dead in the first five seconds if not for her."

Bands nodded.

He tipped his chin at the sling laying over her armrest. "I saw your wing. Are you...?"

"I am fine. But you collapsed, Deni'tri says." She turned the question back on him.

"Bumps and bruises. Mirolah took good care of me."

"You look as beat up as I have ever seen you," she said. "And that's saying something."

"And you look like you're trying to catch someone's eye. Why the fetching attire?"

"I am feeling rebellious today. I dressed the part."

"Is there a reason?"

"No doubt," she said, but did not offer anything more.

He waited a moment, then looked down at his royal blanket. "How fares the kingdom?"

"It stands," she said. "And your legend grows. You won't have trouble finding support now. When no one else knew what to do, you stood up and took charge. Your people will follow you through the Godgate now if you ask them to."

"Does Lord Baerst survive? He was in charge of the other group.... They attacked the last dragon."

She nodded. "The man sails under a lucky star. And Stavark, as usual, was stunning."

"Where is Baerst?"

"Likely passed out in a tavern. He started drinking the moment the battle was done."

"He deserves it. This kingdom owes him. Baerst put himself between dragons and Teni'sia. And they're horrifying." He paused. "No offense to you. I'm just saying, the man has courage."

"I do not take offense," she said. "They *are* frightening."

"This kingdom owes you as well," he said. "For organizing us. For preparing us."

"Maybe," she said. "But what it really needed was you. You galvanized the men and women of Teni'sia. You commanded Mirolah's loyalty, and Silasa's and Stavark's. When there was nothing but defeat all around you, you saw victory."

He shook his head. "I wish I could say that was true. I didn't see victory. All I saw was my own death. I just kept running at dragons."

She smirked. "By the gods, Mershayn, take a bow. I doubt even I would have grasped hold of Kytherflahkin's tail like that."

"Kytherflahkin? You knew him?"

"I knew of him."

"Gods..." He looked down, knotting the blanket in his fists. Slowly, he relaxed and smoothed the wool. "I am sorry, Bands. It must be hard for you, fighting those you've known—"

"I am not sorry," she interrupted. "They began this war, and they are wrong. Avakketh is wrong. I will give my life to stop him. I'm not sad they died in place of those they came to kill. I am only sad they succeeded in taking so many Teni'sians with them."

"But they are your people," he said.

Finally, he saw a reaction. She closed her eyes. "Yes," she said in a quiet voice. "They were. But tell me, did you cry for the Sunriders who died in the Corialis Mountains when they tried and failed to take Teni'sia a decade ago?"

"No."

"And would you weep for one of them simply because you knew his name?"

"No."

"Then you know some of what I am feeling. They came to murder. They lost. I do not weep for Kytherflahkin."

"All right."

They watched one another in silence.

"Well, that's good," he said. "Because I made a decision before I passed out, when I knelt in the wreckage of the dragons' passing."

She nodded.

"If there is another battle, we choose the battleground. We must take the fight to them."

"Good," she said. "Smart. But you know you won't get to Irgakth, right? At best, it's only a matter of days before Avakketh comes south. You've done the impossible, and he'll be cautious. He won't know how you did it, and he'll move slowly. But he will come. He's lost too much now. And his primary reasons have only grown stronger. He fears threadweavers, hates that humans have that power. He will assume that is how you stopped his dragons, but he won't have guessed it was one, lone threadweaver. If he discovers this, he will move to eliminate her. Keep that secret, Mershayn, and you will make the best use of it."

"I will."

Bands shook her head and looked out the window, pensive. "Mirolah is an unknown quantity. Even I don't know how she stole the air from six dragons at once, and I've been studying her every chance I've had. Sucking the air away from a dragon for a few seconds is difficult threadweaving. But depriving six dragons of the power of flight indefinitely?" She shook her head. "I've never seen that, not in all my years. I couldn't do that. Zilok Morth couldn't do that. The only person who might have had the power to do such a thing is the legendary Daylan Morth. And he created the fountain that almost destroyed Amarion."

"She's special," Mershayn said.

"Mmmm." She turned her emerald gaze back to him. "And dangerous. Be careful with her, Mershayn. I've...seen how close you are."

"You're talking about the kiss." He knew that his kiss with Mirolah was one of the many stories circulating about him now. The people liked the idea that their king was in love.

"And the bond she made with you," Bands said.

He raised his chin. How did she know about that?

"It doesn't behoove you to hide things from me," she said. "That's why I'm warning you. I know you trust her, but...she's unpredictable. There's no other way to say it. She could be your undoing if you aren't careful. I just want you to understand that."

"Why is she dangerous?"

She sighed. "Because there's more than one gust in that wind."

"What?"

"Mirolah isn't the only one in her head, and she is on the edge of losing control all the time. Yes, she's powerful. Yes, she favors you, for now. Maybe she even thinks loves you, or she wants to love you. But the real truth is that somehow, she needs you. Desperately. That's different than love, and if her need somehow shifts, if the voices in her head decide to see you as a threat..."

He didn't say anything, and he didn't tell her about the night when Mirolah blasted him into unconsciousness.

"Keep your focus on Avakketh," Bands said. "That's where it should be. But don't look away from Mirolah for too long. And...be careful." She seemed about to say more, but didn't.

Silence fell between them, and Mershayn found himself thinking of Mirolah. If she wanted his life, she could have it. He already owed her his life.

Bands took a breath and let it out slowly, like she was marshaling her courage. He came back to the present and looked at her. He didn't like the sound of that sigh.

"I have news," she said.

"Bad news," he guessed.

"I am leaving," she said.

Cold roots grew in Mershayn's stomach. He didn't know how long he hesitated, stunned. "When?" he finally managed to say.

"Today."

He raised a hand helplessly, then let it drop to the bed. He blasted a resigned breath. "Why?" he asked, before he could stop himself. He sounded like a whiny child rather than a king. How could she leave? The kingdom was on the edge of disaster, and Bands had, through sheer will, held it together. If she left...

She rose and came to sit on the edge of his bed. She took his hand. "You showed me why I must leave."

"By Thalius's beard, tell me how, and I will undo it!"

"Your unthinking bravery. Your willingness to give everything to win. Against impossible odds, that is the *only* way it can be done. When we see the course we must take, no matter how daunting, we must take it without hesitation."

"Yes, fighting Avakketh. So stay and help us fight."

"I can't."

"You *have* to. We can't win without you."

She nodded. "Let me tell you a secret I have kept until now: I did not think we could stop the dragons. I thought you were all going to die."

"What? But you—"

She waved a hand. "I prepared you as best I could. I did

257

everything I thought we might do to keep Teni'sia standing, but as Stavark and I crested the ridge and saw the dragons, I knew that Teni'sia would burn and all her people would die. I knew I would die fighting next to you, or be dragged in chains back to Avakketh. But you...you turned it around because you knew what needed to be done. And you did it."

"Bands, please..."

"Like you, I know what my next step is. I have to get Medophae back. If I stayed, I could help you. We might do better in the short term. In the end, we would lose."

"Why?"

"Because Avakketh is a god. He is a hundred times more powerful than six dragons. No matter how powerful Mirolah is, she cannot ground Avakketh. If she goes toe-to-toe with him, he will destroy her. To fight a god, we need a god, and the closest thing we have is Medophae."

Mershayn couldn't think of anything to say.

"Like you," she said. "I must fly into my enemy's teeth and do what needs doing. I must bring Zilok Morth to heel and recover what he has taken."

"What? That spirit thing that made Stavark..." He shook his head. "No. You can't. That thing can twist your mind and make you—"

"He is not all-powerful, though he would like to think he is. I have tangled with Zilok before, but we have never tested...who is the greater threadweaver. Soon, we will know, and either I will return with Medophae, or you will carry the fight to Avakketh alone."

"There has to be another way."

She watched him. Finally, he bowed his head.

"This will not be the last page in our book, Mershayn, King of Teni'sia," she said. "I will return. And Silasa will remain with you. Stavark, as well. Each is a force you must use wisely. Silasa has the experience of lifetimes, but you're going to have to pull it from her. She tends to see herself as a weapon and not a king's counsel; don't waste her by using her exclusively for hatchet work. And Stavark, though he may appear invincible, is more fragile than he seems.

Keep him close. Do not forget he is a twelve-year-old boy. His spirit is strong, but he puts the world on his shoulders. That is too much for anyone to bear. If he breaks, you will lose a powerful ally. He desperately needs a friend, and he will never admit such a thing."

He nodded. "Okay," he said. "And Mirolah. She's going to stay."

Bands hesitated only a second, but it was enough to set Mershayn's heart to beat faster. "What happened? Where is she?"

"Her battle against the dragons took a toll on her."

No...

"What are you saying?"

"She is...still, but I do not believe—"

"What do you mean 'still'?"

"Seeming dead."

He lurched out of bed.

She held up a hand. "Sit down, Mershayn."

"I have to go to her!"

"You need to listen to me first. Sit down."

Slowly, he sank back to the bed.

"Calm yourself. Mirolah does not breathe. She has no pulse. No heartbeat. But to a threadweaver, her body glows like the sun. Something is happening here. If she was just anyone, I would say she is dead. But Mirolah is not just anyone. She has already done several things I would have thought impossible, and..." she trailed off.

"And what?"

"I think perhaps she has been this way all along, but the intense GodSpill she wields has kept her...moving."

"You're saying she's been dead all along?"

She hesitated, then nodded. "I think so."

"That's not possible. She..." He stopped talking. His head hurt. He and Mirolah had spent a night talking, sharing stories. He had kissed her, and her lips had been alive. How could she be...?

"As I said, she has already done several things that I thought impossible," Bands continued. "If she can bring six dragons to the ground, then animating her own...body...might not be outside her ability."

"To be dead and not dead at the same time."

"Yes."

"What can I do?" he asked.

"Do nothing. Whatever is happening to her has not resolved itself, and I can only imagine what kind of trouble you might bring on yourself—or her—if you interfere. Take care of her body, make certain no harm comes to it, but do not disturb her. She will return when she is able."

Or if she is able. He heard the words she did not say.

She stood then. Light seemed to dance in her white blond hair and on her flawless features, as though it wished to linger on her longer than it would a normal person.

"You did this," he said. "This so-called victory. This...kingship. Me. You made this happen, just like you said you would. What will Teni'sia be without you?" He got out of bed despite the many aches that told him he should lie back down. Clad in nothing but his nightshirt, he hugged her. She embraced him in soft, strong arms.

"We will see each other again soon," she whispered.

"Even when you lie, I want to believe you," he said into her hair.

"Now," she said, letting him go, "before I forget. Your page Casur tried to wake you three times this morning. He is very persistent, but I would not allow it. There is something that requires your immediate attention."

"And it is?"

"There are Sunriders at the gates of the city."

"Sunriders!"

"They claim to come in peace. They have been waiting for hours, and they appear to have ridden very hard to get here."

"What do they want?"

She winked at him. "That, my friend, is your duty to discover."

"By the gods, can we have one day without a calamity?" he said. "Is it an army?"

She shook her head. "They are ten strong, an official ring guard for a Vessel Man. This is unusual for the Sunriders. Their Vessel

Men are precious to them; they would not risk one for a trivial purpose, coming so far into Teni'sia with so small a host."

"Then I will see them as soon as I dress."

She went to the door, then turned back to him. "Goodbye, Mershayn. You exceeded my expectations, to put it mildly. You will do well in my absence. Trust in that. Trust in yourself. Trust in your friends. And, gods willing, we will raise a cup after this business is done."

"Wildmane willing," he joked, trying to sound jaunty over the lump in his throat.

Don't go....

She left, closing the door behind herself.

Mershayn stared after, his heart heavy, then he once again got about the business of being king.

37

MEDOPHAE

"SILLY..." the voice warbled to him.

I'm dead, Medophae thought. Should I be able to hear anything if I'm dead?

"You were supposed to wait," the voice said. "All that swimming... How am I supposed to rescue you if you don't cooperate? Like you could make it to the surface with one breath. Humans can't breathe underwater."

Medophae suddenly realized he could breathe, and that he had been breathing for a while. The crush of the ocean still squeezed his body like a giant's hand, but the water was also moving, slithering past him. Or was he moving through it?

"If you'd just floated, you would have lasted longer," the voice continued. "Do you always fight like that? You just fight and fight. Is that what humans do? Do they fight all the time? I forget so many things."

He blinked his eyes. It was still dark, but a light blue glow surrounded the girl next to him. He could see her face clearly, and her blue hair flowed out behind her. She had his handless arm wrapped around her neck, and she was looking up as the water coursed over them.

"Vee?"

She looked at him. "You're awake?" She let out a breath, and he realized then that both of their faces were connected by a big air bubble. "Are you goofy?"

"Goofy?"

"Creatures who don't live in the water, sometimes when they breathe water, their minds go goofy."

"What happened?"

"You fought Mother. She doesn't like it when people fight her. So she took you to the bottom and left you to die. I think she wanted to prove a point. She always wants to prove a point. But it was a good thing she did that instead of just squashing you. We got lucky there."

"You saved me."

"Again." She winked. "But I'm going to need that favor this time." She had big eyes but petite features. Slender lips, a pert upturned nose, and an almost pointed chin. She looked a little bit like a quicksilver, but without the pointed ears, the alabaster skin, and the silver hair.

"Well, I owe you twice now."

"Actually," she said. "I asked you not to tell Mother about me, and you didn't. That was a favor. So we're even on that one. But...well, now I saved your life again. And I need you to save mine."

"What? How?"

"I know who you are," she said. "I've watched you sometimes."

"On Dandere?"

"Yes. On Dandere. In Teni'sia. In Calsinac, when you were happy with your lady Bands."

"Vee..." he trailed off. That was over a thousand years ago.

"You brought Oedandus back from the dead. I want you to do the same for me."

"Vee, who are you?"

She looked down, her lips pressed together, then she looked back up and said, "I'm Vee, like I told you."

TODO

"If you want to be 'brought back', then you're saying—"

"I'm Vee, but I used to be more."

"Who did you used to be?"

"Vaisha."

Medophae couldn't say anything for a long time. "Vaisha the Changer is dead," he finally whispered.

Vaisha the Changer was the daughter of Saraphazia and Tarithalius. She'd been killed by Dervon before humans even began recording time. Tarithalius had spoken of Vaisha with affection and sadness. He'd said the young goddess had been like a newborn colt, filled with curiosity and passion. She had played with the sentient races to make new creatures, which was how she got her nickname "the Changer." She made dolphins from whales. She made quicksilvers from humans. She made the legendary unicorns and pegasi from equines.

Vaisha's experiments changed the world forever, and the other gods imitated her. Zetu created rocklurs from humans and spine horses from equines. Dervon created dramaths and darklings from humans. He created the dreaded neila, vicious imitations of dragons, and soaked them with GodSpill. They were terribly powerful, and nearly killed all the dragons. It took the combined might of two gods to destroy them. According to Tarithalius, Dervon's neila sparked a war among the gods. It was the reason Dervon and Oedandus began their eternal struggle.

But that hadn't been enough for Dervon. Soon after, he captured Vaisha, killed her, and used her godly life force to create White Tuana. That sparked another war among the gods, which ended with Oedandus defeating Dervon a second time, forever maiming him as punishment.

"But Dervon killed you." Medophae finally got the words out.

"He killed Vaisha," she said matter-of-factly. "Yes. He pulled her apart and used her to create White Tuana. But a few pieces of Vaisha escaped, little tiny swirls of what she had been. Mother caught one and saved it. She put it into a dolphin, and I became Vee. But the other little parts of me, they didn't go into the ocean. They went into the woods, into the mountains, into the winds of Amarion. I wanted to get them back, but Mother won't let me leave the ocean. It's far too dangerous, she says. She wants to keep what's left of me alive, wants it so much that she made me a prisoner. I tried explaining to her. I tried begging her. I even tried to escape, but she's too strong. She cast a spell on the ocean, and it won't let me leave. I learned how to transform myself into this human form so I could have feet that walk on land, but the ocean always grabs me and pulls me back in. But back then I could still feel the other pieces of myself, could see them like stars in the distance. I just couldn't reach them." She paused.

"Then one day, those stars went out. They just vanished, like they had finally died from being away from me for too long. I knew my chance to be Vaisha again was gone, and I cried for a whole year after that." She spoke with such soft intensity. "But I was wrong. They didn't die. They'd just been hidden away, like they'd been shoved in a bottle and corked, because someone pulled the cork, and they've come back now. I can feel them again, but this time they're stronger. They're all stuck together, but they're still longing for me. I can feel their longing. They want me to come back to them, and I'm not going to let them die this time. They whisper so loud along the coast of Amarion that I can almost understand them. I have to go to them. I have to put myself back together!"

"Daylan's Fountain..." Medophae said. "Those parts of you, they got trapped in Daylan's Fountain with the rest of the GodSpill. That has to be it. And Mirolah set them free."

"Mirolah!" Vee said. "This is a person? The whispers speak that word over and over. I didn't know it was a person." She smiled wide and turned her face upward. "I need to get to those pieces of myself. But I never could before because I need you. You're the one. No matter how strong Mother is, you cut me free. Your sword killed Dervon. It can sever Mother's spell—"

Her head jerked to the side, and she stared like she could peer through the bubble and the darkness beyond. "Oh no. She's coming," Vee said fearfully, turning back to him. Her wide eyes beseeched him. "Please. Will you help me?"

"Of course I will."

"I will take you to the coast, but she won't let me go. Cut me free, Medophae. Please."

"You get me to Amarion," he said, feeling a thrill of possibility in his chest. "And I will fight her for you."

She giggled, clasping her hands together. "Hold tight," she said. "No matter what happens, hold onto me. She will try to kill you when she sees you with me. Her greatest fear is that someone will steal me. She won't bother drowning you this time; she'll just kill you."

"Go!" he said, taking a big breath.

Vee transformed into a huge dolphin, but with two large hands on her back that grabbed onto Medophae's arms. She flipped her fin and surged upward. The bubble around his face burst as the water rushed past them. The pressure was so great it pushed his eyes shut. He concentrated on keeping the breath in his lungs. Her hands clung to his arms with superhuman strength, and it felt like her grip and the water pressure might tear his arms off. Something broke inside him, and he tasted blood.

Go, he thought, *go!*

Then he felt light on his eyelids. He opened them to a squint, and he could see sunlight overhead. The pressure lessened from the sides as they neared the surface, but the phenomenal rush of the water continued as Vee sped through the ocean.

They broke the surface, and Medophae gasped, sucking in a wet, rattling breath. Medophae felt like someone had crushed him with rocks. He coughed, and blood came up.

"She is upon us," Vee yelled from her dolphin's mouth. "You must take me with you, Medophae. Don't leave me behind!"

In the distance, a monstrous swell rolled toward them, the tidal wave of the approaching goddess.

"Get me to the coast," he said with a cough.

She dove back into the water, the hands gripping him tightly. Medophae clasped them and held on.

The swell neared, sucking the water out from beneath them, and suddenly they were swimming frantically down the wall of a wave.

"Medophae!" Vee cried, leaping toward the shore, but it was too far away. The crazy hands stretched out of her back into long arms, and Vaisha threw him at the shore. He sailed over the rushing water, flailing to try to land upright. He slammed into the rocky coast. His leg snapped, and he fell down the cliff wall to crumple in the sand.

Get up. Get up, get up!

He spun, lurched to his feet, and went down again from the pain. He clenched his teeth and looked for Vee. She had fallen into the shallows beneath the enormous wave, a hundred feet short of the shore. She had transformed back into her human form and she ran toward him, stepping high through the knee-deep water.

"Oedandus!" he called. In that first split second, he felt a cold waft of despair. He didn't know this shore, and he wondered if the flighty Vee had somehow brought him to a shore that was not Amarion.

Was Oedandus even here?

Then he felt a flicker of awareness, a questing thought touch his mind. His god's dark voice said, "Medophae?"

"Medophae!" Vee shouted. The low surf became tentacles of water, grasping her around the waist, the arms, and the legs. They dragged her back into the face of the wave, and she vanished with a splash.

"Come on," he looked down at his left hand, trying to make the godsword appear.

The wave reached the shore and smashed into him. It carried him fifty feet up the cliff and crushed him into it. His ribs broke. His broken leg twisted, and he screamed at the pain.

The water surged backward, dropping him to the beach. The water tentacles wrapped around his ankles and wrists, yanking him across the rocks toward the ocean.

Saraphazia? the dark voice said in Medophae's mind.

"She's trying to kill me—" A tentacle of water smashed into his face. The water sucked him down the beach, hurling him into the front of the hundred-foot wave that had risen again. The water pushed down his throat this time, trying to drown him. With his feet off the ground, the dark voice of Oedandus vanished. He could see the coastline, but the wall of water withdrew, taking him away from Amarion.

He coughed, and more water shoved down his throat.

"This time, you die," Saraphazia's sepulchral voice vibrated all around him. The water shoved him downward with incredible force, crushing him against the shallow ocean floor. All of his ribs broke this time. His heart fluttered against its shattered cage...then stopped.

A blast of golden fire burned through the water, creating a tunnel straight through the water from the coast, and slammed into him.

The rage of Oedandus filled him, and Medophae felt joy along with the pain. Pain was an old friend, and it was much easier to deal with when he knew that the injuries would heal.

Ribs mended. His heart beat again. His leg twisted around the right way, bones popping into place and mending. The fire repaired his ravaged lungs, his bleeding organs. Golden lightning danced around his stump, as if offended he was missing his hand, and the stump split open. Medophae screamed as a new hand burst from the end of his arm, bones extending, tendons slithering over them like snakes, muscles slithering over the top of that and finally, skin covered the hand like flesh-colored paint.

Oedandus lit him up with fury. He spun, and the godsword flared to life in his new right hand. *You are the hand of justice,* the dark voice intoned in his head.

Time to pick on someone your own size, Saraphazia.

"He tried to steal my daughter," Saraphazia shrieked from the water all around. "Let me kill him, Oedandus. He tried to steal my daughter!"

Tentacles of water shot out from all sides. Medophae spun, slicing each in turn.

He looked for Vee and saw her small silhouette deeper inside the huge wave. He pointed the godsword to the left of her and let loose Oedandus's fury. The fire blasted through the water and created another tunnel. Medophae lunged forward and grabbed Vee's arm. The water went solid, trying to pull her away, but he cut her free like she was in a block of ice.

Vee was sobbing. "Mother, please... Mother, let me go...."

Medophae tucked Vee under his right arm and sprinted up the tunnel. Golden lightning crackled all around them, but the pressure of the water broke through. Tentacles squeezed through, lashing at them. He cut them away and leapt for the shore just as the tunnel cracked and collapsed.

They sailed through the air toward the rocky, sandy shore. This time, Medophae spun, cradling Vee and landing on his feet. Golden fire raced away from him along the ground like a prairie fire, then vanished.

"Stay behind me," he said to her.

Saraphazia, in her enormous whale form, looked down on them from the crest of the hundred-foot wave, which had frozen in place, water surging up and down to support her girth.

"Don't make me!" Medophae shouted, pointing the godsword at Saraphazia's face.

She hesitated. She had been there when Oedandus had burned Dervon to death.

Medophae looked along the cliffs and spotted a crack in the cliff face, maybe a path through. He needed to get Vee away from the ocean. If it got hold of her again, it might whisk her a hundred yards into the deep in an instant. Even Oedandus might not be able to retrieve her that far away.

He slid sideways while Saraphazia hesitated. Every inch might count when she finally attacked.

"Give her to me." Her booming voice echoed against the cliffs. "And I will let you live."

"She doesn't want to stay with you, Saraphazia. Let her go."

"*Never!*" The goddess's voice burst his eardrums. The golden fire filled them, and his hearing slowly returned to recognize Vaisha's sobbing.

"Mother, please... Mother, let me go...."

Saraphazia's mute fury rippled through the water and shook the cliff behind them. A few rocks fell onto the beach, dislodged by the little earthquake. Medophae glanced nervously overhead, but no rocks fell on them. He kept moving.

"Give her back," Saraphazia shouted again.

They were halfway to the cut in the cliff face, and the closer they got, the more he could see. Yes. It was a path.

"Vaisha," Saraphazia said to Vee, "they will hurt you. They will

269

devour you, and then there will be nothing left. Is that what you want? Dervon almost killed you! He took away your divinity!"

"He diminished me, Mother," Vee said with a sob. "But you kept me from finding it again. You have to let me go."

"I saved you!"

"And should I remain the way you wish me forever?" Vee shouted through her sobs. "I was a goddess! I explored. I created. I dared! I want to dare again, but you refuse to let me."

"You are alive. That is what matters."

"It's not *all* that matters!"

A ripple went through the giant wave. "You don't know what you're talking about. That world, that *human* world," she spat. "It would kill you. It will break you, betray you, torture you, and then it will kill you."

"I will take that risk."

"You will stay in my ocean. And you will be safe forever."

They had reached the crack in the rock, and Medophae looked back into it. He could see daylight on the other side, rocks and greenery.

"This mongrel human has filled your head with insanity," Saraphazia said. "He is just a mortal. He doesn't know." She turned her hard gaze on Medophae. "Keep her from me, and we are enemies from this moment forward."

"You tortured me. You tried to kill me. And now you threaten to become my enemy? Swim away now, Saraphazia. Salvage some of your dignity. Let your daughter go with grace, and she may someday return to you."

Saraphazia's cry of rage filled the sky. A hundred water tentacles shot out of the wave and reached for Vee.

"Run!" He shoved her into the crack and sliced the tentacles. Golden fire met water and exploded. Medophae shot a blast straight at the wave, burning the tentacles away.

"No!" Saraphazia screamed, suddenly seeing the tiny crack. The giant wave crashed down, blasting into the crevice. It carried Medophae backward, spinning him around and bashing him into rock walls. He could only hope Vee had used the precious seconds to get as far down the crevice as she could.

270

Medophae grabbed an outcropping, stopping his spin. Golden fire erupted around his hand, giving him the strength to hang on. He slammed against the rock as the current shoved at him, but it was enough for him to get his bearings. He pointed his sword back up the crevice and let loose. Water exploded and hissed all around him, and the blast of golden fire shot straight toward the huge form of the whale with her eye up to the crevice. The blast struck her in her enormous forehead, and Saraphazia screamed, the sound reverberating throughout the water.

Medophae's outcropping tore free from the wall, and he tumbled again in the turbulent water, striking one side of the crevice and then the other.

He shot out the other end in a spray of water that launched him thirty feet. He landed and tumbled on the grassy hill. Water from the giant wave sluiced across the meadow, but it seemed like normal water now. The crevice drained as the wave receded.

"Vaisha!" Saraphazia cried beyond the ridge. "Please, Vaisha! Come back!"

Vee stood in the meadow, wretched, staring down the crevice and wringing her hands together. On the other side, the ocean raged, slamming into the ridge like she would break it to rubble. Sprays of water shot from the crevice, and Saraphazia wailed.

"I hurt her," he said. "I don't want to do it again. We've got to go, as far inland as we can manage, as fast as we can."

Medophae grabbed her hand and ran, towing the girl behind him.

It wasn't wise to make an implacable enemy out of Saraphazia, but Medophae felt giddy with Oedandus crackling through him once more. He had made it to the mainland, and, strangely, the words of the unnamed goddess in his dreams returned to him.

Take my gifts and wield your power for those in need. Gods and mortals alike.

He'd been given another chance, and he wasn't going to waste it. Not ever again.

I won't forget, he thought as he ran, holding tight to Vee's hand. The wails of the goddess of the ocean faded behind them.

I am the protector of Amarion, and Oedandus the hand of justice.

Avakketh, if you insist on harming humankind, then you will have to go through me. And I will show you the rage that destroyed Dervon.

EPILOGUE
AVAKKETH

SEVEN DRAGONS WERE DEAD.

Avakketh sat in his cave, high in Stak-lin Kur Mountain. He looked out over the glorious peaks of his realm, and he seethed.

Seven of his dragons were dead, and the stripling demigod was hiding from him. Pashyli-kest Nadilaz and her sister had returned, reporting that the human city of Corialis Port was destroyed. It was the only bit of good news in a series of unexpected failures.

Dyrfalikazyn and his flight had not returned. Zynderilifakyz, one of Avakketh's own elites, was also missing. And they would have come home by now, if they had been able. Nothing would have stopped them.

Which meant they were dead.

He had not felt this kind of rage since the early days of the world, when Saraphazia was a constant annoyance, Natra walked around making decrees to suit her moods, and Oedandus enforced them, making the others bow to him as though *he* was the Breather of Life and mother of gods.

Now the GodSpill had returned to Amarion. Threadweavers were rising, and the gods were to blame. They'd had two chances to exterminate humankind and passed up those opportunities. When humans first harnessed the GodSpill so long ago, it should have ended right then. The gods should have come together and sucked the life from these vermin who played at being gods. Avakketh had told the others it was an aberration, that it must be stopped. But without Natra to hear his grievance and command the fools, he was forced to speak to his loathsome family one at a time. He was forced to...try to *convince* them.

But they were fools, and they wouldn't comply.

As always, Saraphazia ignored him. As always, Zetu could not be found, and as always, Tarithalius only laughed, eager to see what his little beasts would do with the GodSpill. If Avakketh had come south at that very moment, when the most inept, fledgling threadweavers began playing with the GodSpill, then it would have been over. He could have remove humankind from the world like he was slicing the hide from a carcass.

But no... He had decided to wait. He had decided to watch, to give the humans the benefit of the doubt.

He regretted that decision every day.

The second chance had been mere years ago. After the humans' dabbling in the GodSpill had nearly destroyed them, Avakketh had foolishly waited. He'd reveled in the self-damning justice of their blunder, and been content to watch their own folly slowly destroy them. He longed to see them get what they deserved, slowly sliding into a bestial state like the equines had done before them.

But now, they'd somehow released the GodSpill again. Threadweavers were rising. The threat had returned.

And none of the others had the wit to see it except Avakketh. Fools. He wasn't even going to bother involving them this time. White Tuana could not be counted on as an ally. She was clearly insane, staging her bloody experiments with the half-human tribes in the Spine Mountains.

Saraphazia, of course, thought nothing would ever invade her oceans, and she refused to see the threat. She harbored the illusion that she had created a safe haven for herself and her creatures for all eternity.

And Tarithalius... Well, Tarithalius was an idiot and always had been. He only cared about giving his beastly little humans advantage after advantage to see what they would do with it. He reveled in laughing at their creations or their self-destruction.

But if humans were allowed to harness the GodSpill long enough, eventually they would become little gods. Enough little gods could threaten the original gods. That was unholy on every level. And Avakketh, as the eldest and strongest, had an obligation to purge the world of the aberration of humankind.

And there was only one being who might stop him: Oedandus.

Avakketh could sense when the other gods were near. It took concentration, but he could do it. And so he went looking for Oedandus, feeling for when he concentrated enough of himself in the human called Medophae. Avakketh created a bridge to the human's mind, and sent him visions.

Avakketh had no wish to fight Medophae. The human-turned-demigod was like a dragon hatchling with an adult's fire-breathing. He blasted his power around, always off-balance, striking at random. Medophae had burned Dervon's head off that way.

Oedandus had been unbeatable once upon a time, and no one knew just how much of the old god was left, stretched out across Amarion, and how much resided inside the upstart human. There was always the chance, however slim, that Medophae's reckless fire might hit Avakketh and do what it had done to Dervon.

The dreams Avakketh sent to Medophae, while giving the mortal the fantasy of escape, were actually Avakketh's first attacks. Though Medophae had Oedandus's power, he had a human's weak mind. Human minds could be destroyed, their sanity undermined. Medophae had fallen prey to the attacks. Avakketh felt him slowly weakening.

But then Medophae had vanished. Either he wasn't using Oedandus at all, or he had found a way to hide himself when he did. Now, seven of Avakketh's dragons were missing and likely dead.

So either threadweavers had miraculously arisen in Amarion,

coming to potency more quickly than Avakketh thought possible... Or Medophae had slain the dragons and kept Avakketh from seeing it somehow.

Avakketh gnashed his teeth, and a flicker of fire escaped his nose.

He considered waiting, watching for a better opportunity, keeping his dragons in the north for the moment and waiting for Medophae to surface. But he had waited before, and he had regretted it every—

Avakketh raised his head at the tremor in the great tapestry. It was slight, so slight he would have missed it a month ago. But he had spent so much time concentrating on Medophae lately that he felt the flicker of Oedandus.

Avakketh closed his eyes and focused, sent his awareness through the threads.

There! Medophae was in the Corialis Mountains, and he was battling Saraphazia, of all things. Avakketh could see it like a vision in his head. There were no details, only a glowing gold outline of Medophae's human form fighting the glowing blue outline of Saraphazia's whale form. Another human, small and barely visible, was with Medophae, and together they ran away from the goddess of the ocean.

Avakketh cast aside his doubts. He considered flying directly to Medophae and eviscerating him right now, but that would be hasty. Oedandus was too unpredictable. This must be planned for. Oedandus must be trapped. And now that Avakketh knew where Medophae was, it was time.

I see you, Medophae. It is time for you to die.

Mailing List/Facebook Group

MAILING LIST
Don't miss out on the latest news and information about all of my books. Join my Readers Group:

https://www.subscribepage.com/u0x4q3

FACEBOOK
https://www.facebook.com/todd.fahnestock

AMAZON AUTHOR PAGE
https://www.amazon.com/Todd-Fahnestock/e/B004N1MILG

ALSO BY TODD FAHNESTOCK

Tower of the Four Series
Episode 1 – The Quad
Episode 2 – The Tower
Episode 3 – The Test
Episode 4 – The Nightmare
Episode 5 – The Resurrection (Forthcoming)
The Champions Academy (Episodes 1-3 omnibus)

Threadweavers Series
Wildmane
The GodSpill
Threads of Amarion
God of Dragons

The Whisper Prince Series
Fairmist
The Undying Man
The Slate Wizards (Forthcoming)

Standalone Novels
Charlie Fiction
Summer of the Fetch

Short Stories
Urchin: A Tower of the Four Short Story
Royal: A Tower of the Four Short Story
Princess: A Tower of the Four Short Story
Parallel Worlds Anthology: *Threshold*
Fantastic Realms Anthology: *Ten for Every One*
Dragonlance: The Cataclysm – *Seekers*
Dragonlance: Heroes & Fools – *Songsayer*
Dragonlance: The History of Krynn – *The Letters of Trayn Minaas*

ABOUT THE AUTHOR

TODD FAHNESTOCK is a writer of fantasy for all ages and winner of the New York Public Library's Books for the Teen Age Award. *Threadweavers* and *The Whisper Prince Trilogy* are two of his bestselling epic fantasy series. He is a finalist in the Colorado Authors  League Writing Awards for the past two years, for *Charlie Fiction* and *The Undying Man*. His passions are fantasy and his quirky, fun-loving family. When he's not writing, he teaches Taekwondo, swaps middle grade humor with his son, plays Ticket to Ride with his wife, scribes modern slang from his daughter and goes on morning runs with Galahad the Weimaraner. **Visit Todd at** www.toddfahnestock.com.

Made in the USA
Monee, IL
15 May 2023

444b52d6-8335-4079-bc36-773eeab304a1R01